WHO GOES THERE?

Something had me on 10
idea what I was listen

My eyes were playing as
something wrong with t e
effect all but disappeared

I checked my mailbox. It was empty, which wasn't unusual.

Something was definitely wrong.

I looked around. The fake potted plant by the door to the stairwell didn't look quite right, as if somebody had pasted the area into a picture but it was one pixel off. Then it definitely moved.

The effect was really subtle, and reminded me of that movie with the alien predator who could camouflage himself. My heart rate took off like a fighter pilot who has overshot her landing on an aircraft carrier.

I forced myself to stand in front of the notice board next to the elevator and pretend to read. I concentrated on my hearing.

This was an exercise we'd practised a few times in Krav Maga class. It was a technique used by some blind people to navigate.

Sound bounces off hard objects like walls and produces reverberations. We seldom notice them as our brains filter them out, but they are the reason why people feel stifled in a recording booth with sound-absorbent padding on the walls, and have trouble understanding speech in a gymnasium that's nothing but hard surfaces. Humans can learn how to interpret those echoes to locate objects. Not as well as bats, but well enough. Our teacher assured us that it wasn't difficult. It just required practice.

As I pretended to read I made clicking noises with my tongue. If you were skillful, you could use the clicks like submarine sonar pings. I was barely a beginner at it, but I'd tagged a few people in class when they were trying to sneak up behind me.

Out of the corner of my eye, the potted plant now looked normal. *Click, click, click...*

The change wasn't anything I could really analyze. The clicks suddenly sounded different.

I put both hands against the wall, and mule kicked backward as hard as I could at an average stomach height. My foot hit something extremely hard, and I felt it move. Like kicking a concrete block on ice.

I ran for the stairwell door, yanked it open, and darted through.

I pulled on the handle to get the door to close faster. Something grabbed it and dragging me forward. Whatever it was pulling on the door was strong.

I let go of the door and kicked it. There was a second thump just after my foot landed, and the fire door vibrated. With any luck I'd nailed whatever it was in the face. Assuming it had a face.

ALSO BY G.W. RENSHAW

Odd Thoughts: An Anthology of Speculative Fiction

The Chandler Affairs

The Stable Vices Affair
The Prince and the Puppet Affair
The Kalevala Affair
The True Love Affair (coming 2016)
The Private Investigator's Cookbook (coming 2017)

To Devon,
Have fun. Always! :)
G. W. Renshaw

THE KALEVALA AFFAIR
Book Three of The Chandler Affairs

by

G.W. Renshaw

Javari Press
Calgary, Alberta
2016

The Kalevala Affair

Copyright 2016 G.W. Renshaw
All rights reserved.

Javari Press,
Calgary, Alberta, Canada.
http://www.javaripress.ca/

ISBN: 978-1-895487-09-1 (pbk)
ISBN: 978-1-895487-10-7 (eBook)

First paperback edition, April 2016.
Excerpts from The Kalevala by Elias Lönnrot, translation by
John Martin Crawford

Set in Gentium Book Basic
Printed in the United States of America

PUBLISHER'S NOTE: THIS IS A WORK OF FICTION. NAMES, CHARACTERS, PLACES, INCIDENTS, GODS, DEMONS, AND BUSINESSES ARE EITHER THE PRODUCT OF THE AUTHOR'S IMAGINATION, OR ARE USED FICTITIOUSLY. ANY RESEMBLANCES TO ACTUAL PERSONS, LIVING OR DEAD, PLACES, INCIDENTS, OR BUSINESSES ARE ENTIRELY COINCIDENTAL.

DEDICATION

This book is dedicated to four women whose strength towers over that of the Heroes of legend.

Catherine and Leanne, both of whom survived and have flourished in terrible circumstances.

Kelly, who continues to trust that life and beauty are to be found just around the corner.

And Victoria, who beat all the odds to become one of the most caring, loving, and wonderful women I know.

ACKNOWLEDGEMENTS

No book can be written by a single person, no matter how talented the author. Too many details depend on knowledge gained from others. In particular:

Daniel Berryhill, chef, international performer, and dispenser of obscure and detailed knowledge about Finland.

Swati Chavda, neurosurgeon and author, for helpful information about head trauma.

Plamen Dimov, musician, and leader, for inviting me into the inner world of Nightwish and the Kitee International Music and Art Festival.

Sandra Fitzpatrick, my lovely wife, best friend, and auxiliary brain when mine failed. *Mi amigas vin.*

Leigh Lyle, my wonderful friend, and international woman of mystery, for her expertise in English customs, international travel, and smuggling.

Jenna Miles, who has taught me a great deal about many things, as well as being Lana's creator. *Mi amigas vin ankaŭ.*

Fred van Driel, a man of great and diverse talents, whose help with beta reading and editing is greatly appreciated.

In addition, I wish to thank the late Professor Seppo Nieminen, without whom this book would not have been possible.

Any variances between the information given to me, and what appears in my writing are mine. All mine. I refuse to share the credit with anybody else.

If they want credit, let 'em make their own mistakes.

AUTHOR'S NOTE

Stories must always be rooted in some reality. Even if a novel takes place in a far away galaxy we expect the characters to behave in familiar ways, and to fall when they stumble.

For novels set closer to home, it is easier for readers to relate to a real location, such as Calgary, as a setting even if the people and situations in the book are completely unreal.

In this work, institutions such as the Hawaiian Volcano Observatory, the Karelian Institute, the University of Warsaw, and the Finnish SIS, actually exist in real life, but the characters in this book who are associated with them are products of my imagination, are not based on any real persons, and do not in any way pretend to speak for the real organizations.

Some characters are historical, but never acted as they do in this story. Perhaps this is because they were never tempted by similar circumstances.

Other characters are fictional because their names have been lost to history, and their real contributions remain unknown. For every well-known general or eminent statesman, there are hundreds or thousands of ordinary people who made a difference. Josef Berkowicz and his son Abraham are fictional, but they stand for the many brave people in Poland who fought against the invasion of their country during World War II in ways large and small.

THE KALEVALA AFFAIR

CHAPTER 1

Killer Cranberries

In the end, it's the little things in life that get us. For example, despite what you see on television, the actual number of people who are killed by an asteroid while their town is being attacked by zombies during a volcanic eruption caused by the awakening of an ancient Native spirit is shockingly small.

On Friday night I was being the dutiful daughter, and prepping for the family dinner I was hosting on Sunday. Midnight might seem like an odd time to be cooking, but life's like that.

I might have been safe if it wasn't for the cranberry relish. Cointreau is required for my recipe, and it was well after midnight when I realized that the bottle in my cupboard was empty. Why I'd put an empty bottle back was a mystery. It was time to go on a quest.

Fortunately, the liquor store at Brentwood is open until two in the morning. It wouldn't take me long to run out and get a bottle. At least I wouldn't have to worry about traffic at that hour.

The parking lot was a sparse forest of light poles casting their steady glow over nothing but empty asphalt.

Other than the two employees, the store was deserted as well. I guess Easter isn't a big time for people to get drunk.

I'd seen what happened in parking lots when people couldn't hold their liquor, so I was careful to hold the bottle firmly as I carried it to my car. Once the bottle was safely on the passenger side floor of Binky I could relax.

Yes, I named my white Cavalier Binky because it's my faithful steed. If you don't get it I don't think we can be friends.

Being the wild and crazy rebel that I am, I drove straight across the lot toward the exit. None of this keeping to the lanes rubbish for an intrepid private investigator like me.

The sound wasn't as loud as you would expect. It was a sort of surround-sound crunchy popping. My keenly-trained investigative mind instantly reacted to the event.

Um, why is there a hole in the windshield?

The glass was mostly intact, apart from a small, oval opening hovering like a spider in the middle of its web of cracks. A stream of cold air blew in onto my face. The outside world sounded louder than it should, so I turned to look at the rear window. It was missing.

Weird. It's almost like—crap! Somebody is shooting at me!

I threw myself across the passenger seat and gouged my ribs as they became overly intimate with the shifter. I hadn't seen any movement or muzzle flash ahead of me, so the shooter had to be behind. From my horizontal position all I could see through the windshield were the bases of the looming light posts as they went by. I should be able to get away as long as I didn't drive into one.

There was the sudden flapping sound of a seriously flat tire, and Binky pulled to the right. That aimed me toward the outlying professional building. That wasn't what I had in mind.

Unless I wanted to drive back toward the shooter I needed to thread my way between that building and the main mall. The steering abruptly pulled back to the left, and started wobbling. The flapping was now flap-flapping. The shooter must have taken out another tire.

The only way I could keep Binky on track was to sit up and try to drive normally, but that would expose me to the shooter. The flat tires felt like they were on opposite corners as Binky kept bobbing from side to side like a coracle trying to shoot rapids. The sound of metal rims grinding on pavement became noticeable. With the tires no longer attached to the rims I had to slow to a crawl or Binky would lose all traction, and I'd be even slower getting away.

I had to get out. At this speed the shooter could just stroll up to me and finish the job.

Binky got me as far as the coffee shop near the corner of the building before I had to leave him. The liquor store was the only place open, but it was now at least two hundred metres behind me. Besides, that would just trap me in a store with some innocent bystanders. There was no way I'd let that happen. I was on my own.

I hid behind a garbage can and quickly scanned the area. There was still nobody in sight. Binky probably covered me at the moment, but that safety wouldn't last longer than it took for the shooter to change positions. If ever there was a time to swallow my lone-wolf pride and call the police, this was it.

I unzipped my jacket, and put my hand in the inside pocket where I usually kept my phone. It was empty. I must have dropped it. I looked around, including in the car, and I had a sudden mental image of my coffee table. I was only going out for a few minutes. I'd left the phone at home.

Veronica, you idiot.

Okay, there was no sense crying over it. The garbage can was plastic and wouldn't even stop a bullet from a .22 pistol. I got down on my stomach and crawled toward the corner of the building. Rather than running across another 200 metres of empty parking lot, I hugged the L-shaped mall.

I peeked back around the corner, but I still couldn't see anybody.

I ran along the front of the mall, and looked over the area while cowering as far into the corner as I could by the mall entrance. Still, nothing was moving.

One more long dash and I'd be on Charleswood Drive. Maybe somebody would drive past and I could get their attention.

I took a deep breath and ran. When I was nearly at the far end of the Safeway, one of the plate glass panes in front of the store exploded into tiny shards a metre behind me.

I instinctively ducked, but without cover there was no point in stopping. Maybe the breaking window had set off an alarm. The end of the building was close.

I ducked around the corner, and considered my next move. I could stay on the sidewalk and try to get to the next block, but there was very little cover. If I could make it to the other side of the road I would have a lot more cover that was closer. It didn't hurt that it was the direction of my home.

The good news was that there was no traffic, so I didn't have to worry about being run over or endangering bystanders. The bad news was that there was no traffic. I was still on my own.

Across the street a church backed onto an unpaved lane. I made it to the lane without being shot. I chose to go right, hoping that it would take me closer to Crowchild Trail. There was always traffic on Crowchild, even at two in the morning.

If all else failed I could try hopping fences to get there. I thought about banging on doors, but that would call attention to me and put other people at risk. I wasn't going to involve other people unless it was necessary.

My best bet was the University C-train station on Crowchild where I could use the transit emergency call box to yell for help. The train had stopped running at least an hour before, so the platform would be clear. Anybody else I saw should be the shooter and I'd know to duck.

I skulked down the lane as quickly as possible, turning left at an intersection so I wouldn't be going back toward the mall. The probability was that I'd lost the shooter, but I value my life and wasn't taking chances.

Now that I was no longer running the cold was bugging me. I hadn't expected to be out this long, or to be sweating this much, and had just thrown on a light jacket before leaving home. The temperature had to be around the low side of freezing, which wasn't too bad unless I was out in it for a long time after running for my life. I had to get to that emergency call box.

A right turn from the lane led out onto a street, but it didn't feel far enough from the mall for safety. The next right led onto what I recognized as Morley Trail. Despite its grand name it was just another two lane residential street. Most of the houses were bungalows from the 1960s when big front yards were in fashion.

Now that I knew where I was I jogged along Morley for a block, and cut right at the next intersection. The complete lack of other people, even at this hour of the morning, was a bit spooky. I knew there was a pedestrian overpass on the side street paralleling Crowchild that would take me right to the station. If I could find it.

Castle Road went in exactly the right direction. I could see the stairs of the overpass at the other end of the block on Capital Hill Crescent. Trying to stay warm, I began jogging again.

The straight, badly-named crescent was separated from Crowchild by a concrete noise-abatement wall that was way too high for me to jump. I was almost at the steps leading up to the overpass when something whizzed past my ear, and buried itself in the concrete pillar near the bottom of the stairs. Small chips of cement sprayed me and the area as I ducked and covered my head.

This outing was not going in any way as I'd expected. The object that had hit the concrete wasn't a bullet. It was an arrow.

The stairs weren't the only way onto the overpass; there was a ramp about a block to the left. I scrambled behind the thick bushes planted along the wall, and ran as well as I could through the space behind them that was rapidly getting shorter. Stray branches tried to gouge my eyes out a few times. At least the ramp and wall protected me from the top and right.

The bushes were still leafless in the early spring and certainly not arrow proof, but the shooter would have to find me before he could hit me. When the head room was too small for even me to continue crawling, I fought my way out from between two bushes, and made for the end of the ramp.

Another arrow hit the concrete beside me. *What the hell?* This time it came from the *Crowchild* side of the wall. From the angle it looked like it had been shot from the C-train platform itself.

Give me a break! How is this guy getting around? Or are there more than one of them?

So much for crossing the overpass. I'd be a sitting duck running up the ramp. Even more so when I got to the platform. If I was very lucky somebody might notice the shooter on the station CCTV cameras, but not in time to keep me from becoming a Veronica kebab.

I stayed on the street and ran.

Capital Hill Crescent only curves at the ends. The rest is as straight as the section of Crowchild it parallels. The plantings didn't have much room between them and the wall, but I was small enough to make it through.

The bungalows on the other side of the street all had big front lawns, and very few had hedges or trees. There was no cover there.

I got to an angle where the wall jogged that gave me a bit more concealment from the direction of the overpass. I didn't waste energy being happy about it. I was breathing hard and sweating. I'd have opened my dark blue windbreaker, but I was wearing a white t-shirt underneath. Not good for keeping out of sight at night.

The wall was shorter here, and I could occasionally hear traffic on the other side. I could probably heave myself over, but I'd be a perfect target while I did so. I made a mental note to take up parkour if I survived.

There was still nobody behind me when I stopped for a moment to catch my breath. There was no movement at all. I waited and listened. Apart from those inaccessible cars on Crowchild there was no sound.

I walked as carefully as possible trying not to move the branches and give away my position. A cross street gave me hope for a moment, but there was even less cover in that direction. I kept going.

Another useless cross street came and went. The stress of trying to hide from a murderous stalker was wearing me down. The bushes kept trying to tear pieces off me as well as the branches slashing at my eyes. There didn't seem to be any more intersections for a stupidly long distance.

That would be Twenty-fourth Avenue, another major residential road that should have traffic. Better yet, it intersected Crowchild and there might be at least one car stopped at the traffic light where I could get help. At the least a driver might report a crazy woman screaming and running around the intersection.

Just as the bushes ended another arrow hit the concrete right by my head. I felt a sting on my forehead where a piece of concrete hit it. When I put my hand to my head there was blood. From the angle of the arrow, the shooter was somewhere in front of me.

The last part of the block was a new apartment building with a cafe on the ground floor. Of course it was closed. I ran like hell across the street, and into the adjoining lane. There was a door I tried on the way by, but naturally it was locked. There was no intercom.

Out the other side of the lane, and I was on Twenty-fourth *Street*. Given the direction of the latest arrow, I couldn't risk the open intersection at Crowchild. I headed east into another lane.

This time I was even more careful, moving from shadow to shadow as much as possible. If the shooter tried following me at least I'd see him first outlined by the street lights against the end of the lane.

Again, I listened carefully before each move. There were no sounds except for occasional distant vehicles. Too distant. At this point I was now only about five long blocks from my own home. Once there I could get inside my controlled-access building, and call the police. I also had some weapons with which I could make the shooter very unhappy if he did try to break in. The advantage would be with me; bows are not close-quarters combat weapons.

The end of the lane looked clear, but this guy had followed me too far for me to feel confident that I'd given him the slip.

If there had been help around I'd have gladly collapsed into a sobbing ball and let them take care of it, but I was on my own. I had to keep going. It was a good thing that I'd lucked out in the personality lottery: I tended to go to pieces *after* an emergency rather than during. There would be plenty of time for freaking out when I was safe.

Twenty-third Street looked clear. I sprinted across it into the lane without drawing fire, and resumed my sneaking.

When I got to Twenty-second I took a short breather. All I had to do was to make it a few blocks south and I'd be home.

I hugged the side of the garage on the corner, and looked up and down Twenty-second. There was nobody visible. I waited a few minutes, but there was still nothing moving. There was no traffic at all anywhere that I could see or hear.

I made my way down the block toward Twenty-fourth Avenue and jogged across. Just as I reached the south side there was a loud clang. An arrow was sticking through the steel light post a few metres to my right.

I ran like a pack of demons was after me. I'm in good physical condition, but I'm not a runner. Parkour lessons were looking really good right now. If I lived to take them.

One block went by. Two blocks. Another half block and I'd be...

Another light post was skewered by an arrow, and the light died with the crackling hum of a shorted high-voltage cable followed by a loud bang as something inside exploded.

What the hell kind of bow was this guy using? For that matter, what kind of arrows was he using to penetrate steel and concrete like it was balsa?

My building was just ahead. I dug into the right pocket for my keys as I ran. For an awful moment I thought I'd lost them, but this time I'd put them in the left pocket of my jacket.

I got the key into the lock, wrenched the door open, and almost fell inside. I pulled on the steel door against its closer until it latched with a satisfying click. Gulping air like a beached fish, I stumbled to the elevator and pushed the button.

An arrow came straight through the outside door. It buried itself almost to the fletching in the elevator door in front of me. With its inner and outer doors pinned together it the elevator wasn't going anywhere.

I was really sick and tired of this. I ran up the stairs taking them two at a time, pulling myself up by the railing and ignoring my burning leg muscles. Three flights later I fell out into the corridor and bounced off the far wall. I was running on adrenaline and sheer bloody-mindedness at that point. It took me a moment to get the key into the lock and stumble into my apartment.

My cat, Yoko Geri, had been sleeping on the sofa. He looked at me, and went back to sleep.

I got the door closed, pulled my sweat-soaked jacket off, grabbed my tactical baton from the basket by the door, and my phone from the coffee table. It took me a while to get enough breath back that I could make the call.

"Nine-one-one. What is the nature of your emergency?"

※

This was the second time I'd called the Calgary Police because somebody was trying to kill me, and again attempted murder got me fast service. Six minutes later a car with two constables pulled up in front of my building followed by a sergeant's van.

I think that they were wondering if I was drunk or stoned from what I'd told dispatch. That changed when I buzzed them in, after first confirming who they were on the video camera, and they saw the arrow stuck in the elevator door. The constables made sure my drapes were closed before taking my statement by the kitchen where it would be harder to get a line of sight on me from outside.

Yoko Geri decided this was all too weird, and hid in my bedroom. I wished that I could have joined him.

The tactical team showed up next, followed immediately by the sound of HAWCS, the Helicopter Air Watch for Community Safety. They'd be out looking for the infrared signature of somebody skulking around in the neighbourhood. The shooter would need to have a major miracle on his side to be able to evade them.

HAWCS and the tactical team found nothing. The only evidence that I wasn't crazy was the arrow buried in the elevator door, some holes where I'd said the other arrows had struck, and poor Binky with trashed glass and tires.

I'm told that it took a lot of doing to pull the leaf-shaped arrow head from the metal doors. They had to use a chisel to enlarge the hole.

All the tromping around woke my neighbours, of course, who were not amused at the hour. I didn't blame them. I wanted nothing more than to go to bed with the covers over my head.

During the whole circus my mother arrived.

She flashed her badge at the constable keeping watch outside my door. "Are you all right?" I'd dragged Yoko out of the bedroom, and he was sitting on my lap while I stroked him. We both looked up as she came in.

I had to keep up my appearance of coolness. "Hi Mum. I don't know why they called homicide. I'm not dead yet."

My sarcastic PI/daughter face held for about five seconds before my subconscious told me that my mummy was here to protect me, and the tears started. She sat on the sofa next to me and cradled me in her arms. Yoko Geri seemed to know that I was upset and stayed where he was. I could feel as well as hear him purring.

"We'll be outside," someone said.

Some time later I mostly got myself under control. Mum was stroking my hair. She'd also put the box of tissues from the coffee table beside me. I pulled three of them out, and blew my nose loudly enough that Yoko decided that he'd be safer in the bedroom. The tactical team should have come running.

"Thanks."

"Do you have any idea who was after you?"

I shook my head. "No. I've pissed off a few people during investigations, but none of them badly enough to shoot at me."

"Did you see the shooter?"

"No. The arrows just kept coming out of nowhere."

She had me go over the whole evening once more, in even more detail than the constables had demanded.

"May I use your laptop?" She said when I'd finished. I nodded while drying my eyes.

She brought up the Google satellite view, and had me show her my exact route, where the arrows had hit, and their directions.

"Hmm."

"What?"

"You were a clear target when you got in the car, but that first shot missed. The next two shots took out two of the tires on opposite corners so you'd be forced to abandon your car. Those aren't shots consistent with somebody who misses."

"There might have been more than one shooter."

She pointed out the locations on the map.

"I agree, but look at this. As soon as you were about to get on the overpass a shot hit the wall right in front of you. Yet you weren't bothered while you made your way to the ramp, where another arrow prevented you from using it."

"Damn," I said. She was right. "At each point, the arrows either prevented me from getting help, or goaded me into hurrying."

"I doubt that it was a coincidence that the final arrow missed you too."

"Somebody was *herding* me?"

"Looks like."

That pissed me off. "Why?"

"Do you have any ideas?" she countered.

"None. I don't even know how it could be possible. There must have been at least four shooters, or..." I stopped as a nasty possibility occurred to me. One I couldn't tell her about.

"Or?"

"Um, nothing. Just that there must have been more than one."

Mum looked dubious. Her instincts could smell a lie from across the city.

"You're coming home with me tonight."

"I'll be fine here."

"No, you won't." She used her Motherly Voice of Command. "Think of this as protective custody. It's either come home with me, or I'll lock you up."

"I'm over eighteen. You can't put me in protective custody without my permission."

She switched to her Hurt Mother Look. "Please."

Damn it, I wasn't going to win this one. "Yes, Detective. Let me get an overnight bag."

⁂

"You're being unusually quiet," she said as she drove south toward my parents' house.

"I'm tired," I said. In fact I was exhausted, but that wasn't the whole reason for my silence. Somebody who might be able to appear and disappear at will, coupled with the weird choice of weapon, had me wondering if this had anything to do with the Blakeway affair of last year.

So far I'd avoided telling Mum about the outcome of that case, and I intended to keep that from her as long as possible. It wasn't every day that you had your nose rubbed in the reality of demons walking the Earth. I thought I had a small handle on the supernatural world, but until I knew more it probably wouldn't do her any good to know about it. Knowing might also get her in big trouble.

There was also the problem of getting her to believe me.

"You know more than you're letting on," she said. Damn. Are all mothers this psychic, or just the ones who are detectives?

"Not really. Mostly I'm trying to figure out who could be after me. I just hope you're right about this not being attempted murder, but if it isn't that then I have no idea what it is."

"You and me both."

Dad was waiting up for us when we arrived. I didn't know how much Mum had told him, and I didn't feel like going over the story one more time, so I just said I was exhausted. I didn't get away without a long hug, not that I wanted to.

Dad had turned down the bed in my old room. I took off my still-damp t-shirt, dirty jeans, and shoes. That was all I had energy for.

It still took a while for me to get to sleep. It surprised me how much I missed Yoko Geri curled up with me under the covers.

I woke up to my phone ringing on the bedside table. The alarm clock said 1:17. Since I hadn't gotten to bed until almost 4:30, I assumed that it was after lunch. I felt like I hadn't been to bed yet. I'm really not a morning person. Even when it's afternoon.

I said something into the phone. I believe it was *mmmff*.

"Are you okay? What happened?"

"Hi, Kali. How's my favourite sister?"

"Don't stall. Dad left a message saying that you'd been shot."

No wonder she was freaking out. "No, I was shot *at*. They missed. Lots of times."

"Who was it?"

"I have no idea." I told her the whole story. I was getting good at it.

"Do you think it was anything to do with, you know, the demons?"

"I don't know. I can't figure why they might be after me a year after our last encounter."

"Who knows how they think? Especially Beleth. She's nuts."

"Good point. And thanks for that comforting thought."

"Where are you now?"

"At Mum and Dad's place. She won't let me go back to my apartment until they catch the bad guys."

"You are going to anyway, aren't you?"

"Nonsense. Whatever would make you say that? "

After lunch I found Mum in Dad's home office working at the computer.

"I thought you'd be at work."

"I *am* at work. I'm going over the evidence while guarding you."

"I'll need to go home to feed Yoko Geri."

"That's taken care of. I went this morning."

"Kali could..."

"I'm not letting civilians near the scene until we resolve this."

I knew that tone of voice. The discussion was over.

"Has Ident gone over my car yet?"

"Yes. There was nothing other than the obvious. They think they found where the first arrow hit, but there was no sign of it. The shooter must have collected it afterward."

"I'll need to get Binky fixed."

"That's taken care of too. I had them tow it to a place that Doug recommended."

Doug was my genius mechanic, but he didn't do glass. Any place he recommended would be good.

"Thanks. I was wondering if they found a bottle of Cointreau on the floor by the front seat."

"Not that anybody mentioned."

She tapped a number into her phone.

"Ray? This is Janet Chandler. Did you find a bottle of Cointreau in Veronica's car? Front seat... Okay, thanks."

"No," she said. "No bottle. Somebody must have stolen it before we got there."

"Damn. All night running around being shot at, and now I've lost a new bottle of Cointreau. My life sucks."

"It could be worse," Mum said. I raised one eyebrow.

"So my big win is that I'm not dead? You sure know how to cheer me up."

"That's what mothers are for. Go have a shower and I'll make you some breakfast."

"That's nice of you, but I've already survived one attempt on my life."

"Fine. I concede that you and your father are the great master chefs. You can pour your own cereal."

CHAPTER 2

Staycation

After a week I was still living at my parents' house. Dad and I had cooked Easter dinner together. He not only supplied the missing Cointreau, but also baked an apple pie for dessert.

Apart from the parental units and me, there was Kali and George. Kali was technically my BFF, but all of us considered us to be sisters. She'd inherited an gigatonne of money from her parents. As usual she was wearing a black Romantigoth gown that made her look like Queen Victoria mourning Prince Albert. This dress had purple lace trim and matched her black hair with purple tips.

George had been her boyfriend for over two years, and was such an astoundingly nice guy that I actually approved of him. Not that I'm overly protective or anything. He had a scholarship to the University of Toronto, and he was only here during school breaks until he graduated.

"How's the investigation going?" Kali asked as her boyfriend passed her the spouts. It being an active case, Mum said nothing.

"Not well," I said. "The only evidence was the damage to my car, some holes in concrete and lamp posts, and one arrow buried in the elevator door. That's not much to go on."

Our eyes met and I could see the question in hers: *Demons?* I scrunched my mouth: *Not now.*

George missed the psychic girl by-play. "How long are you going to hang around here before going home?"

"No longer than necessary," I said pointedly, looking at Mum.

"I think we can find another topic," Dad said.

"Fine. How's Toronto, George?"

George sighed. "Not bad. The program at the U of T is great. I just wish I was closer."

George and Kali gazed fondly into each others eyes, and she trailed one finger over the back of his hand. I could see the hairs on his wrist come to attention as he shivered delicately. Kali's lips parted slightly. The moment could only be described as smouldering. It surprised me that they didn't jump each other right then.

That reminded me that I was currently between boyfriends and my hormones were not happy about it.

"More potatoes?" Mum asked, waving the serving spoon.

⁓

On Monday I was reading in the living room when Mum came out of the office, and flumped on the sofa next to me. That worried me. I thought only Kali flumped.

"I just got an e-mail from the lab," she said, then paused.

"Oh?"

"They can't figure out what the arrow is made of."

"How is that even possible these days? Tell them to cut a piece off and feed it to a mass spectrometer." Yes, I watch cop shows too. I think every investigator does, if only to make fun of them.

She paused again. That wasn't like her.

"You're beginning to freak me out. Don't just sit there, say something."

"The arrow was one solid piece of something metallic-looking. Even the fletching seemed to be part of the shaft. The whole thing was ridiculously rigid. Even the feathers refused to bend under any conditions they tried."

"Seriously? They're feathers. Did they try poking them with a finger?"

"You know Ray in Ident?"

"Yeah. Big guy. Used to play football I think."

"When they were sure that nothing they could do would get any useful evidence from it, he put the arrow on the floor in the basement and took a five pound sledge hammer to it. The feathers didn't budge. In fact, they left cut marks in the head of the hammer as well as chipping the concrete."

"You're kidding." She pointed at her face, giving me the "does this look like I'm kidding?" sign. "That's ridiculous. Nothing is that strong."

"That's *one* reason why they're confused." She paused again. "The other is that the arrow disappeared before they'd completed their testing. It wasn't lost or stolen. The technician swore that he turned away for a moment to make a note and the arrow just—vanished from the bench. Most people don't believe him, but there's no sign that anybody but him entered or left the lab, and they searched the lab. The arrow isn't there."

Sadly, I believed it. "That's—strange."

"And you're still hiding something."

I sighed. She was right, of course.

"It's nothing that will help solve the case."

"So you say."

"Please, just drop it. I'll tell you when I'm ready."

The look she gave me made me feel even worse than I already did. The whole unbending/disappearing arrow thing was exactly what I'd expect from demons. Especially Beleth—she was bug-house nuts.

Very few people in the world knew that demons were real. Kali and I were two of them. Sure, lots of people took demons as an item of faith, but it's whole a lot different when you meet them face to face.

With their powers, if demons wanted me dead I'd be dead. It seemed like they were just playing around for some, as usual, unknown reason.

I suppose in some way that was mildly comforting.

A week later Mum left me in the house by myself while she went shopping. Binky was back from the shop—good as new and sitting in the garage so he wouldn't be visible from the street. She was taking no chance that a would-be assassin might find me.

I'd been indoors for over two weeks. If I didn't get outside soon my head was going to explode. There were some things I wanted from my apartment, and if nothing was happening to me here it wasn't likely that anything would happen if I just popped out to get them.

Okay, to be truthful, I was on edge the whole way there. My eyes locked on every moving object, and I almost went nuts trying to memorize each vehicle behind me on the road in case one was following me. I wasn't as cool about this trip as I had thought.

Tenant parking is around back, and I kept looking around as I unlocked the door to my building. People make fun of paranoia, but trust me, it's not fun at all. Especially when somebody *is* out to get you.

I was beginning to think that this was a really bad idea, but it's patience I'm short on, not stubbornness.

The hallway between the back door and the lobby was empty except for the quiet hum of the overhead fluorescent lights. There was nobody in the lobby. The only unusual thing was the OUT OF ORDER sign on the elevator. The front door to the building had either been replaced or patched really well.

I jogged up the stairs as quietly as I could. There were no other people around.

My black, furry sidekick looked up from the couch as I opened the door to my apartment. He must have been expecting Mum, but when he saw me he trotted over and bunted my legs while purring loudly.

"I missed you too, fuzz butt." Before I could pick him up, he meowed and trotted into the kitchen where he looked at me accusingly. Sure enough, his bowl was empty. I repaired that matter before grabbing my things.

The apartment was a lot cleaner than when I'd left. Apparently Mum had tidied as well as looking after the fur ball. She'd even watered my potted herbs.

I jumped when my phone rang, then felt stupid. It wasn't like an attacker was going to call me before shooting at me. I expected it to be Mum, demanding to know where I was, but it was a man.

"Ms. Chandler, my name is Jack Hoag. I would like to meet to discuss a case with you."

I'd been so braced for parental displeasure that his voice confused me for a moment. A shot of adrenaline ran through me as I wondered if he had anything to do with my shooter. Damn it, I wasn't going to let some bad guy prevent me from living my life.

"Ms. Chandler?"

"Yes, sorry. I have some time right now if you'd like to come to my office."

"Excellent. I'll see you in ten minutes."

He hung up before I could give him my address. It's not listed because it's also my apartment. Oh well, either a former client had given it to him, or he'd be calling back. Either way, I had enough time to check my mailbox downstairs.

○○○

Something had me on edge. I found myself straining to listen with no idea what I was listening for.

My eyes were playing tricks on me too. It was almost like there was something wrong with the lobby, but when I looked directly at it the effect all but disappeared. Maybe it was time for an eye exam. I wondered what I'd look like with glasses. Would the hot librarian look work for me?

I checked my mailbox. It was empty, which wasn't unusual.

Something was definitely wrong.

I looked around. The fake potted plant by the door to the stairwell didn't look quite right, as if somebody had pasted the area into a picture but it was one pixel off. Then it definitely moved.

The effect was really subtle, and reminded me of that movie with the alien predator who could camouflage himself. My heart rate took off like a fighter pilot who has overshot her landing on an aircraft carrier.

I forced myself to stand in front of the notice board next to the elevator and pretend to read. I concentrated on my hearing.

This was an exercise we'd practised a few times in Krav Maga class. It was a technique used by some blind people to navigate.

Sound bounces off hard objects like walls and produces reverberations. We seldom notice them as our brains filter them out, but they are the reason why people feel stifled in a recording booth with sound-absorbent padding on the walls, and have trouble understanding speech in a gymnasium that's nothing but hard surfaces. Humans can learn how to interpret those echoes to locate objects. Not as well as bats, but well enough. Our teacher assured us that it wasn't difficult. It just required practice.

In class, the idea was to tell when somebody was sneaking up behind you by detecting differences in the ambient sound. Human bodies absorb a lot of sound.

As I pretended to read I made clicking noises with my tongue. If you were skillful, you could use the clicks like submarine sonar pings. I was barely a beginner at it, but I'd tagged a few people in class when they were trying to sneak up behind me.

Out of the corner of my eye, the potted plant now looked normal. *Click, click, click...*

The change wasn't anything I could really analyze. The clicks suddenly sounded different.

I put both hands against the wall, and mule kicked backward as hard as I could at an average stomach height. My foot hit something extremely hard, and I felt it move. Like kicking a concrete block on ice.

When I turned I couldn't see anything, but whatever it was had to be between me and the front door. I ran for the stairwell door, yanked it open, and darted through.

I pulled on the handle to get the door to close faster. Something grabbed it and dragging me forward. Whatever it was pulling on the door was strong.

I let go of the door and kicked it. There was a second thump just after my foot landed, and the fire door vibrated. With any luck I'd nailed whatever it was in the face. Assuming it had a face.

I ran up the stairs like I was being chased by invisible demons.

Exactly like that.

⁓⁕⁓

Seconds after I slammed my apartment door the downstairs buzzer sounded, which didn't help to calm me at all. The security camera showed an ordinary looking man wearing a suit and carrying a brief case.

There was no way I was calling the police and trying to explain invisible assailants. Both times when my attacker had shown up I'd been alone, so keeping my appointment was probably the safest thing to do. I buzzed him in.

Mr. Hoag was short, slight, and all business. At least that helped me focus.

"I represent a consortium of collectors who wish to acquire an historical artifact," he said, opening his brief case on the coffee table. "All the information we have on it is in this file."

I skimmed through the folder while he patiently waited. It was all background information about something called the Sampo. The name sounded fake to me.

"This is very interesting, but I don't see anything about where it is now."

He smiled coldly. "That's why we need you. Nobody knows where it is."

I picked up the executive summary page.

"According to this, the Sampo was mythical. And it was destroyed at sea. By gods."

"If you read further, there are reports that the Sampo was seen in historical times. It's quite real and, at that time, seems to have been intact."

I pushed the file back toward him. "I'm a private investigator, not a thief. Even if I locate it, you will need to buy it from its present owner—if any—and probably get permission to take it out of whatever country it's in."

"All of that can be arranged once it is located. We certainly aren't asking you to do anything illegal. We merely want you to find it for us."

I was trying not to let on how excited I was. According to the file, the Sampo had last been seen in Sweden which meant it was probably somewhere in Europe, unless a collector from elsewhere had acquired it. The chase could lead anywhere in the world. This was not my usual cheating spouse or runaway child.

Besides, it had been a few weeks since my last case. I could use the money. I could also use a distraction from my alleged attempted homicide.

Chasing a mythical artifact could be exciting. I already had a fedora. Maybe I could get a bull whip to go with it. *Whoa, girl, take it easy. This sounds too good to be true. Especially the "we merely want" part.*

"There are some practical difficulties. I'm only licensed as an investigator in Alberta. Anywhere else I'd just be a private citizen."

"We're hiring your expertise, not your credentials."

"That's another thing. I'm relatively young. Why not hire a more experienced PI? Why me?"

"Let's just say you come highly recommended."

"Really? By whom?"

"Your former clients speak very highly of you."

"How would you know who my clients are?"

He shrugged. "One person mentions you. They also mention that they recommended you to a friend. The friend recommends you to someone else. Despite your youth, your chain of satisfied customers is quite long. My clients were impressed."

The flattery was nice but it wasn't going to get me to give in that easily. "The biggest difficulties in this investigation will be time and money. It probably will cost you tens of thousands of dollars in expenses, and I don't have the resources to front that."

He reached into the brief case again. "My principals anticipated that. I'm to give you this if you accept the job." He placed a card on the table. It was a corporate credit card with a familiar logo, but it was plain white rather than the more familiar gold or platinum. "You'd operate on an expense account."

"What's the limit on this card? Of course I'll be as economical as possible, but I need to know if I'm getting close so I'm not stranded."

"It doesn't have a limit."

That sounded preposterous, both because I'd never heard of a card with no spending limit, and because he was offering it to me. "Even if the card has no preset limit, how much is your client willing to spend?"

"As much as is necessary. I'm told that your normal rate is $75 per hour?"

"That's correct. With a two thousand dollar retainer." I'd recently raised my rate as I became better known.

"We also understand that a breakthrough might happen at any time, day or night, so I'm also authorized to offer you twice your normal hourly rate, charged 24 hours a day until you find the Sampo. That's $3600 per day."

Holy crap. Calm down, girl.

"That takes care of my fee and expenses, but what if I don't find it within your expected time frame?"

"We're giving you three months. If you haven't located it, and there are no current promising leads, then you can pocket approximately three hundred twenty-four thousand dollars and walk away with our thanks for your efforts. Of course if there *is* a promising lead we'd be happy to extend your contract for as long as necessary."

My too-goo-to-be-true meter was still quivering right near the top of the scale.

"Let me get this straight. You are willing to give me an unlimited expense account, and a three month head start. What's to prevent me from taking a cash advance of a hundred million and disappearing?" I figured I'd name an outrageous sum to shock him into giving something away. I hadn't had much experience with big players.

"There's no chance of that happening," he said calmly.

"How do you know? A hundred million is awfully tempting."

"For one thing, you are too intelligent to bring that up if you really intended doing it. For another, you have a reputation for scrupulous honesty, and devotion to your clients as long as they play fairly with you. We are playing fair."

"It still seems too good to be true."

"I assure you, the offer is genuine. As is the offered reward."

"Of course, you'd say exactly that even if it wasn't."

He nodded, conceding the point. "As a final incentive, my employers have authorized me to offer you the full three-month pay regardless of how long it takes you to find the Sampo. If you find it on the first day, you still get the full three hundred twenty-four thousand dollars. My clients are quite wealthy, and even the full amount represents a small investment to them."

I wished he's quit saying three hundred twenty-four thousand. That would buy a lot of cat food.

"I take it that there will be a written contract?"

"Of course." He pulled a small stack of paper from his case.

I read it over very carefully. It was too simple to contain much trickery. Everything he'd mentioned was there, including the detail that my payment in full would be placed in trust pending the completion of the contract. I'd heard of the law firm that was named as the trustee. They were a big name and highly reputable. I tried my cynical best, but I couldn't find anything wrong with the agreement.

Besides, this could help me out with my other problem.

I got out my pen. "All right, when do I start?"

⸎

I walked Mr. Hoag out of the building, just in case my invisible friend was still here. Before we left my apartment I took a few moments to put the items I'd gathered in a bag: the case file, the red phone from my night stand, my knife roll from the kitchen, and my tactical baton from the basket on the book shelf by the front door.

I opened my bedroom door so Yoko could get out, and I took a moment to scratch his head.

"I'll be back as soon as I can," I said to him as he lay on his back purring. "Be a good boy."

He was slightly affronted when I stopped petting him and left.

I listened carefully as we walked down the stairs. There didn't seem to be any weird echoes to our footsteps. Nor were there any predator-like shimmers.

"You didn't answer my question. When do you want me to start?" I asked.

"As soon as possible. While I would not presume to tell you how to investigate, may I suggest that you start with Professor Seppo Nieminen."

"Who's he?"

"The world expert on the Kalevala, currently working at the British Museum. The Kalevala is the nineteenth century Finnish epic poem that mentions the Sampo. The details are in the file."

We got to the lobby. As far as I could tell we were the only ones there.

"There's one further detail," he said at the front door. "The PIN for the card is your birthday: eight digits, year, month, and day."

"How do you know when my birthday is?"

"Please, Ms. Chandler. We wouldn't offer you this job unless we'd thoroughly vetted you. Good luck."

We shook hands, and I drove to my parents' home as quickly as possible. If I was very lucky Mum would still be out when I got there.

⁓

My mother wasn't home. Detective Chandler was, and she let me know the moment I opened the door that she was not at all amused.

"Are you insane? Going out without telling me? Somebody is trying to kill you!"

"There's been no threat for two weeks."

"Yes, because you have sensibly stayed out of sight in the house!"

"I'm going nuts sitting around all day. I needed to go outside."

She shook her head and looked disappointed. "You waited until I went shopping so I couldn't stop you. What was so important?"

I fished the knife roll from my bag.

"I wanted my knives."

"They're exactly the same as your father's."

"No, these are *mine*." She raised an eyebrow. "It's a chef thing. Besides, I got a call from a potential client while I was out. You don't want me to be a dead beat, do you?"

"You took a *phone call*? You *are* insane. What if he was the one who shot at you?"

"I'd have flattened him."

"Just because you are good at Krav Maga doesn't mean you're invincible."

"I met him in my living room, not in a dark alley, and a bow isn't a close-combat weapon. I had my baton nearby."

"Do you know how many cops are shot with their own guns? Again, a baton isn't a magic wand that makes you invulnerable."

I was almost stupid enough to say "whatever," but I really didn't want the argument to get completely out of hand. I compromised.

"Maybe, but at least having a new client will free you from babysitting me, and let you get back to your life."

"Oh? And how do you figure that?"

"I'll be heading for London as soon as possible. That should keep me out of the shooter's way."

"Seriously? Ontario or England? What's there?"

"England. A professor who's an expert in nineteenth century Finnish epic poetry."

She gave me that dubious look. "It must be one weird case."

I thought about my suspicion that demons might be involved. "I hope not. It's just property recovery. I'm told that he knows where it is."

"You've never been outside Canada. I hope you know what you're doing."

"Mum, I always know what I'm doing. I already have a passport."

She snorted, which I thought was quite unattractive. "You be careful. Please."

"When am I not careful?"

She didn't even bother to answer. I very sensibly shut up, and went to my room to read the case file more carefully.

CHAPTER 3

Flight of Fancy

Mum and I were a bit cool toward each other for the next while. It would have been less awkward if I could have left immediately. Unfortunately, when I did a bit of research on international travel there was this thing called an International Driving Permit that I'd need if I wanted to drive in other countries. It was available from only one place, and getting it would take two to three weeks.

At first I wasn't going to bother, but the more I thought about it the more it made sense as a precaution. That put my departure off until May 21.

I contacted Mr. Hoag who didn't seem to care about the delay. In my experience, clients aren't that understanding about a several week delay in starting a case. My nagging worry that this case was too good to be true returned.

While I was waiting I dug into other things that might come in handy, including reading the whole Kalevala. There weren't a lot of details in it about the Sampo except for the poet having a real fascination with its lid.

The permit arrived only ten days later. Mum grudgingly agreed that my apartment was probably safe for civilians, especially if I wasn't in the country, so Kali agreed to take care of Yoko while I was away. I changed my reservations to the fourteenth, packed, and contacted the British Museum to make an appointment with Professor Nieminen on Friday.

Dad drove me to the Calgary airport, and Wednesday evening I was on a plane bound for London. My client's credit card had worked perfectly, which rather surprised me. I had to pay a penalty for the last minute reservation changes, but again my client didn't care.

As an airplane virgin, I was too excited to do any sleeping while we were in the air. My first disillusionment as to the joys of air travel was a three hour layover in Toronto. How much excitement is there in Pearson International Airport at six in the morning? Just enough to keep me from getting any sleep.

We landed at Heathrow at around nine p.m. local time. By the time I deplaned I had a pretty good idea what *jet lag* and *stiff muscles* meant.

My first task was to find the outside world. I followed the signs to baggage reclaim even though I'd crammed everything into my carry-on. It wasn't like I would need a dozen pairs of shoes and an evening gown for this trip.

Three hundred metres later I got to passport control which was a huge hall with those tape stands you see in banks so customers can snake their way to a teller. One set of lines was labelled "UK/EU Passports" and the other was labelled "All Other Passports." I guessed that meant me. I joined the end of a line behind a man in his early thirties.

To keep myself awake I said, "is the line always this long?"

He looked amused. "First time at Heathrow?"

"First time outside Canada."

"This is nothing. During busy times I've seen lines over two hours long. We should be through this in twenty minutes."

He seemed nice, and under normal conditions I'd have kept asking questions to see if he might be interested in an assignation. Now that I was in England it seemed as though I should have an assignation rather than merely hooking up with a hot guy.

For once, I was too exhausted to be interested no matter how cute he was. I let it pass.

He was wrong. It was only about fifteen minutes before I was standing before the counter. I handed all my papers to the Sikh officer who did various things with them, asked me some questions, and then handed the documents back with a smile.

"Welcome to the UK."

The next ordeal was customs. Amazingly, there was actually a line for "nothing to declare." Given that my entire luggage consisted of a change of clothing, toiletries, and extra underwear, I was through in seconds.

I was now officially in England. There were a lot of people going in all directions, but I finally found a sign pointing me down a ramp to the Underground. Another 500 metres on a moving walkway, and I came out at *Heathrow Central Terminals 1, 2, 3*. Honestly, that's the name of the station.

A colourful train arrived a few minutes later, and the first thing I noticed in the car was that, unlike the C-train at home, the seats had armrests. There weren't many people on the train, so I flumped into a seat and tried not to doze off during the 45 minute ride.

The Tube only stayed underground for a few minutes, then became a regular surface rail line. After a long time it submerged again, and after another long time we pulled into Green Park station. The names of the stations themselves sounded English rather than Canadian: Hatton Cross, Acton Town, Turnham Green, Hammersmith, Earl's Court, Baker Street. It wasn't until I saw the Baker Street station that London began to feel real to me.

At Green Park I transferred to the Victoria Line heading south. According to what I'd read online we actually passed *under* Buckingham Palace to Victoria Station. Cool.

I was definitely not in Canada any more. Victoria Station was huge and, well, Victorian with a thin overlay of modern. My hotel was supposed to be next door, so I ignored the information counter and braved the streets.

My first steps outside only drove home feeling of foreign soil even more. The cars had unfamiliar license plates. The buses were different. A double-decker bus went past. Even the smell of the city was different. Everybody who was talking was speaking with an English accent.

The hotel I'd picked was central to a lot of things. If it had been another client I'd have spent a lot of time comparing rates to find somewhere cheap. As it was the rates didn't seem too horrible, and the online reviews made it sound good.

I think I was expecting something like hotels I'd been in at home with modern decor. Nope. This was an historical romance. Passing through the revolving doors I was in a marble lobby. The walls were marble, the floor was marble, the columns were marble except for the pseudo-Egyptian capitals which were gold. It was real gold, not just paint.

There was a huge area rug covering most of the floor. In front of me was a grand staircase with—you guessed it—marble steps and railings. The balusters appeared to be onyx. It was like walking into a palace. A sign to my left said "Reception."

For a moment I wondered if I'd come to the wrong place, but there couldn't be two Grosvenor hotels next to Victoria Station.

The young man at the reception desk gave me a friendly-but-professional look. "Good evening. May I help you?" I felt under-dressed for the part, but I couldn't resist.

"I have a reservation," I said in my best Daniel Craig manner. "Chandler. Veronica Chandler."

He consulted a discretely-placed computer, and his friendly look slipped. "Ah. One moment, please."

"Is something wrong?" Damn it, I knew this was too good to be true. I was about to fall asleep on the lobby carpet.

A woman in an immaculately tailored suit came out of a back office, and glanced at the computer screen. "Good evening, Ms. Chandler. I'm afraid there was a mix up with your reservation."

"Oh, crap," I said, which may not have been the most elegant response imaginable. Where the hell was I going to find a bed in a strange city at an hour before midnight?

She didn't even bat an eye. "Please don't be distressed. We take full responsibility for the error. At the moment we don't have any of the standard single rooms you requested available. As it was entirely our fault, we'd like to offer you the Cora Pearl Suite for the remainder of your stay at same price. Would that be satisfactory?"

I felt my adrenaline start to fade, which only left me feeling more tired. At least it sounded like I'd get a bed. "Perfectly."

I had no idea who Cora Pearl was, but I certainly knew what she looked like. A huge portrait of a sultry woman hung directly above the king-sized bed. The whole suite was decorated with what I suspected were real Victorian antiques. There was a subtle BDSM vibe to the place.

The bathroom was huge with a separate room for the toilet. I made a note to have a good, long soak in the claw-foot tub after as many hours of sleep as I could manage.

Exhaustion made it hard even to get undressed and brush my teeth, even though my body thought it wasn't yet supper time of some day or another. I did remember to ask for a wake-up call at eight o'clock the next morning. My appointment with the professor was at ten.

I don't even remember rolling over once my head hit the pillow.

∽

An annoying sound woke me. I fumbled for the phone beside the bed, and grunted into it.

"Good morning, Ms. Chandler. This is your wake up call. We'd like to remind you that breakfast is available to you in our Club Lounge."

I cleared my throat, hoping to mimic human speech. "Thanks." That was welcome news. My stomach was letting me know very clearly that it had missed supper.

The Club Lounge looked just like you'd imagine: A Victorian gentleman's club with wing-backed leather chairs and a fire place. Fortunately, this club wasn't reserved for men only. They also had wonderful, creamy scrambled eggs with sausages, toast, jam, and two cups of coffee.

The hotel had free Wi-Fi, so after breakfast I e-mailed Kali and Mum on my phone to let them know I was still alive, and that nobody had tried to kill me yet.

The concierge called me a real London black taxi to take me to the British Museum. I tried not to bounce up and down and squeal like an idiot as he wove through traffic while my nose was glued to the window.

He seemed amused. "First time in London, miss?"

"Does it show?"

"Only to a seasoned observer such as myself. I'm sure nobody else would notice at all."

I was in an entire country of Englishmen and the driver looked to be in his twenties. Have I mentioned recently how sexy an English accent is?

To get into the British Museum you pass through ornate wrought iron gates into a huge forecourt, then into what looks like an immense complex of Greek temples. Inside the front door was the Great Court: two acres of space with an amazing tessellated glass dome overhead. I suspected that the entire Glenbow Museum at home would have fit into the Court.

The information desk was obvious, and a nice man smiled as I approached.

"May I help you?"

"I have an appointment to see Professor Seppo Nieminen."

"Your name?"

"Chandler. Veronica Chandler."

He spoke on the telephone for a few moments. He wasn't smiling when he turned back to me, the handset still by his ear.

"I'm sorry, but Professor Nieminen is no longer with the Museum."

"What? When did he leave?"

"I wasn't told."

Crap. Now what? "Is there anyone from that department I could speak to?"

He relayed my question.

"Doctor McGuffin will be down as soon as he can."

I wandered aimlessly for several minutes, peeking at the exhibit halls that branched off from the Court before a man in his forties approached me.

"Ms. Chandler? I'm Fionn McGuffin. I understand you had an appointment with Professor Nieminen." I found his Irish accent lovely.

"Yes. I was going to consult with him regarding his work on Finnish mythology."

"I hope you haven't come far. He had to leave rather abruptly."

"I flew in from Canada yesterday evening," I said.

"Oh dear. I'm dreadfully sorry that you've wasted your trip." *No kid-*

ding. I could have slept in this morning.

"Is there any way I can get in contact with him?"

He shook his head. "Seppo is a bit of an odd duck. He's private even for a Finn. He doesn't use telephones unless he must, and he doesn't believe in e-mail at all."

"Did he return home?"

"Yes, I believe so."

"Can you get me his address? It's quite urgent that I speak with him."

He hesitated. "I'm not sure I can do that. Please don't take this personally, but you must understand that I have no way of knowing if he wants you to contact him. I'm sure you understand it's a matter of respecting his privacy."

"He *did* make an appointment with me for today. Unless you think he left the country just to avoid me." I tried to look as innocent as possible.

He hesitated again, then said "you can try contacting the Karelian Institute at the University of Eastern Finland in Joensuu. I'm afraid that's as much as I can do for you."

I thanked him, and wondered what I was going to do now. According to my phone there was a flight leaving for Finland in 70 minutes. It would take a major miracle and a teleporter for me to catch that one. The options after the weekend were much better.

Oh dear, whatever would I do in London by myself with three days to kill?

∞

I spent the next several hours wandering around the museum. There was no hope that I could see all eight million exhibits in one day. The size and scope of the collection was overwhelming.

On my way out I stopped at the gift shop and bought Kali a statue of Isis for her goddess collection. It hoped that it would fit into my luggage and I wouldn't have to buy another suitcase just for souvenirs.

Another taxi took me to the one place in London that I considered absolutely mandatory for me to visit: The Sherlock Holmes Museum at 221B Baker Street. It was everything I'd hoped it would be. Of course I bought matching deer-stalker hats for myself and Mum in the gift shop.

On the way out I paused to get my bearings, and noticed a young man on the other side of the road intently looking at a shop window. He stood out because he didn't look like the kind of man who would be fascinated by a nail salon, especially with the way he was trying to hide in the popped collar of his jacket. He looked like he'd have been more at home selling drugs in a school yard.

Once he had my attention, I also saw that he wasn't looking at the inside of the shop. He was using the window as a mirror to observe the museum. As soon as he saw me looking at him he suddenly turned away and started reading a magazine he pulled from his pocket. If I was paranoid, say for example because somebody had recently tried to kill me, I might think he was surveilling me.

It's almost always better to think about a situation before acting. If he was watching me, how had he known I'd be there? Even I didn't know until part way through my tour of the Museum, and I hadn't told anybody but the cab driver.

I'd expect someone connected with my would-be killer to be on a roof top looking at me through a rifle scope, or at least a crossbow scope.

I decided that I was being paranoid. Maybe he was just girl watching. I didn't think it likely, but it could happen. There were a few easy ways to see if he was after me.

As long as I was on a busy street I was safe. Baker Street is one-way, so it was easy to jog across the road between traffic, pull out my phone, and take a panoramic photo of the museum and surrounding street just like any other tourist. The man wandered away from me up the street, then leaned against a lamp post a few metres away to read his magazine again.

I took the panorama shot from left to right, sweeping across the museum, and ending with a picture of my possible stalker. As soon as the camera got close to him he quickly raised the magazine to cover his face. It was an instinctive reaction on his part, but awful tradecraft. It told me that he really was watching me.

Perhaps there was somebody else on the street who was under surveillance, but it was unlikely. Wouldn't *that* be a coincidence!

It was getting toward supper time, even if my stomach wasn't used to the new time zone yet. The Baker Street Tube Station was just over a hundred metres down the street, so I strolled away from him. As I went I did some research on my phone.

Rather than trying to use shop windows to see if he was following me (it's much harder than you think), as soon as I had my answers I used my phone held down at my side to take a picture behind me.

The man was indeed following me. He didn't even know enough tradecraft to walk on the other side of the street, and was about ten metres back.

I stopped, and looked at shops on the other side of the street. He stopped and went back to his magazine. Nobody else on either side of the street appeared to care about either of us.

I needed to know if he was part of a team, so I re-crossed the road during a gap in the traffic. If he had partners, he would stay on his own side and let his partner on this side pick up the tail.

He crossed the street. Whoever he was, he was either working alone or he had no idea at all how do conduct surveillance.

Who would be tailing me? Mr. Hoag hadn't mentioned that anybody else was after the Sampo, but that didn't mean that there wasn't. It might be somebody affiliated with my would-be murderer, but that didn't seem likely. It was expensive and unnecessary to send an assassin to England. If they wanted to try again they could just wait for me to return to Canada.

Enough of this. I took another photo of him as I came abreast of the Tube station entrance. I stopped, and my new friend predictably took out his magazine again.

Eat my dust, amateur.

When there was a gap in the traffic with more coming I suddenly darted across. It would take him at least a few seconds to react, find another gap, and follow me. I'd established that my client's credit card worked for touchless payment, and I hardly broke my stride as I went through the turnstile.

Some parts of the London Underground almost seemed to be designed to allow somebody to throw off a tail. Baker Street served *five* different Tube lines on as many levels. I wanted the Bakerloo line which was two levels down. Needless to say, it's a very busy station, and my height was an asset. Once I was in a crowd I was almost impossible to spot.

It was near the beginning of rush hour. The crowd was thick but not shoulder-to-shoulder, so I ran, dodging and weaving like a street urchin until I reached the escalators. I think I startled a few people, but my passage didn't disturb the flow of people enough to point me out to my pursuer.

Once on the platform, I buried myself in another group of commuters. I was invisible from more than several metres away.

When the train arrived there was no sign of my shadow. Either I'd lost him, or just possibly he'd been after somebody else after all.

At Oxford Circus I got off, and stood beside the Help Point, ready to push the big green Emergency button if he appeared. Between that, the CCTV security cameras on the platforms, and my willingness to defend myself with extreme prejudice I wasn't in much danger. By the time the train left there was still no sign of my possible stalker. I transferred to the Victoria line to take me back to my hotel.

Before having supper I made a list of attractions I wanted to visit, and made arrangements with the concierge to get me tickets for Saturday morning. There was no way I was letting a stalker keep me from enjoying my sightseeing. I just wished I'd been able to bring my baton with me on this trip.

The Saturday morning wake-up call was easier to take. That's my story and I'm sticking to it.

Again I braved the Tube to get to Westminster station. Crossing Westminster Bridge I took pictures of the Houses of Parliament, the London Eye on the far shore, and anything else that looked interesting.

Everything in London looks interesting.

The London Eye was just as huge as it looks in movies. It never stops rotating unless a wheelchair passenger is getting on, and one revolution takes half an hour.

I'd paid extra for a ticket to go to the head of the line, regardless of when I arrived. It wasn't long before I was getting into the slowly moving capsule.

The capsules have seats, but you can also walk around to see the view from various directions. I spent about half my time looking out at the scenery, and half taking pictures. It's a good thing my phone has a large memory card. To me, everything in London was scenic.

When my capsule got to ground level the doors opened, and we all reluctantly filed out.

There was another landmark I wanted to see nearby. At least, nearby in Canadian terms. As this was what I was told was an unusually sunny day, I took the Queen's Walk south, enjoying the sights along the Thames.

As I made for the Queen's Walk I saw my stalker loitering nearby. His technique had marginally improved. I wouldn't have noticed him if I hadn't seen him before, if he hadn't been wearing exactly the same outfit, and if he wasn't reading the same magazine.

Using the same phone trick I watched him follow me. I decided that he needed a name; I would call him Algernon. He was a lot further back than he'd been the day before. That made me a bit nervous. It might mean that he now had a team. I couldn't spot anybody else tailing me, but that didn't mean they weren't there. For all I knew they had somebody with binoculars watching me from the other side of the Thames.

About a kilometre from the Eye I left the Queen's Walk for the Albert Embankment, which despite its name is a street. Algernon was still behind me. Ahead I could see a tall building that looked like a hotel except for the forest of antennas on its roof.

When I got closer I saw that the building was surrounded by a wall topped with an iron fence. The tops of the bars were bent outward, which suggested that casual visitors might not be welcome. A solid steel gate labelled OUT faced onto the street and reinforced that impression. It was entirely functional, with no attempt at decoration. It gave the decided impression that the inhabitants took things extremely seriously.

I was getting that giddy fan girl feeling again. After a few dozen metres a car with blacked out windows turned into another gate just ahead of me which opened at its approach. I wondered how that worked. Probably some really clever encrypted radio signal, or perhaps just a guard pulling on the gate. It hadn't closed yet as I passed by, and the gentleman blocking the entrance wore a black uniform with a white belt. He carried an assault rifle, and didn't return my smile. I had the good sense not to take a picture of him.

Turning west onto the Vauxhall Bridge, I took several photos of the building from the Thames side where the stone, steel, and glass façade of the Secret Intelligence Service headquarters, also known as MI6, looked like a stepped castle. I could identify the windows near the top where, according to at least one of the movies, Q Division was located. Not that I believed it for a moment. I wasn't completely irrational.

But that didn't matter to the Canadian fan girl who got odd looks from pedestrians as she giggled and jumped up and down with excitement.

Gods, I can be so geeky at times.

At the far end of the bridge I crossed the street so I could flag down a taxi. So far I hadn't minded too much as Algernon following me at a discrete distance, but I wasn't going to let him have his own way all afternoon.

He never had a chance. He was still on the north side of the bridge when I caught the cab.

"Where to?"

I felt whimsical. "Some place good for lunch."

"Do you mean good as in posh, or good as in yummy?"

"Yummy. Definitely."

"Any preference as to nationality? Sit down or take away?"

"No preference. I'm going on the Jack the Ripper tour this afternoon, so somewhere between here and there would be good."

"Right. You have plenty of time, so sit down Indian it is."

༺♥༻

The outside of the Khushbu Grill House was painted a startling purple, but on the inside it was all gleaming chrome and modern tables. The staff were friendly, and my lamb curry, rice, and sweet lassi were delicious. The serving dishes were traditional iron ones with big loop handles. I finished in lots of time to make it to my tour.

I could have taken the Tube and been there in five minutes, but the online map insisted that it would only take 15 minutes to walk.

Everywhere I went in London there was history, and nothing was quite like it was at home. The traffic drove on the left, road signs were different, the road markings were different, and buildings centuries old rubbed shoulders with new ones. I could have happily spent weeks exploring.

The walking tour of Jack the Ripper's haunts begins at the Tower Hill Tube station. There were several companies, and I'd picked this one specifically because the world expert on the Ripper was their tour guide.

The only thing that detracted from the tour was that I tended to keep watching for Algernon. There was only one possible way that I could think of that he had found me on Baker Street and at the Eye, and that was that the concierge at my hotel had told him. I would be having words with the manager about that when I got back. What I couldn't figure out was how he knew where I'd be staying in the first place, and what his game was.

Forget it for now, I told myself. *Enjoy the tour.*

It was just as fascinating as I'd expected, a combination of early forensics, investigation, and living history. Being there, actually walking the same streets and lanes, gave me a sense of belonging that I'd never gotten from history classes in school. I was *there*, breathing the same air. It was also interesting how the city had changed in the past 127 years. One of the murder sites was now in the middle of a car park.

The Ten Bells was a public house where prostitutes and a variety of unsavoury characters drank—at least in Victorian times. Two of Jack's victims were known to have been clients: Annie Chapman and Mary Jane Kelly. It is said that Mary used to pick up customers just outside, and was quite abusive to any girls who tried to intrude on her territory.

These days the pub caters to hipsters and other gentry of the now trendy Whitechapel and Spitalfields.

I ended up at a table with an American couple who had also been on the tour.

"Hey, I'm Herb and this is my girlfriend..."

"Danita," she said.

"Veronica. Did you enjoy the tour?"

Danita was a gusher. "It was *awesome*! This is our first time in England and everything is so *amazing*!"

"I know the feeling. I spent most of the day yesterday at the British Museum, then I went to the Sherlock Holmes Museum."

"Have you been in a taxi yet? They're *just* like in the movies!"

"Yes. A couple of times. Have you been on the Eye? The view is spectacular."

"Not yet. We actually saw MI6 headquarters. I thought it was just made up for the movies, but it's *real!*"

Danita didn't seem to be able to speak without exclamation marks. Normally it might have annoyed me, but it perfectly mirrored my own feelings about London.

"I saw that today. A car was just arriving at the back and I saw one of the guards."

"Oh my God, we'll have to try that! I wonder if we'll get in trouble if we hang around for a while?"

Herb decided to get in a good edge-wise word. "Next week we're going to Cardiff to tour the locations where they film Doctor Who."

"*Now* I'm envious. I'd love to see that."

"On the way we're seeing Stonehenge."

That was it. I had a small geek meltdown. Britain was too full of things to see. I'd have to come back as many times as I could manage.

I was sipping the last bit of my Truman's Budburst when I noticed a familiar and unwelcome face loitering outside the pub on Fournier Street. My slight amusement at seeing him earlier vanished.

"Excuse me a minute."

I casually got up from the table, and sauntered over toward some people at another table as if I was going to join them. Instead, I put my empty glass down, and bolted out the door. He didn't have time to run before I'd pinned him against the stone window jamb with my hand on his throat. In case he was armed, I was ready to crush his throat while kneeing him in the stomach.

"Who the hell are you and why are you following me?"

He made a weak gurgling noise. I released the pressure slightly so he could talk. His eyes darted toward something over my shoulder and got bigger in a mixed expression that was a combination of fear and relief.

I pushed him into the jamb and ducked. A foot whooshed through the space where my head had been and damned near took Algernon's head off instead. I pivoted on one foot, the other outstretched in a sweeping kick.

From my split-second view of a black dress and long hair I assumed that my assailant was a woman. By the time I swept her leg, she had almost recovered from her kick. Damn, she was fast.

Not quite fast enough. She went down on the pavement as I jumped to my feet. Hipster bystanders scattered in all directions and formed a perimeter. She did a sort of break dance manoeuvre, and was on her feet again almost as fast as I was. Out of the corner of my eye Algernon was running away on Fournier Street. Clever lad.

We paused for a half second. Now that she wasn't spinning in midair, I could see that my attacker was maybe a few years older than me, and appeared to have Japanese ancestry. Her long black hair was tied back in a pony tail, and she was not looking friendly.

I got time to say, "Who the hell are *you*?" before she began weaving back and forth in a weird little dance I'd never seen before. Her arms were waving in front of her like a preying mantis in a three count as her feet stepped right and left in a sort of shallow lunge stance in a two count. It was creepily mesmerizing.

On one of her steps she jumped into the air, spun around and I found myself with another foot heading toward my face. My back was almost against the pub window which made it impossible for me to duck and sweep again.

I burst forward and with my arm I caught the inside of her knee as it swept across. Pivoting and bringing my arm down caused her leg to rotate. That flipped her over while in flight, and her other foot caught me hard across my chest before she landed face first on the pavement where I could jump on her.

That was the theory. In practice she managed to pull her head in and land on her shoulder. She rolled, narrowly missing a bollard by the curb, and sprang to her feet again.

The whole situation was going on too long. We had gathered a crowd who might decided at any moment that this was a real fight rather than some kind of performance art.

As long as nobody called the police I should be all right, but since I had no idea who she and Algernon were, or who they worked for, I might end up staying in England longer than I wanted as a guest of Her Majesty.

"Look, just tell me what you want," I said as she resumed her dance. I dodged to one side to spoil the timing of whatever she had planned. She moved her dance in the same direction.

At that exact moment something hit the side of the pub hard. Whatever it was gouged a deep hole and shattered the stone facing. I felt the sting of several specks of rock hitting me.

I was facing more or less southwest, and in the growing twilight I caught the muzzle flash on top of the Barclay's diagonally across from the pub. If we hadn't moved the bullet would have hit one or both of us.

We both stared at the hole for an instant, then she took off at a crouching run up Commercial Street. Despite being maybe ten centimetres taller than me she was dodging and weaving through the crowd as well as I could. By staying low she was using the crowd as human shields. That wasn't as evil as it sounds; sniper rifles have a limited number of shots, so they can't just shoot an entire crowd out of the way to get to a hidden target. They wait for the clear shot.

The bystanders were bystanding, still thinking that this was some kind of street theatre performance and applauding our moves. I could stay there and maybe get shot, or follow her and maybe get some answers. I followed.

As I ducked through the audience we got another polite round of applause.

She passed a pizza shop, and darted right into a lane called Puma Court. I swung myself around on the traffic bollard as I rounded the corner after her, then nearly bowled her over as she stopped. She was trying to get her breath back. Score one for me. The altitude of Calgary is over a kilometre higher than London. I wasn't even breathing hard.

"Somebody's shooting at us," she said in what I thought was a fairly upscale London accent.

"I saw a muzzle flash from the roof across the street. Are they after you or me?"

"I have no idea. Who are you?"

"You attacked first. Who are *you*?"

"We're out of the shooter's line of sight, but we need to move."

"Agreed. Where?"

She jogged along Puma Court. I kept enough distance between us that I could take her down if she turned to fight.

"Why was Algernon following me?"

"Who?"

"That guy I was about to question when you showed up."

"His name's Natt, not Algernon. He's my assistant and friend."

"All right, why did you attack me?"

"Obviously, because he's my assistant and friend. I tracked his phone and arrived just in time to see you choking him."

"Why has he been following me for two days?"

"Has he?"

"I spotted him yesterday at the Sherlock Holmes Museum, today at the Eye, and here."

"It certainly wasn't on my behalf. Unless..."

"Unless what?"

"It's possible that he thought I wanted you followed. My brother left a note that you were coming to London. Natt got hold of it before I did, and it seems that he decided to keep you under surveillance without telling me. When I got the message I traced his phone. You know the rest."

"Why would you want to follow me?"

"I have no idea. My brother and I have a—complicated—relationship. The subtext of his message wasn't obvious."

We came out onto Wilkes Street and turned north, then east on

Princelet. I was trying to keep track of where we were in case she got away from me and I had to make my way back by myself.

She pulled out her phone and speed dialled.

"Lana here. There's been an incident. Pick us up at the Old Truman Brewery."

I stopped walking. "Enough of this. What is going on? Who are you? Why are we going to a brewery?"

She turned to face me. "As to the former, the Old Truman Brewery is a trendy arts and club complex just up the road that, obviously, used to be a brewery. We should be safe in the crowd until we can get away. My name is Lana Reviere. I'm an independent criminologist and investigator. And you are...?"

"Veronica Chandler. You should teach Natt better tradecraft; I spotted him the moment I came out of the museum. You really have no idea why your brother would care that I'm in London?"

"Female investigators in our age bracket aren't common. I take it that your trip triggered some kind of alert, although I've never been clear about where he gets his information. Why are you in London?"

"At the moment I'm just sight-seeing until my flight leaves."

Princelet Street was—eclectic is the only word I can think to describe it. All the buildings were identical three-storey brick and were probably built in the 1700s. The ground floor was always a business of some kind, and those ground floor facades were anything from 300 year old red brick, to beautiful dark wood, to modern stucco and blonde wood. The street was just wide enough for a line of cars parked on our left, and a single lane just wide enough for a mini-van. The sidewalk was protected by the painted iron bollards that seemed to be everywhere in this area. I hadn't forgotten that we were fleeing from a sniper, but the architecture of London continued to amaze me. Besides, we were moving away from the shooter on what I hoped was an unpredictable route. There were no pedestrians, which meant we had less cover but also fewer potential casualties.

At the end of the block we came to Brick Lane. Despite its name, it was another narrow, one-way street like Princelet. I was still getting used to the street names being on signs attached to the buildings rather than on separate posts like they are in Calgary.

"Where now?"

Neither of us spotted anything unusual in any direction. Lana turned left and crossed to the east side of the street while I followed.

"You don't seem surprised that we were shot at," I said.

"I've been the recipient of similar attention in the past. You don't seem surprised either."

"As you said, similar things have happened to me before. Who do you think the bullet was meant for?"

"There's no way of telling at the moment. Is your entire trip a holiday, or are you working on a case as well?"

"A bit of both. The person I came to see has left England so I thought I'd catch some sights before following."

She stopped abruptly in front of a restaurant. From the shop signs it looked like this was the Indian quarter of Spitalfields.

"This person—he wouldn't happen to be Finnish, would he?"

"Son of a bitch."

"Professor Nieminen?"

"What are the odds that two people meeting by chance just happen to be investigating the same case?"

"Until a minute ago I'd have said slim to none."

"Shit. This is ridiculous. Let me guess—you have been asked to locate something unusual."

"An ancient artifact."

"Shit. Okay, so we're looking for the same thing, which means that either somebody is after one of us for other reasons, or they don't want one or both of us to find the—item."

"Obviously. Do you have anybody who would want you dead?"

"Maybe. There was a half-hearted attempt on my life before I left home. You?"

"I'm afraid so. My sister's father would love to see me turn up floating face-down in the Thames so he can—repossess her."

"That sounds like an interesting story."

"One for another time."

"I wonder if this is why your brother thought my arrival was significant to you?"

"Possibly."

A yellow brick structure spanned the road ahead. Above the arched windows I could see TRUMAN on the wall. I assumed that this was the old brewery. As we approached I saw a big orange sign that let me know we were no longer in the best of neighbourhoods: PLEASE USE THE TOILETS PROVIDED.

Lana was right. The area was packed with people. Unless the sniper caught up with us and found a lucky high perch there was no way for anybody to take a shot at us. Even then it would be difficult, especially if they were after me. Sometimes, being short is useful.

She led us into a narrow loading area. Although we had no exit, it would be almost impossible for a shooter to get at us.

"Did you speak with Professor Nieminen at all?"

"Not as much as I'd like," I said.

"Neither did I." We looked at each other. Translation: Both of us had completely missed him.

Ten minutes later a black cab pulled up. Natt was peering out the side window. Lana got in without hesitation, pushing Natt to the far side, and I followed her.

Natt looked like I made him nervous. Good. He must have already given the driver an address; we left without anybody speaking.

"Where are we going?"

She kept her eyes on the road. "My flat in Paddington."

"No, we aren't. You are dropping me off at my hotel. I'm willing to accept your explanation for now, but I'm not going anywhere in the dead of night with people who have been spying on me and trying to beat me senseless." I noticed the driver perk up as he heard that. I knew that London cabbies were supposed to be "of good character," and I hoped that he'd act on my behalf if he thought something was amiss. For my part, trying to fight an expert in the back of a cab, even if Natt didn't take part, sounded like an experience I could live without. At least she wouldn't be able to kick me.

Lana looked at me steadily for a few seconds. I glared back at her just as hard.

"Very well. Driver, please take us to the..." She glanced at Natt.

"Grosvenor Hotel," he said. So he knew where I was staying. That did not improve my mood.

The driver relaxed slightly. "Right you are."

⁂

It had been an icily quiet ride. I got out in front of my hotel, and the taxi took off into the night before I could offer any money. If Lana and Natt wanted to pay the whole fare that was fine with me.

I briefly thought of calling the police to report the shooter, but that would have led to a lot of questions and delay for not much gain. If it was the same bad guys who had taken potshots at me back in Calgary they was unlikely to have left any evidence.

Now that I knew somebody else was after the Sampo I had to move quickly.

If the concierge was feeding information to Natt and Lana I might be able to use that to my advantage. On my way into the lobby I stopped by his desk, and asked him to find out when I could get a flight back to Calgary on Monday afternoon. Just to be mean, I also had him find me a small suitcase for my souvenirs, and gave him a deadline of ten p.m. to have it delivered.

Once in my suite I made online reservations for the next flight going to Helsinki, which was a British Airways flight leaving at 11:25 the next morning. I also made reservations for the connecting flight, a hotel reservation in Joensuu, and a car rental.

Despite my horror at the hour, I also arranged a wake up call for six o'clock. I wanted to be gone long before Lana and Natt would think of setting up surveillance on me.

To save time I packed, and had a large supper in The Brasserie just off the lobby so I wouldn't need breakfast.

When I got back to my suite I soaked in the tub for a long time. Lana's kick had left a bruise in the middle of my chest that made deep breathing painful, but otherwise wasn't too bad. I knew I'd been lucky. That girl kicked like a psychotic ostrich.

When my new luggage arrived I transferred a few pieces of clothing from my carry-on, and filled the empty space with fruit from the gift basket in the suite. I had no idea if anything would be served on the flight and I wanted to avoid starving if possible. If they confiscated it at the Finnish border it wouldn't really matter.

I didn't sleep well, and six o'clock came much too soon. As quickly as possible I checked out of the Grosvenor, took the Tube back to Heathrow, and checked in for my flight to Helsinki. Once I was in the boarding hall I was safe from Lana and Natt's interference.

In due time we boarded the jet. There were a few empty seats, one of which was beside me. I hoped it stayed that way so I could sprawl, even if it was only a three hour flight. Who knows? I might even get more sleep.

I was gazing out the window watching the ground crew doing the mysterious and complex things they do before take off when I felt somebody sit in the aisle seat beside me.

"Good morning," Lana said. "Lovely day for a trip, isn't it?"

"What," I said, "the hell."

"We're both working the same case, and as we don't know who shot at us or why, it seemed to me safer if we work together. At least until we find the Sampo. Then I suppose we can always flip a coin for possession."

It was time for some good Colombian swearing. "*Pichar*," I said quietly as I watched us thunder down the runway.

I like working alone. At least if I'm relying on myself I don't have to guess at other people's skills and reliability.

We didn't say anything more until the seat belt sign went off when I took the initiative with a bit of sarcasm. "Lucky for you that you just happened to get the seat next to me."

The sarcasm seemed to go right by her. "As they say, fortune favours the bold. I called the airline and told them that my sister-in-law and I were going to Joensuu, but she'd probably forgotten to get us seats together. They were very accommodating."

"And how did you know I'd be on this flight?"

"It was a reasonable deduction. Professor Nieminen is from Joensuu, and this is the first flight to Finland since last night."

So much for my misdirection with the concierge.

"Have you ever been there before?"

"Finland? Never. You?"

"This is my first time outside Canada. I don't suppose you are ready to tell me who your client is?"

"I can't share his name, but he's a research fellow at Oxford. He caught wind that the artifact had been seen in historical times, and hired me to look into it for him. You don't need to know more. And yours?"

"A group of collectors."

"It does sound like giving the artifact to my client would be more ethical than giving it to yours. Mine wants it for open research. It won't be hidden away in a private gallery."

"You don't know that. My understanding is that pieces that are being studied live in the back rooms where the public never sees them. Maybe your client just wants the academic props that come with bagging a rare object. Since my client is a consortium, it's not clear that they would be hiding it anywhere, unless you believe that they have a communal private gallery, or will be moving it back and forth between their secret vaults."

She waved dismissively. "Perhaps. We can discuss this later. In the meantime, what shall we talk about for three hours?"

We both tried to get a feel for each other by talking about normal thing: music, movies, and literature. We had a surprising amount in common. Lana was widely read, and an interesting person who loved to learn as much as she could about the world. It would be easy for me to forget that we were rivals.

When she wasn't trying to play soccer with my head, that is.

It's funny how we subconsciously picture foreign places. I didn't realize that I had a mental image of Finland until we landed. Helsinki Vantaa was laid out almost identically to every other airport I'd seen (all three of them), which is to say a long walk, baggage reclamation, passport control, and customs. We then checked back in with the airline for our connecting flight. The decor of the terminal was a cross between the Crystal Palace and an IKEA showroom.

Being used to Alberta, it felt odd to me that there were no mountains in the distance. We couldn't see the city itself from the airport, but various posters strewn about the walls showed a city that in many ways was like London but with fewer tall buildings. Contrary to my assumptions, there wasn't a single Nordic chalet or reindeer in sight. Nor was everything covered in snow.

I took the opportunity to change my hotel reservation to a double room so I could keep a closer eye on Lana. Just because I was beginning to like her didn't mean I trusted her.

It was now almost 5:30 local time, and we had three hours until our flight left for Joensuu.

We'd crossed two time zones, so it was two hours later than I thought it was. My stomach, still trying to adapt to London time, now thought it was three o'clock. The fruit I'd brought hadn't made much of a lunch for the two of us.

The examples of the Finnish language that I saw on signs and posters made me thankful that most of the airport signs were accompanied by icons, and sometimes by English. None of the words looked anything like Spanish, which was the only other language I really knew. It was time to swallow my pride.

"Can you read Finnish?"

Lana frowned. "Not a word. It doesn't even look vaguely familiar."

"If we're going to be working together we should pool our resources. What languages do you speak?"

"English, of course, as well as Japanese, French, and German."

Crap. I was on the short end again. "I know English and Spanish. A bit of French, of course, being Canadian." I doubted that *fromage fort* would get me very far. "Let's find something to eat."

Weirdly enough, the first place we found was called O'Leary's. Lana had a salad while I gorged on a burger and fries. The Finns love coffee, so I was able to top up my caffeine tanks.

"Keep eating," Lana said about half way though our meal. "There's a man watching us who is sitting three tables behind you."

I swallowed. "Are you sure? Maybe he's just getting up his nerve to try to pick us up."

"Not everything is about sex."

"I can dream, can't I?"

"He came in after us and I saw him specifically ask for that seat so he can observe us."

"Maybe it's coincidence."

"He has a book with him, but he hasn't turned a page since he sat down. Either he's the world's slowest reader, or he's watching us."

I resisted the urge to turn around. "There's something even more troubling. We're on the air side of the terminal, so he must be catching a flight. How could anybody have known where we'd be?"

"I didn't take any special precautions when booking my flight. Did you?"

"Nothing past making my own reservations online. I misled the concierge because I thought he was feeding information about me to Natt."

She seemed startled by the thought. "At the *Grosvenor*? A concierge there would probably die before betraying a client. It's a very traditional establishment."

"Then how did Natt find me on Baker Street?"

"I have no idea. Perhaps my brother told him. I'll have to ask him when we get back."

I dabbed my mouth again with the napkin, then made a small show of looking around without actually turning to look at our watcher.

"Any idea where the washroom is?"

"Over there." She pointed behind me. I'd already spotted the WC sign when we came in. The acting was for our watcher's benefit.

I stood up, and ambled past the guy's table without obviously looking at him. He kept his eyes on his book the whole time. For my part it was a wasted effort; I'd never seen him before. There was no sign that he was carrying a weapon, but unless he was something like an air marshal that would be difficult in an airport anyway.

It was hard not to stare at him. He looked like a wrestler who had taken up body building. His long hair somehow looked like an affectation. His face would have looked more at home with a buzz cut.

When I returned we finished our supper, and went to our departure gate. Our flight would leave in an hour. Fifteen minutes before boarding our watcher showed up again, and casually sat reading in our boarding area.

"He seems to have read a lot in the past hour," I said. He was at least a hundred pages further into the book.

"I noticed."

"I wonder if he has a weapon in his checked luggage. Any idea how difficult it is to get a gun in Finland?"

"My understanding is that normally it's quite well controlled. It probably isn't difficult if you have the right connections. The Russian border is only 75 kilometres from Joensuu. There's undoubtedly a black market in weapons, especially with the political situation where we're going."

"What political situation? I don't remember anything on the news."

"The border between Finland and Russia has been—fluid—for a long time. Part of Karelia currently belongs to Finland, and part is Russian. Karelian nationalism has been flaring up recently."

"And Joensuu?"

"Is in North Karelia."

Compared with the rest, Joensuu airport was quaint: one runway, and a single storey terminal with a control tower that had to be all of ten metres high. They rolled out a mobile stair, and we walked across the tarmac to the building.

Our friend with the book had a car waiting to pick him up. It was a relief to see that he was a false alarm.

It turned out that making a car rental reservation was even cleverer than I'd thought. There was only car rental agency at the airport, and it was unmanned unless a customer was on their way.

The town was eleven kilometres from the airport. There was a shuttle, but a car would give us more options depending on what we needed to do in town. For all I knew Professor Nieminen lived on a farm half way to Russia.

Lana didn't have an international driving permit, so it was up to me to be the chauffeur. Finns drove on the same side of the road as North Americans, so I was the logical choice anyway. She offered to split the cost of the rental which was nice of her. If she hadn't I was going to ask for it anyway.

My major problem with driving was that the road signs were a lot different from those I was used to. I'd studied them on the flight, but there's a big difference between recognizing something after thinking about it, and recognizing it when you have to make a snap decision while flying down the highway.

I'd asked the rental guy how to get to our hotel. His English wasn't great, but he drew us a little map with the road numbers and names on it. It looked easy enough, especially since we had an hour before dark.

Regional road 501 was easy to find, being the only one leaving the airport. It was one lane either way with almost no shoulders. Having no idea how zealous Finnish the police were I stuck to the speed limit.

After several kilometres we reached an overpass where we turned onto road nine. It was what we'd call a divided highway. All we needed now was the sign telling us where to exit.

I let Lana navigate so I could keep my eyes on the road. An important-looking sign went by.

"What did that say?"

"*Keskusta, Linnunlahti, Kapykangas.* Nothing about Joensuu. What's our distance?"

"Eight kilometres. We must be getting close."

"That could have been it."

North American road signs tend to be big, which means that they have to be far from the road so nobody hits them. The Finnish signs were tiny in comparison, but they're also much closer to the road. Neither of us saw one that mentioned our destination.

A little later there was another sign.

"Well?"

"Some kind of announcement, but at least it included the name Joensuu."

"That's promising."

At 9.6 kilometres there was another exit. I made a command decision.

"I'm taking this one."

"There's no sign."

"I know, but we're supposed to be there in another 1.4 kilometres. If I'm wrong we can just get back on the highway."

The ramp ended in traffic lights. "Great, this goes to *Keskusta* again."

"Turn right," Lana ordered, looking at her phone. "*Keskusta* isn't a place name. It translates as centre."

"As in city centre?"

"I haven't the foggiest idea. At least we may find somebody we can ask."

"There's a sign coming up. *Areena, uimahalli, jiahalli,* something."

Lana's fingers flashed over her phone. "Arena, swimming baths, ice rink. I didn't catch the rest."

"That sounds like we're getting closer."

I remembered that a sign like a city skyline meant that we were in town, and town speed limits applied. Most of the buildings looked like short apartment blocks. Maybe they were a holdover from when this was Soviet territory. There were a few pedestrians, but there was no parking on any of the roads. There was too much traffic for us to just stop and have a conversation.

Lana was staring at her phone. "I think I've found us. Turn right."

We were among more apartment blocks, and the street was narrower. "This doesn't look good. Now what?"

"Try turning left as soon as you can," she said just as I passed a street.

"Too late. I'll take the next one."

Blocks passed. The blocks in Joensuu are *long*. A bigger street came up. "This looks major."

"*Siltakatu*! Turn left!"

"Silwhat?"

"Just turn left!" I did as I was told.

"Now where are we?"

"This is the street our hotel is on."

I saw a sign with some icons. "What's a *Carelicum*?"

"I can't find a translation. The symbol looks like it could be an information booth of some kind, though."

"I'll follow the pointer. If it's a tourist information place we'll ask there. We don't even know if we're going the right way."

"That's fair. Turn left! I see another sign for *Carelicum*."

"I can't see any other signs."

"Did we pass it?"

"Do I *look* like I know what a *Carelicum* looks like?"

"Forget it. Turn left. Maybe we can get back on *Siltakatu*."

We passed a large building with a banner on the front in English. "At least we've found the art museum," I said.

"What's that on the right?"

"The park?"

"No, that building on the corner."

"Wait, is that our hotel?"

"It's our hotel."

"Oh my god," I said, "I don't believe it! We've found our hotel!"

"Well done. Now, where's the parking?"

"Surely that can't be it." We'd finally found one place in this town with on-street angle parking. It was full.

"Try this lane way on the right."

"Oh yes! A parkade!"

"You mean an underground car park."

"That's right. Correct my English."

"I wouldn't have to if you weren't a bloody colonial."

I found a space and turned off the engine. We'd made it to Joensuu.

Why was I not surprised when the standard twin room looked exactly like an IKEA showroom with two beds?

Monday morning arrived in due course. Lana was out of bed before me. I didn't care.

"Good morning," she said from the room's desk where she was holding her blue phone. "I found Professor Nieminen's office."

"Uh. We should get breakfast first. How far away is his office?"

"About 800 metres."

"Seriously?"

"If we'd turned right at the first exit last night we'd have driven through the middle of the university on *Siltakatu*."

I yawned. "Who knew?"

She was annoyingly awake. "Breakfast is downstairs in the dining room."

I treated myself to a piteous moan before getting out of bed.

I'd never heard of the University of Eastern Finland. My ignorance didn't prevent it from being a famous and respected institution with several campuses.

Professor Nieminen was in the Karelian Institute, which in turn was part of the Department of Social Sciences. If UEF was anything like the University of Calgary, parking on campus would be impossible. We walked from our hotel.

We were in luck again. The sign pointing to the Karelian Institute looked almost the same in Finnish as it would in English. The receptionist was an older woman who looked up as we entered. I hoped she spoke one of our languages.

I tried English first. "We're looking for Professor Nieminen. Is he here?"

She put her hand up, palm forward, and said "*Anteeksi!*" It sounded like a command, whatever it meant. She called louder, "*Aino!*"

A much younger woman poked her head up from behind a partition. "May I help you?" I repeated my question.

She looked puzzled. "Do you mean Professor Nieminen?" Her pronunciation was a lot different from mine. Less like Neeminen and more like Nee-ehmeenen.

"Yes. Professor Seppo Nieminen." I did my best to copy the way she said it.

She looked at us like I'd just asked to take her toddler to the park without supervision. "He's very busy now. Do you have an appointment?"

"I was supposed to meet with him in London before he left, and was hoping to speak with him here."

She seemed displeased, and I wondered what I'd done. It was probably something to do with Finnish social customs. "Who are you?"

I gave her our names. "Come."

Professor Nieminen had an office that looked like most other university offices: a desk, two chairs, a computer, and a ton of books and papers strewn everywhere. He was slowly packing things into boxes.

I had an immediate suspicion as to why he had left the British Museum so abruptly. He was probably around forty years old, but he was emaciated, completely bald, including his eyebrows, his eyes were sunken, and he moved as if he was in pain.

Our guide introduced us. "Professor Nieminen, Ms. Veronica Chandler and Ms. Lana Reviere."

"Professor," I said, extending my hand. He didn't move as we stared at each other. I slowly took my hand back. Lana remained silent.

"I have no appointments today. Goodbye."

"Sir, you had an appointment with me in London. I came from Canada to discuss your work, only to find that you had left before we could talk."

Again we had a staring contest. He awkwardly sat in one of the chairs.

"I'm sorry, you are right. What can I do for you?"

I sat in the other chair, leaving Lana to fend for herself. We might be warming to each other, but she was still a rival.

"I'm told that you can help us find the Sampo."

I saw a flicker of surprise. "What is your interest?"

"We are private investigators. Our clients have hired us to locate the artifact."

Professor Nieminen laughed, a dry, brittle sound that rapidly became wetter-sounding and turned into a cough. For a moment I thought we might have to call for an ambulance. After a while he recovered enough to keep going.

"I'm sorry, but your journey has been in vain. I cannot help you."

Lana sounded impatient. "Why not?"

Professor Nieminen began coughing again, but refused our help. The younger woman, appeared outside his office door with a glass of water for him. She said something in Finnish, but he waved her away.

"My apologies. My health isn't what it once was."

"You're dying," Lana said. I was horrified by her bluntness.

"Yes. That is why my research is not complete. I don't know where the Sampo is and cannot help you."

"We'll do it for you," I said.

"What?" Both of them said in unison.

"We've been hired to find the Sampo, which as I understand it is the point of your work. Give us a copy of your research notes, and we'll finish your research for you."

"How do I know I can trust you not to give the Sampo to some collector who will keep it hidden in a vault?" Lana gave me a blatant *I told you so* glance.

"That isn't out intention. We both agree that it should be available."

She handed him her card. "We're staying at the Cumulus hotel. Contact anybody you know in London, and ask about my reputation."

I wasn't going to be outdone, and handed him my card as well. "You can contact the Calgary Police Service about me. We'll be in town until you can give us an answer either way."

We left him sitting in his office holding our cards in his hands.

∽

The walk back to our hotel was nice. The temperature was about what you'd expect on a late spring day in Calgary.

"What do we do now?" Lana asked.

"I suppose we wait. If we don't hear back from him by Thursday we'll have to nudge him."

"He didn't look like he'll survive until Thursday."

I stopped walking. "What made you tell him that he's dying? I don't know how you were raised, but my parents would call that a screaming lack of tact. I expected him to throw us out after that."

"It was a calculated risk. The Finns value politeness and privacy, but also honesty. He wasn't going to mention anything other than vague generalities about his health, so I reminded him that he has a strictly limited amount of time available to him."

"What if he decides that talking to us is a waste of that time?"

"That's why it's called a calculated risk."

I just shook my head and continued walking. Lana was not doing anything to change my opinion about working alone.

Back at the hotel I sent three e-mails. It would be about 4 a.m. in Calgary so I didn't expect any immediate replies. I gave Mum a rundown on what was happening, leaving out the sniper, and asked her to run a background check on Lana Reviere. I told Dad I was having fun and would try to bring back some European recipes.

The message to Kali was a lot longer, and contained all the details I'd left out of the e-mails to my parents, including the London sniper. I'd learned through painful experience that if I lied to her or tried to protect her she'd hand me my head. She had a very Latina temper.

Once I'd sent my e-mails there was little else to do. All the movies that were playing would be in Finnish, as were the television shows, and probably everything in bookstores. I played some games on my phone for a while, then did some random research. One fun thing about the Finnish language is that it's phonetic. Once you know what the letters sound like, you can actually read things out loud. That seemed like a handy skill for ordering food. Especially since the words for "and" and "please" were so easy.

That reminded me, the hotel restaurant was nice but I wanted to find somewhere more interesting for a celebration supper if the professor cooperated. There was a highly rated restaurant only two blocks away that sounded good. In particular, I could feel myself salivating over the thought of a moose steak.

Lana was lying on her bed looking at her phone as well. Weren't we the industrious pair of investigators?

Around 4:30 I was about to ask Lana if she wanted to go out for supper when my phone rang.

It was the younger, protective woman. "Aino Korhonen here. Professor Nieminen will see you tomorrow at nine o'clock in the morning."

"Thank you. We'll..." She hung up before I could say anything more.

Lana looked up from her phone. I told her what was going on.

She frowned. "Does that mean he'll cooperate?"

"I hope so. I can't see him asking for a meeting just to brush us off, but we should probably hold off on celebrating." I got off my bed. "Let's get some supper."

There was a poster in the lobby with a rather striking picture of a musical conductor gesturing like a magician. It had the word *Konsertit* in large letters, which despite the language barrier seemed obvious.

The man at the desk was helpful. "The concert is tonight at the university in the Korelia Hall. It starts in 90 minutes."

"What kind of music are they performing?"

"Mostly choral. Some instrumental." He hand-drew a map so we could find the venue.

I turned to Lana. "Wanna go to a concert after supper?"

"It's probably better than playing Pokémon all evening."

"Such enthusiasm."

I turned back to the clerk. "Where do we get tickets?"

"Either at the door, or at the *Carelicum,* but they close at 5:00."

He handed me a brochure that showed where the mysterious *Carelicum* was. It was three blocks away. If we left immediately we should just make it.

"I hope this is worth it," Lana said as I paid the nice lady ten Euros each for the tickets.

"It has to be better than playing Pokémon all evening." I was being snarky because, as far as I was concerned, almost anything was better than Pokémon.

We took a pedestrian-and-bicycle-only street called *Kauppakatu* south to *Suvantokatu.* Lana pointed out that we were going in the opposite direction to the university.

That was because I had a diabolical plan. We soon found ourselves outside *Ravintola Kielo.* From my vast knowledge of Finnish (about ten words), I knew that *ravintola* meant restaurant.

Lana peered suspiciously at the menu while I sat there looking knowledgeable. She finally puzzled out what she was having just as the waiter arrived.

"*Blini ja sienisalaattia ja hirven ulkofilee.*" I said.

"*Kahvi?*"

"*Kyllä.*"

Lana glared at me. "Since when do you speak Finnish?"

It possible that I may have been looking somewhat smug. "Since I had several hours to kill this afternoon."

Fortunately for her, the waiter also spoke English, and she managed to order a salad with local fish.

I can honestly say that it was the best moose steak I've ever had.

◦∞◦

It was a lovely early evening to walk off some of our supper on the way to the university. There was a slight breeze and the temperature was perfect. I was feeling mellow and a bit romantic. If Lana had been a guy, or if she'd given any indication at all that she was feeling similarly, I'd have held her hand.

After all the chasing around I'd been doing lately, the thought of just quietly sitting and listening to music was appealing. The concert hall was next to the building where we'd met Professor Nieminen, and it was built like a lecture theatre. Despite a reasonable audience we had no problem finding seats.

The master of ceremonies gave an introduction; we were going to listen to music from Nightwish, whoever they were. At the risk of being rude I Googled them while he was speaking.

They were a symphonic metal band from Kitee, about 100 kilometres south of Joensuu, and *what the hell was symphonic metal?* This could have been a mistake. The stage was bare except for a grand piano and some microphone stands. It didn't appear that we were about to be blasted by what I usually associated with metal bands.

It startled me to realize that the MC was doing his introductions in several languages. Did everybody in Europe except me speak multiple languages?

The MC left the stage and the audience clapped as a young woman came on wearing a pink dress. She looked like she was going to a school graduation dance.

The music was a recording, and definitely symphonic. I could easily imagine it being used for an adventure film. Her voice was pure and operatic with an incredible range. Another surprise was that the words were in English.

If this was symphonic metal it wasn't anything like I expected. The songs varied in style from show tunes to folk songs, instrumental pieces, ballads, and a cool piece sung by a woman in a Steampunk costume. One woman played the violin. Another singer was pretty redhead in a wheelchair. The only male performers were playing the piano and acoustic guitar. If this was metal I'd been missing out.

Then there was the choir.

After almost two hours all the performers, plus a few extra men, came out and arranged themselves across the small stage with four soloists in front. The pianist began playing a ballad that turned into a really stirring anthem with intricate key changes. Between each verse the soloists swapped out with other choir members. I had heard live music before, but I'd never felt it like that.

Then there was the choir.

The MC gave them their notes on the piano, and they began the least expected piece of the evening, at least for me. The song was performed *a cappella* and it was a hymn. I guessed that the language was Finnish.

I felt my eyes sting, tears running down my cheeks, and I had no good idea why. It was a beautiful, gentle, haunting melody with exquisite harmonies. It was triumphant.

By the time it ended I found myself actually crying. I had no idea what the words meant, but the melody itself insisted that my heart understood everything it needed to. Why did it affect me so much?

After that somebody made a speech and hugged all the performers. The pianist played one more piece with the choir that was a song of farewell, and the concert was over.

I didn't wait to see what Lana wanted to do. I wiped my tears on the backs of my hands and went down to the stage where the performers were slowly filing out into the wings.

The redhead I'd noticed earlier was bringing up the rear. "Excuse me."

"Hi," she said. Her English was as good as mine.

"Um, I hope I'm not intruding."

"Not at all." A man with a long ponytail and goatee came back to see what was going on.

"I just wanted to tell you how much I enjoyed the concert. What was that song near the end? The hymn."

"Finlandia," the man said. "It's sort of the unofficial national anthem."

I couldn't figure out how to tell them how much it had affected me, so I fell back on the time-honoured conversational ploy of saying something stupid."Your English is very good."

She snorted and tried to hide her smile. "Thank you," he said. "We're from Canada."

"You're kidding. I'm from Calgary. Veronica." We shook hands.

"Daniel. This is my wife, Bailey Dawn. We live in Edmonton. Are you here on vacation?"

"Work. I'm a private investigator."

"Are you investigating us?" Bailey Dawn asked.

"No, we just saw the concert poster and decided to come."

"We?"

I turned. Lana was standing by the stage, obviously waiting for me. "My colleague and I." Bailey Dawn waved to her. Lana ignored her.

The MC said something to Daniel and Bailey Dawn. It sounded like English but the grammar was—unusual. The two Edmontonians didn't seem to have much trouble decoding it.

"We should go. I'm glad you liked the concert," Bailey Dawn said.

"The hymn made me cry," I blurted, then felt foolish.

Bailey Dawn put her hand on my arm. "It does that."

"A lot," Daniel agreed. "There isn't a day that goes by that the song doesn't run through my head."

When I got back to Lana I asked her how she liked the concert.

"It was all right. They did a good job with the Sibelius."

"The...?"

"The *a cappella* piece at the end. It was written as a political statement before Finland gained its independence from Russia."

My eyes teared up again. "I thought it was the most beautiful thing I've ever heard."

"Most Finns would agree with you."

∞

Another thing the Finns *really* appreciate is punctuality, so we made sure we were at the Professor's office three minutes before nine. This time he had an extra chair for us.

He didn't beat around the bush. "I have checked your credentials. They are impressive."

"Does that mean you will help us?" Lana asked.

"Yes. Would you like coffee?"

"Yes, please," I said. Lana said she preferred water.

He called to Aino, and in a few moments later she arrived with a tray holding two cups of coffee and a glass of water. She gave us a restrained dirty look. I wondered what her deal was.

After she left he got down to business.

"What do you know of the Sampo?"

"Just what I read in the Kalevala." I said. "It's a magical item with a colourful lid that's supposed to create things. In particular salt, grain, and money."

"You've read the entire Kalevala?"

"Yes."

He looked at Lana. "And you?"

"Selected parts."

"Like everybody else you saw but you did not understand." He spoke quietly, and it was obvious that he was reciting from memory.

> Then the blacksmith, Ilmarinen,
> Sought a place to build a smithy,
> Sought a place to plant a bellows,
> On the borders of the Northland,
> On the Pohya-hills and meadows;
> Searched one day, and then a second;
> Ere the evening of the third day,
> Came a rock within his vision,
> Came a stone with rainbow-colours.
> There the blacksmith, Ilmarinen,
> Set at work to build his smithy,
> Built a fire and raised a chimney;
> On the next day laid his bellows,
> On the third day built his furnace,
> And began to forge the Sampo.

He stopped and looked at us. "Do you understand?" Lana looked as blank as I felt.

"There are a variety of local ores that are multicoloured. Many of them are compounds of elements that are used to produce modern electronic devices."

Lana frowned. "So you are saying that the Kalevala should be interpreted literally?"

"Of course not, but our ancestors thousands of years ago were not scientifically sophisticated. They described things as well as they could within their experience. Those descriptions have been further changed to fit the poetic style of the runes, and again by Elias Lönnrot when he collected them."

"If I understand correctly, what you are saying is that the Kalevala is a mythic account of real events," I said. "That the Sampo was an advanced technological device."

"Exactly."

Lana raised an eyebrow. "There were no electronic devices a thousand years ago. Who do you think built it? A blacksmith god? Or perhaps aliens?"

In that moment a really nasty suspicion laughed evilly in my mind. I tried to ignore it before it coloured my investigation. It was probably untrue, completely unwelcome, and would explain so much—demons.

"That I don't know. An object fitting the description of the Sampo was found in the early 1600s by a fisherman on the coast of what is now the Barents Sea. I believe that the dark land of Pohyola mentioned in the poem is the island today known as Svalbard. That would fit the poem. I had hoped that an examination of the Sampo itself would tell us who built it."

"So you don't know where it is now?"

He sighed, and closed his eyes. "No."

"I must say, your evidence doesn't seem particularly compelling," Lana said.

"Do you know how microcircuits are manufactured?"

Her eyebrow raised. "No, not in detail. I know that sand is turned into purified silicon to which various other elements are added to form the actual circuits."

"That's more than most people know." He indicated one of the shelves. "Bring me the small display case."

The case was a shallow wooden box with a glass front. Inside were neatly labelled mineral samples. Again he recited.

>The eternal magic artist,
>Ancient blacksmith, Ilmarinen,
>First of all the iron-workers,
>Mixed together certain metals,
>Put the mixture in the caldron,
>Laid it deep within the furnace,
>Called the hirelings to the forging.
>Skilfully they work the bellows,
>Tend the fire and add the fuel,
>Three most lovely days of summer,
>Three short nights of bright midsummer,
>Till the rocks begin to blossom,
>In the foot-prints of the workmen,
>From the magic heat and furnace.
>
>On the third night Ilmarinen,
>Bending low to view his metals,
>On the bottom of the furnace,
>Sees the magic Sampo rising,
>Sees the lid in many colours.
>Quick the artist of Wainola
>Forges with the tongs and anvil,
>knocking with a heavy hammer,
>Forges skilfully the Sampo;
>On one side the flour is grinding,
>On another salt is making,
>On a third is money forging,

> And the lid is many-coloured.
> Well the Sampo grinds when finished,
> To and fro the lid in rocking,
> Grinds one measure at the day-break,
> Grinds a measure fit for eating,
> Grinds a second for the market,
> Grinds a third one for the store-house.

"What do you notice about the top row of samples?"

We examined them for a moment.

"They certainly are colourful," I said. "I particularly like the bismuth crystals."

"The samples below them are the elements that are derived from those minerals. Many of them are used in modern microcircuit fabrication. How would you describe them? In particular, the sample of silicon."

That was harder. "Less colourful?"

"Metallic," Lana said.

"Exactly. Colourful stone that is smelted into a mixture of 'certain metals,' even though some of them, such as silicon, aren't truly metals."

"My search began with the assumption that the overall mythology described real events. That would put Pohyola somewhere to the north of Finland. I found a clue in the research done by an anthropologist among the Sami people. Are you familiar with them?"

We both shook our heads.

"They are a nomadic people native to northern Finland. Some have an oral tradition of a mysterious object that was drawn from the northern sea by a fisherman. Details vary, of course, but all versions agree that it had a lid of some kind that sometimes shone with various colours."

Lana was content to let me keep him talking. "What happened to it?"

"Their shamans said that it was not of this world, and should be given back to the spirits. When a missionary came to try to convert them to Christianity, he was given the artifact. Shortly afterward he decided to return home so that his religious superiors could examine the artifact."

"The missionary was Finnish?"

"No, that would have been extremely unusual. He was Swedish. Finland was part of Sweden at that time. I found a record of him passing through Tornion kaupunti, which is a small port at the northern tip of the Bay of Bothnia. Being Swedish he'd have taken the artifact to Uppsala, which is still the seat of the Archbishop of Sweden."

"I take it that you haven't had a chance to contact Sweden about this missionary."

"Of course I have. I even have his name: Johan Agnetason."

CHAPTER 4

The Confession (translated from Latin)

The name given to me by my mother was Johan Agnetason. That was many years ago, and it cannot be long now until the just Hand of God reaches out to take me to whatever reward I deserve. I feel that I must record my life in this chronicle to confess the sins that I have hidden from mortal men.

Though I have lived many years in this land, I was born in Sweden in the Year of Our Lord 1578 in the village of Testa. My mother, Agneta Gunsdotter, was a prostitute. Neither of us knew my father. As a boy I learned many skills necessary to my survival: how to relieve someone in a crowd of his purse without detection, how to shoot, how to protect first my mother, and later other women, with a club, pistol, knife, or my fists.

When my mother passed to her heavenly reward I was 20 years of age. By then I commanded the loyalty of a small band of men whose bond of brotherhood was the belief that we should assist those more fortunate than ourselves in sharing their considerable wealth to those of lesser means. Although our efforts often seemed to trouble our patrons, there is no doubt that we were doing the Lord's work as we would then in turn donate our new-found wealth to tavern keepers and such women as drew our custom.

Such was my life for the next several years during which my men and I roamed the area south and west of Upsala. It was a good life until 1603, when we found ourselves in the village of Dalby. There we were spreading our wealth, much to the joy of the inhabitants. None of our beneficiaries would think of turning us in to the king's men.

It was in Dalby that I met the young woman who was to have such a profound effect on my circumstance. As she entered the tavern she was notable to me for remaining wrapped in a plain travel cloak despite the summer heat. It took her a few moments to look around, after which she headed directly for the table where I sat.

"I'm Brita," she said as she sat by me. Beneath her hood was a woman about my age with golden hair and blue eyes. Her lips were full and she licked them slowly as she looked at me. Just above her cloak clasp I could see the beginning of a costly dress.

"Johan," I replied. "What can I do for you?"

"A great deal, I suspect." Below the table I could feel a delicate hand on my thigh. After a moment it explored further.

I could think of no reason why I shouldn't take her up on her clear offer. A noble woman would hardly offer herself as a trap for the likes of me, and the softness of the hand now seeking a way into my breeches, as well as the quality of her dress, told me that this was no peasant.

Brita's boldness in the common room promised a woman of an exceptionally lusty nature. That promise was fulfilled in my room. Indeed, she left many scratches and bruises upon me that led to some later teasing by my men. She would not say where she lived, but promised that she would meet me again in a week.

The next week we met as arranged, and twice during the week after that. The only two difficulties were that we both wished for more frequent meetings, and my men were getting restless from being in one place for an extended period. Every day we stayed near Dalby was another day during which the King's soldiers might find us. Our greatest protection lay in us calling nowhere our constant home.

Knowing the futility of ordering my men to do something to which they would never agree, we again began moving from place to place. As much as possible I kept us south of a line between Enköping and Ekolsund. Most of the time it took me only an hour or two by horse to get to where Brita and I had agreed to meet. Frequently this was in the woods, and we slaked our appetites for each other on a bed of moss. Both of us understand the need for secrecy in our trysts.

After several weeks I discovered that I was falling in love with my enigmatic lady, and to my regret I resolved to find out more about her.

After a particular assignation I followed her as skillfully as I could manage while leading my horse through the woods. Less than half an hour later she reached a track where she met another woman tending two horses.

Although I was too far away to hear their conversation, the bearing of the second woman strongly suggested to me that she was Brita's servant.

I had no suspicion of how ill things were for me until she took out a travel cloak and fastened it about Brita's throat. On the back of this cloak was a device of a red cross on a silver background with two gold stars and a silver crescent moon on a blue background across the top.

I recognized it immediately, as anyone would whose business was to keep track of the comings and goings of the nobility. My lover was Brita Pontusdotter, of the family De la Gardie.

The wife of Gabriel Oxenstierna.

I followed at a distance as they returned to Ekholmen Manor, only a quarter *lantmil* south of Dalby. A man wearing a sword met them at the door, and there ensued a heated argument during which the servant was dismissed along with the horses. After more shouting Brita stormed off in the direction of the woods.

Leaving my horse tied, I made my way toward her.

When I was close enough I spoke. "Why didn't you tell me?"

She was startled at the sound of my voice.

"What are you doing here?"

"I followed you to find out who you are." The words did not come easily to me. "You have stolen my heart."

"I thought you had the wit to know that I desire you only for your prowess as a lover."

Before I could answer the sound of shouting came to us from the direction of the house. Her husband had re-emerged and seen us. He was charging in our direction, calling for his men as he ran. She removed a purse from her belt and tossed it to me. I caught it without thought.

"Strike me!"

I saw at once that she meant to provide herself with an excuse for our conversation, casting me in the role of a mere robber. Though I loved her, the slight she had dealt me caused my hand to fly true, and she fell at my feet.

Her husband's initial outrage had left him in a bad position. In order to catch me before I regained my horse he would have to be mounted himself, or at least my equal in woodcraft. He must also see to his wife, whom I had left unmoving, and whom he must return to the safety of the manor before he could set out in pursuit.

I had only a brief time to make my escape, and I knew that my old life was at an end. A man of his standing would never let the matter rest. Rather than bring my misfortune to my men by leading my pursuers to them I set out for the Grystavik, a shallow bay of Lake Mälaren that is nearly pinched off by a narrow strait near its mouth. Over the ploughed fields a horse could not manage more than a canter without risking injury, but the distance was short and it was enough. My horse easily crossed the narrows that were no more than sixty feet wide, and it took me little time to find a fisherman who was willing to take us on his boat. Brita's purse divulged 30 silver German thaler which was more than enough for my escape. The Biblical implication was not lost on me.

We set out at once, and after several hours we approached Ekolsund at the north end of that arm of the lake. It was fortunate that I had trained my horse to lie down on command. This was a useful trick both when hiding from pursuit in dense forest, and for mounting after being injured. In this case, it made the boat less likely to dump us all in the cold water.

My goal was to get to Upsala, and 30 thaler would allow me to get there more quickly than mounted pursuit could follow. There should be enough silver left over for any bribes necessary for my plan to succeed.

At Ekolsund we disembarked, and I paid the fisherman another thaler to ensure his silence. I was sure that two weeks good wages for a few hours work would ensure his loyalty. After letting my horse walk off his stiffness from the voyage, we made for the village of Nyby on the shore of Lake Ekoln. There I found another fisherman who was willing to trade silver for passage, and again we were sailing northward.

For me, this was the difficult part of the journey. We were now outside of the lands that I knew, and I was at the mercy of the fisherman to know how to get me to Upsala. Fortunately, he was either honest, or didn't believe that betraying me would be in his best interests.

By supper time we had reached Flottsund where the Fyrisan flows into the lake. Again I paid an extra thaler for silence after we had landed.

My destination was the cathedral. A passing woman told me that I could scarcely miss it if I kept to the western side of the river.

While on the boat I had several hours in which to make my plans. Whether Brita confessed to her adultery with me, her husband would be looking for a brigand. My hope was that he would never think to look for a monk. Certainly she would never describe me thus.

All I had to do was to convince the priests at the cathedral that I had a true vocation, and that they should accept me into their ranks. A generous offering of silver should help them with their decision.

With God as my witness, I believed that this course was forced upon me by circumstance. If I had known her identity, I would not have committed adultery with the wife of the brother of Axel Oxenstierna. When I thought upon the nature of the men involved in this matter I would count it as nothing less than a miracle, and a sign of Divine Grace, if upon my capture they merely killed me.

The cathedral was much more impressive than any castle I had ever seen. The red brick building had square towers on either side of an entrance in white stone. Scaffolding atop the towers showed where the spires were under construction. I could easily believe that it was the tallest building in Sweden, if not in the whole world.

Having never been in a church before, at first I was at a loss to know where to go. The sanctuary at the far end of the aisle seemed like an important and the most obvious place. Huge brick columns on either side of the aisle supported the roof far above.

We had all heard rumours that a criminal who made it this far could ask the church for sanctuary and, if granted, was then secure from the agents of the law, but I had no desire to spend my entire life in this building with Oxenstierna's men waiting outside. If I could become one of many monks and be sent on a ministry to some distant place I could start a new life.

This is to show how my thoughts have changed since I was a young man. God's plan for my life turned out to be far more wonderful than I could ever had imagined at that time.

Eventually a priest came to speak with me as I sat in the front pew. To my current shame, I told him that I had a dream in which God had revealed to me that I was destined to minister to the heathen Finns. This was the furthest place I could think of.

I was taken deeper into the cathedral and told to wait. After some time I was called into the archbishop's presence.

Olof Mårtensson was not the frail old man I had expected from one bearing the title of archbishop. Instead, he was a large man, strong and of keen intelligence.

"I'm told that you want to minister to the Finns," he said. From his voice alone I suspected that he could have won at wrestling with Big Jörgen, the member of my band who lifted logs into place to block roads for our ambushes.

I kept my eyes down. "Yes, Archbishop. God has granted me a vision."

He looked at me for a long time while I sweated. "Hmm. I don't believe you."

I tried not to panic. I could not risk being cast out.

He leaned forward over his desk and steepled his fingers. "What did you do?"

"Do, Archbishop?"

"You might be surprised at the number of criminals who attempt to evade justice by joining the church."

I could feel the sweat running down my chest and back under my shirt.

He sat back in his chair. "How well do you know the Bible?"

I relaxed slightly. My mother had taught me to read and the Bible was the only book we had.

"I've read it, Archbishop."

"We shall see."

For the next hour or more, he asked me questions about the Bible and

I answered them to best of my ability. At the end of it I felt like I'd run all the way to Stockholm with Big Jörgen on my back.

"Very well, you show an adequate understanding of Our Lord's word. Now I will hear your confession."

That could take a long time. "Archbishop?"

His eyes narrowed. "I hope that your discomfort with the act of confession of sin doesn't indicate any *Calvanist* leanings on your part?"

"Uh, no, Archbishop. It's just that..."

"You are undoubtedly wanted for an entire constellation of crimes, and you expect me to turn you over to secular justice. Let me ease your mind somewhat. I have a task in mind for which I believe you may be well suited. I would hate for all that potential to go to waste at the end of a rope." He moved around to my side of his desk. "Kneel before me."

I had no choice. I told him my entire history, as nearly as I could remember it. When I finished he waited. I didn't know what else to say. All of my life had been taken up in concealing my deeds. It was the first time I'd confessed to anything to anyone, let alone a priest.

"Repeat after me: I am sorry for all of this and ask for grace. I want to do better."

When I had said it, he said, "God be merciful to you and strengthen your faith. Do you believe that my forgiveness is God's forgiveness?"

I guessed at the answer. "Yes."

He put his hand on my head. "In the stead and by the command of my Lord Jesus Christ I forgive you all your sins in the name of the Father and of the Son and of the Holy Spirit. Amen."

He returned to his side of the desk, and smiled at me. It was not a comforting smile.

"Well, well. Oxenstierna's wife. I can see why you would be tempted." Not knowing what else to do, I rose from my knees and sat in my chair.

The Archbishop's absolution felt—strange. I'd spent all of my life being a highwayman. I'd killed a few men who displayed less wisdom than most when we set upon them. And yet, loving Brita seemed to have opened a door that I hadn't even known was present in my soul. Her treachery might have swung it partially closed, but the Archbishop's forgiveness had opened it again. I didn't know whether I liked the change in me or not.

He sat. "Your former life is behind you now. From this moment on you will live a blameless life. At least, that's our intention, is it not?" I nodded.

"Now, as to your ministry. I understand you want to convert the Finns."

"Yes, Archbishop."

"I think we can use your particular talents best in Lappland."

My knowledge of the wide world was limited to a few things I'd heard of the Germanies, Poland, and the province of Finland. "I've never heard of such a place."

"Don't worry. You'll have excellent guides."

⁓

Pål was the biggest man I could ever have imagined. He made even the Archbishop look sickly. If the old god Thor appeared on Earth I'm certain that he would have looked like Pål.

Ander was more my size, but for all my skill in a fight, I doubted that I could have bested him. They were both experienced soldiers who had been in many campaigns in distant lands, and yet were still alive and possessing all their limbs. They were familiar with Lappland, and had little good to say of the place.

"The people are called the Sami," Ander told me. "They worship their own gods and speak a language unlike ours. Be thankful that we're travelling in the summer. In the winter the sun disappears completely for weeks at a time. Of course, it will take us two months to get there so you'll get to see that for yourself."

Nothing was said on the matter by either man, but it was clear to me that they had been given instructions by the Archbishop, and would be greatly displeased with me if I tried to escape from their care.

Our journey began pleasantly enough by riding to Stockholm where we boarded a ship going north to the Finnish town of Tornion kaupunti, or *Duortnus* as the Sami called it. From there we walked north through a land that was empty and flat. We were unable to use horses as the footing among the bogs was frequently too treacherous.

The Sami are a friendly people. Most of the ones we met barely came up to my chest, and their skin is a peculiar brown-yellow colour. These nomads do not create cities, towns, or even villages. The majority of them do not farm, but either follow the herds of reindeer from place to place or they fish.

I understood not a single word of their speech, and if not for Ander and Pål with their rudimentary knowledge of the language I would have been as lost in speech as I would have been in this trackless landscape.

After we had journeyed for several weeks the land of forests, bogs, and lakes gave way to a land of small shrubs, grasses, bogs, and lakes. The weather continued to get colder, and before we reached the sea we had to deal with snow.

At the beginning of October we reached a fishing settlement on the Murmans sea. These Sami were expert in building light boats of wood sewn together with deer sinew, and in these they fearlessly went to sea.

As I slowly learned their language, I tried my best to explain Christianity to the inhabitants. Even with help from Pål and Ander the language difficulties seems insurmountable. No matter how I tried to explain the sacrifice of our Lord Jesus Christ what I said failed to get through to them. There was something that was not being communicated, and I was at a lost to know what to do.

They seemed to regard Christianity as merely part of their own foolish superstitions. For my part, I tried to understand their religion in an attempt to bridge the gap between the two, but as nearly as I could discover, they believed that everything was God: sky, people, fish, reindeer, moss, sea, and stones. It made no sense.

One day in December when the sea was a churning mass of crashing waves below a dark grey sky filled with howling winds from the north, a fisherman named Bierdna came to me. Fearless as they were, even the Sami would not venture out to sea in such weather.

It was clear that Bierdna was afraid of something, and when I saw what he had brought to me wrapped in reindeer hide, I understood his fear.

He said that he had caught it in his net while out fishing. It was unlike anything I had ever seen before, of some smooth white stone that would not be marred by anything we had with us. Even the point of Ander's sword would not make a mark on it, though he was rightfully very proud of the quality of its steel.

The object was shaped much like a wheel of cheese, albeit a small one that I could easily encompass with my arms. It weighed somewhat less than what one would expect from a stone of that size as if it might be partially filled with wood.

The curious thing was its lid. This was the thickness of my thumb, and rotated freely as if it was screwed on, or turned on a central spindle like a potter's wheel. Yet no amount of turning or prying would loosen it further.

The lid also appeared to be of the same white stone until touched with the hand. Then it glowed without heat and symbols in many colours appeared. The writing, if it indeed was writing, was unknown to any of us. A few heartbeats after one's hand was removed the symbols faded.

Bierdna insisted that I take the thing.

The question that absorbed my companions and I for many days was what to do with it. We could have taken it out to sea and consigned it to the depths, but Bierdna swore that his nets did not touch the sea bottom, and we were all at a loss to understand how this thing had become tangled in them. We all felt certain that sooner or later it would be found again; that it *wanted* to be found.

It was now February, and my companions and I were thoroughly sick of Lappland. In all honesty, however, it was not this that prompted us to wrap the object securely in leather and begin the long trek back to Upsala.

The matter was this—we could not decide among us whether this thing was Divine or Demonic in origin.

That it was not natural was obvious to everyone. Nothing in nature glowed as this did, with the possible exception of the lights that danced in the northern skies. The shining symbols that appeared on its lid spoke of an intelligence, and that implied a purpose. What that purpose might be, and whether it was for the greater glory of God or an artifice of Satan to tempt us to sin was beyond our understanding.

We therefore resolved to take it back to the Archbishop in the hope that he could make sense of this mystery. We were also much heartened by the though of getting away from a constant diet of fish.

Our journey south was much the same as our outward trek although, the season being earlier, we were able to use a sled for part of our journey. This was good, as none of us were anxious to carry the object for any length of time in fear that it would do us some harm, and it was heavy enough that it would have been all one of us could do to carry it alone for any great distance.

Nearly two months later we boarded a trading ship in Tornion kaupunti that was bound for Stockholm. We arrived there ten days later.

The Archbishop was at first not pleased to see us, but when we revealed what we had found he forgave us for abandoning our ministry.

He even praised us for bringing it back to be examined.

CHAPTER 5

Swedish Archives

Professor Nieminen gave us the rest of the information about his research. The wonderful thing about Christian churches is that they love to keep detailed records. On occasion they are even more meticulous about it than tax collectors.

"Okay, we have a Swedish cleric named Johan Agnetason. What's his story?"

"There's no information on him before his mission. When he returned the artifact was examined by the Archbishop's people and declared to be demonic. I was unable to find more information than that."

I tried to be tactful. "Was that because of a lack of records?"

"No, my health, although his last name indicates that he was a bastard. He was exactly the kind of person who would be ignored by history."

"We need to go to Uppsala," Lana said. "Did you have a research assistant while you were there?"

"Yes, Doctor Karen Lindberg from the University of Uppsala. She is fluent in seventeenth century Swedish."

"Can you write us a letter of introduction? It would be great if she can help us to target promising areas of the archives that you didn't get to."

"Yes, I can do that. I'm sure she'd be willing to help. When I left she said it was like reading half a mystery novel and she wanted to know how it turned out."

"Maybe we'll be lucky and she's continued the research on her own," I said.

"It's possible."

"Do you have copies of what you've found so far?"

He handed me a USB drive. "Of course." He cleared his throat. "My doctors tell me that I have maybe two or three months to live. You can't imagine how wonderful it is to have my research continued. Thank you."

I pocketed the drive. "Don't give up yet, Professor Nieminen. It's possible that we might find the Sampo soon. You've already done the hard part."

"I hope you are right." He had another coughing fit. "I'm sorry, but I must go home and rest."

⁂

I made the collect call to the University of Uppsala from the professor's office, after Aino confirmed that I was using a credit card and not leaving them with the bill. I finally decided that she was feeling overly protective toward the professor.

It was nice to make a call to a place in the same time zone for once. The person at the university switchboard spoke English, and gave me their e-mail address so we could send them a copy of our letter of introduction from the Professor.

An hour later Dr. Lindberg called back.

"Of course, I would be delighted to work with you. I do hope Seppo is well."

"Unfortunately, no. I really hope that we can finish his research in time for him to see it. When would you be able to start?"

"I have few social obligations at the moment, so any time when I am not teaching is at your disposal. We could start tomorrow if you can make it."

"We'll figure out the airline schedule and let you know."

Lana and I had an early lunch at the university cafeteria. I spent part of the time with online booking. "Okay, I got us two seats to Uppsala. We have a stop-over in Helsinki, but that can't be helped. I don't think Joensuu has direct flights to *anywhere* except Helsinki."

On the way back to our hotel we were walking beside a park when Lana shoved me forward. As I stumbled I saw a big man rushing toward us from the direction of the trees. He was holding an impressive-looking knife in a way that told me he wasn't an amateur with it. He was wearing a ski mask.

Seriously? A ski mask? How cliché.

Lana had backed away and was starting her dance. Since I was on the ground he ignored me for the moment it took him to try to figure out how to attack Lana. That gave me a chance to spin around and drive my foot into the side of his knee. He shifted his attention back to me just in time, slashing the knife downward toward my leg. I felt it catch on my jeans, then my foot connected.

His knee buckled with a nasty sound and he grunted. The knife stayed in his hand as he fell. His noise-making didn't last long as Lana launched herself into the air almost simultaneously and nailed him on his temple with her heel. Her dress billowed out gracefully, and it would have looked spectacular in slow-motion. I don't think he appreciated the sight before he became extremely unconscious.

Lana looked completely unruffled as she held out her hand to help me up. "Are you all right?"

"Yeah." That's when I noticed some blood on my leg. His knife had been sharp enough that the cut wasn't hurting yet. Through the slice in the fabric it didn't seem too bad.

She checked his neck for a pulse. "He's still alive."

I kicked his knife further from his hand. "That's a relief. I don't envy him how he'll feel when he wakes up."

Lana peeled back his mask. "How interesting."

It was our book worm from the Helsinki airport.

"What do we do now?" Lana said.

"I'm not sure. What's the emergency number in Finland?"

"Try 1-1-2. That's the European Union emergency number."

I'd just gotten my phone out when a police car coasted to a stop beside us. A young constable got out with a wary eye on us.

"*Mitä tapahtui?*"

"I'm sorry, we don't understand," Lana said.

He switched to English. "What happened?"

"This man attacked us with a knife. We defended ourselves."

He examined our assailant, still keeping us under observation, and made a radio call.

Of course he wanted more details. While we were filling out our witness reports an ambulance arrived. They put a bandage on my calf, and told me in stern terms not to do anything strenuous for a few days. They also took our assailant away.

Neither of our witness statements hinted that this was anything but a random mugging of two innocent tourists. Clouding the issue with extra details would only make us more likely to miss our flight.

The knife went into an evidence bag. It was the first time I'd gotten a good look at it. It was definitely some kind of military knife.

I was amazed at how few people even glanced at what was going on, other than walking around us. Finns were seriously into personal privacy.

It took them half an hour before the circus was finally over. The nice constable gave us a ride back to our hotel so I wouldn't have to walk with an injured leg.

We spent the next two hours in our room discussing the whole thing, and not getting anywhere. Lana announced that she was going to take a shower.

There was a small detail that I'd wanted to investigate, so as soon as I heard the water running I started rummaging in her pack. It was sitting by the wall, and there was a cord leading to the power outlet on the wall. Her phone was on her night stand, so that wasn't it.

I carefully went through her things, following the cord. What I pulled out surprised me more than anything else that had happened.

Twenty minutes later she came out fully dressed. She stopped when she saw what was on her bed—a red telephone.

"How *dare* you go through my belongings."

"It's a pity we didn't go through each others stuff earlier. It might have saved us some time."

She grabbed the phone and examined it for damage. Her brow furrowed. For once I was ahead of her and I was enjoying it. I could see confusion as she realized it wasn't her phone.

I pulled her phone out from behind me. "I think we both have some explaining to do. I had no idea you were also a member of the BSI."

"How were you recruited?"

"Believe it or not, the head of the BSI is also my psychotherapist. What about you?"

"My parents were members before they were killed. I was recommended by the inspector who is my primary contact with the police."

"What about Natt?"

"He knows about the organization, but he hasn't been invited to join. Come to think of it, he may have undertaken to follow you to try to prove how useful he is so he can become a member."

We exchanged phones.

"I'm inclined to trust you rather more now."

"Same here," I said. "Especially after you saved my life."

In a dazzling display of good timing, my personal phone rang before we got all mushy or something.

"Ms. Chandler? This is Detective-Sergeant Laakso. We'd like you both to come to the police station to answer a few more questions about your attack."

"Certainly, though I don't know what else we can add."

"Your attacker has been identified as a Russian national who is of interest to the Special Intelligence Service."

What the hell? How was MI-6 involved? I was playing way out of my league. "All right, but we don't know where the police station is."

"I've sent a car to pick you up." At that moment there was a knock on our door. "Purely as a courtesy, of course."

"Of course. We'll see you soon."

I told Lana what was going on. Neither of us believed that they were just clearing up a few details.

The constable at the door was extremely polite but firm. He had a colleague with him in a slightly different uniform who was carrying an MP-5 like he was ready to use it. That didn't bode well.

―⁂―

"I'm Detective-Sergeant Laakso. Please have a seat."

Laakso was in his late forties and looked like a children's show host: all crinkly eyes and sincere smiles. The interview room was very nice. No intimidating mirrored windows such as you see on American TV. Upholstered chairs. No file folder for him to slap on the table as he came in. His uniform matched the officer with the MP-5.

"As I said on the phone, we've identified the man who attacked you as a Russian by the name of Grigor Lubikov. We believe that he works as an independent contractor who has been implicated in several homicides. To the best of our knowledge nobody has ever managed to get away from him before. Perhaps you could explain how that happened?"

"It's all be the witness report," I said.

"Ah yes." He consulted his tablet. "'I kicked him in the knee. Lana kicked him in the head. He collapsed. The police arrived.' I must say, Ms. Chandler, you have a talent for brevity."

"Thank you. I understand that Finns don't like people who talk too much."

He smiled. "Perhaps a *bit* more detail?"

Lana leaned forward on the table. "I saw him a moment before Veronica did, so I pushed her aside and began the *ginga*. That's the basic movement of Capoeira." *Ah, so that's what that was.*

"The *ginga* confused him for a moment, so I took the opportunity to kick his knee. He got me in the leg with his knife before he went down," I said.

"As soon as I saw Veronica distract him I did a spinning kick to his head. He couldn't block both at once."

"How is it that you both happened to be so skilled?"

"My mother is a detective. I began taking Krav Maga classes with her when I was nine."

"I've been studying Capoeira for ten years," Lana said.

"I see. So a known Russian assassin-for-hire just happened to—I think the word is 'mug'—a random pair of foreign martial artists?"

Oh crap. This interview was about to get messy. The Detective-Sergeant would next ask us why we were in Joensuu, and that would involve the Professor, our jobs, and almost everything else. Lana must have come to the same conclusion.

"We have no idea why he attacked us," Lana said. "We were on our way back to our hotel after having lunch at the university cafeteria."

Nicely played, Lana.

"Why were you at the university cafeteria?" *Shit.*

I waded in. "We had a meeting with Professor Seppo Nieminen about his research on the Kalevala. The professor is not well and said that he was going home. When you verify our story may I ask that you contact Aino Korhonen of the Karelian Institute instead. She can confirm that we were at the meeting and brought us coffee."

"That's quite thoughtful of you. Excuse me."

He left us alone. I caught Lana's eye and flicked a glance toward the corner of the room. She gave the slightest of nods. I wasn't the only one who had noticed the camera.

We sat in silence. Lana looked to be completely at ease. I tried, but I was too aware of time ticking down toward our departure.

I also remembered something she'd told me earlier, about a resurgence of Karelian activism. Could somebody have hired the Russian to stop us from finding a national treasure? Or did they think that we already had it? Was he related to the sniper, or was that someone *else* who was after us?

There were too damned many players in what was supposed to be a simple game. So far there we had my client, her client, the unknown sniper, and now the Russians involved.

I *knew* it was too good to be true.

⁂

Laakso came back about 20 minutes later.

"You'll be happy to know that Ms. Korhonen has verified your story, as have the staff of the university cafeteria. She doesn't like you very much."

"She feels protective toward the professor, and seems to think that we were imposing on him. I don't know why it matters to her."

"Yes, you mentioned he's not well. Why did you need to see him?"

Yup, that would be the sound of the other shoe dropping. There was no point in keeping anything back now. Any lies we told would come back to haunt us very quickly.

"We're private investigators. Our client has asked us to locate an historical artifact, and Professor Nieminen had information we needed. We are leaving tomorrow morning for Uppsala to continue our investigation."

"That may not be possible. We need to ascertain exactly who Mr. Lubikov is working for, and how you two fit into that. You may be in further danger if his attack is related to your case."

"My apologies," Lana said. "I don't speak Finnish, but by any chance does the badge on your sleeve have anything to do with the Special Intelligence Service?"

"Why, yes," he said far too politely. "Why do you ask?"

So he wasn't a local cop. His accent didn't fit though. "I thought all MI-6 agents were British."

He sighed. "The similarity is an accident of language. The Finnish SIS is not the same as the British SIS."

"SIS is their national counter-terrorism squad," Lana said.

Oh crap. They thought we were involved with the Karelian separatists. We could kiss our trip to Uppsala goodbye for now.

"Do you mind if I make a phone call? I need to cancel some reservations."

CHAPTER 6

Oh, Those Russians

Over the next few hours we answered a boat load of questions, and by boat I mean supertanker. Our answers were truthful. The only thing we didn't mention was the sniper attack, or any suspicion that this attack might be related. If we had, we'd have had to explain why there was no police report on the incident. There was a possibility that this could bite us in the ass once the Russian started answering questions, but it was all we could do.

In retrospect, reporting the shooting to the London police might have been the wise thing to do. Hindsight is always 20/20.

Laakso seemed intrigued by our story that the Sampo was a real object, but he didn't let the fantasy elements of the case distract him from trying every trick in the book to poke holes in our story. He got nowhere with either of us.

Grigor Lubikov woke up about four hours after the attack, but the SIS wasn't getting any joy from him either.

His knee would need orthopaedic surgery if he was ever to walk again. He'd tried to gut me with his knife, so I wasn't in the least bit sorry. The Detective-Sergeant told us he was wanted on suspicion of 17 counts of murder. It served him right.

The big problem was that Lana had fractured his skull. As such things went his doctors didn't think it was too serious. I hoped he had a truly epic headache for the trouble he was causing us. The news also made me grateful that I'd mostly managed to deflect Lana's kicks when we fought.

Laakso would have concentrated on interrogating Grigor, but the Russian wasn't talking. Literally. At least, he wasn't making any sense. The fracture had given him aphasia, so everything that he tried to say was gibberish. The neurologists thought that it might be temporary, but they had no idea how long it might last.

Lana didn't react when we were told, as if giving somebody brain damage was of no consequence to her. This whole mess made me think of the guy I'd killed when I was sixteen. That was not a pleasant memory.

I assumed that the SIS were looking for anything in our lives that might point toward terrorist affiliations. As far as I knew we were both clean except for our BSI cell phones. This was not the time to be explaining why we had high-security encrypted phones if Laakso didn't have one of his own.

What probably sealed our innocence was when Dr. Lindberg called back the next morning. All I could provide to the police was her office number, and the university in Uppsala refused to give out her private number to a foreign agency without the proper paperwork.

At least we got to spend part of the night in our hotel room rather than a jail cell, albeit with several burly officers armed with MP-5s outside the door. The Detective-Sergeant told us they were there to guard us in case Grigor had an accomplice. We pretended to believe him.

I didn't blame them for the MP-5s. Given what we'd done to a trained military assassin in about three seconds, if I was him I'd find us freaking terrifying too. Of course we'd been lucky. If Lana hadn't seen him when she did, or if we'd been any slower, it could just as easily have been us lying on the pavement. It wouldn't pay to get cocky.

What concerned me was that I wasn't sure how to feel about our new reputation. On the one hand, it was cool to be considered such a bad ass. On the other, it brought back dreams about what I might do under the wrong circumstances. Sleep was slow in coming that night.

On the positive side I was definitely warming up to Lana—she was a good person to have at my back in a bad situation. Being a member of BSI also meant that she was trustworthy, at least to a certain extent. Her lack of a reaction to the mayhem bothered me, though.

How our relationship would change if and when we found the Sampo was something I didn't want to think about until later. It was likely to get very, very messy.

The sky was beginning to lighten when something woke me. It was a muffled noise coming from Lana's bed that sounded like someone trying to cry quietly. I never let on that I was awake, or that I'd heard her.

That made me feel better. It seemed that Lana wasn't a complete ice maiden after all.

∽

Laakso decided that we weren't terrorists after all. Dr. Lindberg must have been quite persuasive.

It turned out that there was a second flight to Sweden that day, and I was able to make reservations to leave at 9:40 p.m. We'd be in Stockholm just before midnight, but Dr. Lindberg still insisted on picking us up. Uppsala was about a 40 minute drive from the airport.

Apart from our trips to and from the Joensuu airport our rental car had sat in its parking stall the whole time we were there. We asked Detective-Sergeant Laakso to have his people go over it from bumper to bumper before we got in, just in case. We didn't want a car bomb to be our first clue that Grigor had friends who also didn't like us. He was a mercenary, which meant that *somebody* had hired him to attack us.

Before we left I had a chance to ask the Detective-Sergeant about the lack of road signs. He looked surprised.

"It's simple. Joensuu is the largest town in this area, which is also called Joensuu. I think you'd call it a county. Once you are in Joensuu county of course there are no signs leading to Joensuu: you are already here. That's why the road sign said Keskusta which means Centrum."

"That's—unusual."

He shrugged. "It's that way all over Scandinavia. We're used to it."

Getting out of town was much easier than getting in. *Siltakatu* went through the university and continued up until it met the highway at that first exit we'd ignored on the way in. From there we just retraced our steps to the airport.

In spite of being attacked and suspected of being a terrorist, I was going to miss Finland.

I found myself humming the Finlandia hymn. There were far worse ear worms.

⁓

Stockholm was yet another airport. One of these days I'd have to come back and actually visit these places. My preconceptions of Scandinavia were still making a fool of me. As we came out of the arrival hall I pictured Karen Lindberg as a tall, statuesque Valkyrie, but the woman holding a hand-printed sign reading CHANDLER/REVIERE was brunette, fortyish, my height, and pleasantly plump. On the way to Uppsala she brought us up to speed on the research.

"Seppo and I pieced together most of the information about Johan Agnetason from various church financial records. There was an allowance given to his guards for food, lodging, and transportation on his mission to Lappland. We also found a detailed description of the artifact he brought back and the Church's opinion of it. That description is what really excited Seppo."

"Did you find any sign of where the artifact went?"

"Not yet. There are some accounts that show Agnetason and his two guards going to Stockholm, but I couldn't find any further mention of them."

"What do we do now?" Lana asked.

"Let me explain the situation. The actual documents are stored in a climate-controlled facility. Unless there is a need to handle them, most scholars work with photographic reproductions on microfiche. There's also a fairly recent project to store them digitally, but that's less than half completed. I've been concentrating on the digital copies because they are easier to search. Now we need to look at the reproductions for any mention of our monk."

I could already feel my patience eroding. "Sounds exciting."

"I'm afraid that scholarly research rarely is. One set of documents that has recently become available is the personal papers of the archbishop from that time. If anybody knew what happened to the artifact, it would be him."

"That sounds like a promising place to start," Lana said.

Our hotel was about a kilometre from the university library where we'd be working. Dr. Lindberg said she'd pick us up at eight o'clock.

My e-mails home were very short that night. Morning was going to come early. Again.

The next two days consisted of getting out of bed, putting spools of film into a viewer, looking at old documents, and going to bed. We grabbed quick meals when we could. We knew the date when Johan had returned from his mission, so all we had to do was look at the Archbishop's papers dated after that. That was still a ton of documents.

Dr. Lindberg was only there about one third of the time, but she'd left us a list of keywords and phrases to look for. I was still feeling paranoid that Lana and I would miss something through ignorance.

On the morning of the third day there was an unexpected visitor waiting for us. Blond, blue-eyed, and fit beneath his uniform, he actually looked Swedish.

"Lana Reviere? I'm Chief Inspector Lucas Ljung of the Uppsala Police." They shook hands.

"I called Detective-Sergeant Laakso of the Finnish SIS to ask him if I could borrow some of his people for a case, and he mentioned that you were coming to Uppsala. I also learned that you are employed on occasion by the Metropolitan Police as a consultant."

"That's true. Is there something I can help you with?"

"We have a time-sensitive case that needs all the resources we can muster. Would you be willing to work with us? We would, of course, pay you for your time."

"If you need resources then we should include my associate in any discussions."

I extended my hand. "Veronica Chandler, private investigator."

He shook it. "Ms. Chandler. We would be happy to have all the help we can get."

"What sort of case is it?" Ljung looked at Dr. Lindberg, who picked up on his unspoken wish for privacy.

"Please, feel free to use my office," she said graciously. She went back to the microfiche reader she'd been using the day before.

Once we were in the office and the door was closed, the Chief Inspector got right to the point.

"Just before midnight last night three young women were kidnapped on their way home from a party."

"Has the kidnapper contacted the family about ransom yet?" Lana asked.

"No. There's been no word."

She frowned. "Almost nine hours without a ransom demand? That's unusual. Were there any witnesses?"

"No. The car and its occupants have completely disappeared. The GPS tracking system has been disabled."

I was thinking of alternatives. "Are we sure they were kidnapped? Maybe they just took off on a trip without telling anyone."

"We looked into that. Two of the girls have asthma, and one of them left the medication she requires at their home. Their mother said they'll sometimes share an inhaler if they are going out. If they had left of their own accord they would have taken it with them."

"All right," I said, "we'll assume kidnapping for now, but I don't see what we can do until the kidnappers make contact. They could be anywhere within a thousand kilometres."

"That's what we're afraid of. Kidnapping is a rare crime in Sweden, and when it does happen it rarely follows the predictable pattern that is seen in other countries. The women may have been taken for ransom, but it is more likely that they are being kept as slaves or for some other non-monetary reason."

"We understand," Lana said. "How can we help?"

"We have every available officer working to find leads, but I understand that you have a reputation for creative thinking that may be of benefit here. We need analysts and people to generate new lines of enquiry. Frankly, at this point I would almost consider using psychics."

"You *must* be desperate," Lana said.

"I take it that there aren't many leads," I said.

"At this moment, none. The longer the women are missing the less likely it is that we will recover them before anything worse happens to them."

"I'm more than happy to give whatever assistance I can."

"Hell, yes," I said.

"Thank you. I have a car outside, if we can leave now."

I answered Dr. Lindberg's curious look as we left her office. "We're assisting the Chief Inspector on a criminal matter. We'll be back as soon as possible."

"All right. I'll keep looking for our elusive Johan."

The Chief Inspector rated a driver, so he was able to answer our questions while we rode in the back of the car. The first things he gave us were copies of the case file. They had been translated into English in case we agreed to help. Judging by the weird bits of grammar here and there the translation was done by software.

Elsa, Alice, and Maja Blomgren had gone to a party at a friend's house. The girls were 16-year old triplets which made the case even more unusual. Did the kidnapper target them because they were identical? Their pictures showed them to be quite pretty, which also might or might not have something to do with why they were abducted. Their parents were financially comfortable, but not enough to be considered at high risk of being targeted. Sadly, that increased the chance that this was a human trafficking abduction, revenge, or perhaps something else. At this point we couldn't rule anything out.

Maja had called home 30 minutes before midnight to say they were on their way. That was the last anybody had heard from them.

Sweden didn't have government CCTV cameras, but a lot of businesses had them and were willing to share the recordings. Cameras along the most likely routes the girls would have taken were being searched for anything useful.

"I see that you have imposed a news blackout," Lana said after about five minutes of reading. "May I suggest the opposite tactic. Put the event on every television and radio station, as well as the newspapers."

"We were hoping to find a lead before alerting the kidnappers that we were after them. We don't want to provoke them."

"Normally I would agree, but it says here in the background information that Swedish kidnappers tend to travel a long distance to their hideout."

"Yes, in the last such case the kidnapper kept the victim about 500 kilometres from the abduction point."

"At this point it hardly matters. The kidnapper hasn't instructed anyone not to involved the police, so he has to take that as a given. If we make the car stand out he'll have to go to ground much sooner. That makes the search radius smaller. If he can't use the car he can't move them."

"What if he has another vehicle?"

"We do what we can. If the public is looking for any vehicle with three identical teenage girls in it, he'll have to be more creative in his transportation plans. He won't be able to afford to slip up in any way."

Ljung thought for a few seconds, then pulled out his phone and gave some orders.

"Here's another suggestion. In the news release ask merchants to keep an eye out for people who are making unusual purchases; a known bachelor buying meals for four, buying women's clothing, tampons and such like. Anything you can think of that might indicate that a single man is now taking care of three women. Make it difficult for him to hide them."

"I can see a difficulty with this. Suppose he decides to abandon his scheme and kill them?"

"Regardless of his reason for taking them, that's unlikely," I said. "He went to the trouble of abducting three women, but he hasn't made any demands. That may mean that he wants them for something besides money. He'll wait as long as possible before killing them, trying to make his plan work. Abducting more women will be much more difficult after this."

"And what is his plan?"

"I have no idea. Probably a psychotic delusion or a human trafficker. What are the chances of a trafficker in Sweden?"

"If your are talking about procurement, it's very low. We have perhaps 20 to 30 cases of trafficking a year, but those are all receivers. The people originate elsewhere. I've never heard of a case where Swedes were kidnapped for trafficking."

The command centre was in a big white building on the other side of the Fyris River that was the police station, prosecutor's office, traffic police, and police training area.

When we arrived we were given security badges and introduced to the staff. We were also given a small desk in a corner where we could do our brainstorming. The desk had a computer so we could do research as well as sending and receiving official e-mails. Of course any e-mails were in Swedish, but we could cut and paste them into a web browser for translation. Enough people in the centre spoke English that we could as for clarification if necessary. It wasn't a great system but it worked.

Once we got settled I went through the file again. "Something bothers me about this abduction."

Lana looked up from her file. "Apart from the fate of the three women?"

"Do you agree that there's only one kidnapper?"

"I agree that it's most probable. They were driving a Peugeot 308, which is not going to fit more than five adults. Four if you want to sit in the back and still have room to be a credible threat to all three of your captives."

"Okay, one kidnapper in the back seat. I looked up the specs on their car. It has a GPS panic button. Why didn't they activate it?"

"The kidnapper has a weapon."

"Or is so terrifying they don't dare to stand up to him."

"What could make him that terrifying?"

I was keeping notes as we talked. "I don't know. Appearance? Threats? 'I'll kill your family if you don't come with me?' The girls would have no way of knowing if he could make good on the threat."

An e-mail arrived from a Senior Police Constable with a video from a gas station just west of Uppsala. It was timestamped 23:50 which was consistent with the phone call from Maja plus travel time. It showed one of the girls filling the tank. She looked terrified. Judging from the time she was there, she only put a small amount of fuel in the car, which was odd. Either the tank was empty and she added very little, or the tank was full and they wasted time topping it up.

I sent an e-mail to Ljung: *Is it possible to find out how much fuel was in the car when the girls started for home?*

It only took about 20 minutes for somebody to phone enough of the people who had been at the party to get the answer. One of the triplets told her friend that they had to leave early so they could stop for fuel on the way home. Otherwise they might not make it.

Home was about 3.5 kilometres from the party, so if they were worried they'd probably been running on empty for some time. The gas station was about five kilometres away, and in the opposite direction. The girls must have been abducted somewhere between the two.

I e-mailed our findings. Ljung already had people combing the route trying to find a witness. We also had him contact the SPC who had gotten the video to find out how much gas the girl had bought.

The SPC was still at the station, so the answer came back almost immediately. The owner remembered her because she'd paid for five litres in cash and looked scared. A little research showed that a 308 should be able to go about 68 km on that much fuel.

Either they stopped for more gas almost immediately, which would increase the chances of being noticed, or the car was within 70 kilometres of the gas station.

We watched the video, and the girl kept looking at the car as if somebody was talking to her. I could imagine the kidnapper telling her to hurry, that they didn't have far to go. It was possible that the guy had a second vehicle stashed somewhere nearby.

Another e-mail came in. A constable had found a piece of jewellery on the street. She included a picture of it so the family and friends could be asked if any of the girls owned it.

From the look of the gloved hand holding it, the silver pendant was about three centimetres across. Letters were spaced evenly around the perimeter—ARZEP? The design in the centre looked like a Grecian lyre with pitchforks sticking out the sides. From the jagged edges it was clearly cut with a saw rather than cast.

My stomach dropped. I recognized the style, if not the design itself, from my first case. I copied it on a scrap of paper and told Lana that I was going to the washroom.

Once I had privacy in a stall I compared the design with the sigils in a copy of the Lesser Key of Solomon I had on my phone for situations just like this. It only took me a few seconds to find it.

The pendant was the seal of the demon Zepar. According to the book, he was a great duke who appears clothed in red and armed like a soldier. His speciality was to cause women to love men and to bring them together. He also could make women barren, which seemed like a strange side line. Unless you were a delusional kidnapper who wanted three sex slaves who couldn't clutter up the house with children.

What the hell was it with these guys and lust demons?

My own history with the demon Sitri came flooding in and washed over me. I had trouble catching my breath.

I sat on the toilet and cried for at long time while the terror and revulsion went through me. The last time I'd encountered a demon he'd used some kind of mind control to make me insane with lust for him. If I hadn't been badly injured and tied up I might—no, I *would* have—given in to the feelings without question. It was the most horrifying feeling possible. It wasn't that he overcame my resistance. There was no fight; no chance that I might win. As though a switch had been thrown, I suddenly wanted him unconditionally.

It had taken a long time for me to learn to handle the sense of violation, to the extent that I was handling it. The problem was made bigger by the fact that I couldn't share it with my therapist. Not unless I could convince her that demons were real. So far only Kali knew.

If my suspicion was right, those three girls could be going through that same thing right now. They'd have no idea what was happening. They'd have no way to save themselves.

I manged to turn around and kneel before I threw up into the toilet.

After a while I calmed down enough to stop crying and remember that Sitri wasn't the only demon I'd encountered. While Beleth wasn't sane or safe by any stretch of the imagination at least she was sometimes female and she hadn't tried to take over my mind. Maybe. For some reason she also seemed to like me, in her own sociopathic way.

Sitri had told me that all the fancy rituals and props magicians used to summon demons didn't matter. In particular, the magic circles used to protect people from demons didn't work. Demons could just walk straight through it, but they seemed to like playing the game with humans.

Did that mean that I could just call on Beleth? Would she be pissed off if I did? Or was there a chance that she could help me find the girls before horrible things happened to them?

Or would she enslave me the way she had turned two men into human dressage horses against their wishes?

The intensity of my emotional storm finally leached away. I was back on the seat, wiping my eyes with toilet paper when there was a knock on the stall door.

"Veronica? Are you all right?"

How long had I been in here? "Sure, Lana. I'll be out in a minute."

She was gone when I came out. I quickly splashed some cold water on my face, hoping to hide the signs of my tears. I could still hope that we'd find a lead to crack this case before I seriously had to consider seeking demonic help. That had to be our last resort.

When I got back to the command centre not much had changed. The family couldn't remember seeing the pendant before, so the police were trying to find out who might have sold it. Technicians were at the family home collecting finger prints in case we got ones to match. Nobody had made the demonic connection yet, although they were also running down every combination of the letters on the pendant in case it was the kidnapper's name or at least lead somewhere useful.

I had a sudden, encouraging through. At least I could add something to the thin list of leads. I'd been lying to Mum and Dad about this stuff for years. Fooling the Swedish police should be a piece of cake.

"I think I've seen something like that pendant before."

"Really?"

"I think the guy made it himself. If I'm right, it's a demonic sigil."

Nothing gets you attention during an investigation like claiming there are demons involved. For show, I used the computer to look up the Lesser Key.

"Yup. Zepar."

Lana looked over my shoulder. "How does this help us find the kidnapper?"

"Look for a single guy who has bought jewellery making supplies in the past few months. This also means the girls are still relatively safe."

Lana sat down. "Now you've lost me."

"The whole point to these pendants is that the Key says you have to wear one when summoning the demon. If this guy thinks some demon is going to make them want him, he needs to summon Zepar *after* he has the women, so if the kidnapper lost the sigil he'll need a replacement before he can do the summoning. This also confirms that the kidnapper is male."

"Because...?"

"Because the biography for Zepar says 'his office is to cause women to love men.' He doesn't work with lesbians."

"Surely you don't believe in this sort of thing."

"Of course not." *Until it happened to me.* "It's what the kidnapper believes that's important."

"Even if you're right, it couldn't take more than a few hours to make another pendant. It's a simple design."

"Ah, that's where his beliefs trip him up. You can't just whip up a magical tool. It has to be done at special times and under special circumstances."

"How long do we have?"

"I don't know. I'd have to read up on it."

Chief Inspector Ljung thought the new interpretation was plausible, and set his people to interviewing suppliers as well as jewellers. I also suggested concentrating on buyers to the west of us. There was no reason why he'd have forced the girls to drive west just for gas. His hideout was in that direction. Of course, so was a big chunk of Sweden, not to mention.

I hoped that at least one of the girls was thinking clearly enough to play along with his delusions. If he thought they were glad to be with him without demonic influence he might slip up enough for one or all of them to escape. If you are captured by a psychotic you only buy yourself trouble by constantly telling him he's crazy, but you might catch him out if you play along.

The police had a good handle on the investigation. It should be only a matter of time before we nailed this guy without demonic intervention.

Unless he summoned Zepar *before* the abduction and lost the sigil *after* the demon had put the whammy on the girls. That would explain how he captured them and it would be bad. I had no idea if the mind control could be undone by anybody but the demon. Maybe Beleth would know.

That scenario didn't work, though. If the girls were slaves before the abduction the one pumping gas wouldn't have looked so frightened.

Unless she was afraid that she'd be taken away from him if they were caught.

There were too many possibilities.

In the early afternoon we broke for a late lunch. After that I napped in one of the chairs for a while to let my subconscious mull over the case.

I don't know if Lana napped or not, but she was up when I got back to our desk.

"What did I miss?"

"We believe that we've found the silver supplier. Unfortunately, the buyer paid cash and we don't have his name."

"Do we have video or a sketch to add to the news broadcast?"

"Not yet. We're hoping he comes back for more silver to make a second pendant."

"I don't think that's wise. He may already have enough supplies to make a second one. Did anybody get the amount he bought?"

Lana skimmed through the e-mail file updates. "Yes. I'd estimate that he bought enough silver for three such pendants. But he may have spoiled several before he got it right. Or he might have made pendants for various demons."

"Or he might not. The pendant isn't hard to make even for an amateur if you're careful. At the time the Lesser Key was written, *everything* was made by hand. There are no extra points for artistry."

"Any idea how long it would take him to make the new pendant?"

I went back to the computer and started reading. It took a while to work through the directions that sometimes assumed you already knew how to do most of it.

"He can only work on the pendant during hours 1, 8, 15, and 22 on Sunday or Monday. I'm going to guess at two hours to do the actual work. If he starts working at one a.m. he could be done by nine a.m."

"That means we have until sometime tomorrow morning."

"I just found something else. For some reason, the Key says that Dukes can be summoned only between sunrise and noon in clear weather. That means he'd have about three hours after finishing the pendant to do the ritual."

"Is that long enough?"

"Yeah, unfortunately. It is."

Shit, this was not looking good. This meant that we had to rescue the girls by ten o'clock on Sunday morning at the latest, assuming that the weather held. I checked the weather forecast. Damn. There was no chance of rain on Sunday.

It was now mid-afternoon on Saturday.

We were running out of time in a big way. Was there any way to extend the deadline? I couldn't think of one. We had no sure way of reaching the guy to reason with him. The enslavement of the girls by Zepar would happen as sure as sunrise if we didn't get a major lead in the next few hours, and I was the only one who knew it.

I could convince the police that we had a deadline approaching, but not why it was imperative that we beat it. They'd see my point about his "delusions," but assume that if the ritual didn't work he'd just try again the next day.

I wondered if the BSI could do anything for me, but I had no idea what. If we'd had evidence that needed processing, sure. But how could they reliably get in touch with the unknown kidnapper when we couldn't?

Oh fuck. I'm going to have to do it. My courage wandered around looking for a sticking place and not finding it.

I grabbed my copy of the case file, and cleared my throat. I could still hear the unsteadiness in my own voice. "Lana, I'm going to be busy for a while. Call me if I'm needed."

"Where are you going?" I pretended not to hear her as I walked away. *If it were done when 'tis done, then 'twere well it were done quickly.*

The first thing was to find somebody in the centre who spoke English. After my third try I found a young Constable Trainee.

"I need the use of a small room with a door that locks."

"What for?"

It sounded a bit stupid, even to me, but it was all I had. "I want to meditate about the case. See if I can come up with anything else to help us identify the kidnapper."

I had to explain 'meditate,' which hadn't come up in his English classes.

"How much time do you need?"

"An hour or two?"

He looked dubious, but the Chief Inspector had told everybody to cooperate with us on information requests. The trainee decided this must count.

He led me to a small combination shower room and toilet. It was spotlessly clean, but somehow looked like nobody had used it for a long time.

"This was built for visiting officials, but everybody just uses the locker rooms."

"Thanks. It's perfect."

He gave me another confused look, and closed the door. I sat cross-legged on the tile floor, and put down in front of me the copy of the case file I'd brought.

Now I just needed to get Beleth's attention. I had a copy of the ritual on my phone, but none of the props. If the ritual truly didn't matter, then as long as she was listening I should get through.

I felt ridiculous talking to an empty room, and terrified that it wouldn't be empty for long.

"Beleth, this is Veronica Chandler. Can you hear me? I need to talk to you about something important. Beleth, can you hear me?"

I kept up the monologue, with variations, for almost an hour. At any moment I expected somebody to either pound on the door or let themselves in with a key to find out what I was doing.

I was beginning to relax, thinking that it wasn't going to work anyway and this was a pointless exercise. Even if Beleth was getting the message, why would she come talk to me?

Mist swirled before me and became a tiny woman wearing a micro skirt and an unbuttoned blouse tied under her DD breasts. Like me, she was sitting cross-legged. Standing, she'd be a hand-width over a metre tall.

Something jumped off her lap and I almost freaked out before recognizing it. It was a miniature horse, about ten centimetres tall. It snorted, and trotted out to explore the room. It was hard for me not to watch it, and the tiny hoof taps on the tiles were distracting.

Weird piled on top of strange. This was Beleth, all right.

"You rang?" she said, leaning back on her arms.

I tried to find some moisture in my mouth. "I have a problem, and I was hoping you could help."

"Since it's you asking, I suppose I could spare a few moments. Who do you need killing?"

"Nobody. I don't need anybody killed. I just need some information."

"Bo-ring. Nobody ever wants to be bothered with dead bodies any more. Or sex. There isn't enough sex in the world, but I hardly need to tell you that. Do you need help with a man? Men? I can get them for you by the dozen. Guaranteed fresh."

I *so* didn't need that at this moment either. "Somebody has kidnapped..."

"Three girls. Yes. I know."

"You do?"

"Of course. I'm not completely out of the loop. Besides, I keep an eye on Zepar with his pathetic 'oh, look at me! I'm a big, bad soldier!' routine. Like that's going to get the women any more interested in him than they are now. Which, I don't mind telling you, is not at all." She made a circle with her thumb and forefinger. "Zip. Nada. Can you imagine the ironic pathos of somebody whose speciality is getting people to fall in love who isn't getting any?" She looked at her finger circle, then poked her other forefinger through it repeatedly. "He needs somebody to take him in hand. Show him the ropes. Or maybe take him in..."

"Could we get back on topic for a moment?" Now that she was actually here and prattling on as she usually did, I felt less terrified that she was going to do something unnatural to me. It could still happen without warning, though. I didn't understand her or her motivations, and given her power that ignorance made her insanely dangerous.

She folded her hands demurely in her lap. "As you wish." Creepy.

"Do you know if the girls are all right?"

She looked absent for a moment. "Yes, they are. If you discount being frightened and tied up in a basement by a lonely psychotic."

"They're in a basement?"

I swear, she rolled her eyes. "Well of *course*. Where do *you* keep your captives?"

"Where is the basement?"

"Under the house."

Goddamned literal demons. "Under *what* house?"

"The house that Matteo Bjorklund built. First on the left as you come into town." She though that was hysterically funny.

"Great. And where is this house?"

"In Testa, of course. That's where he lives. Where else would he build it?"

Now for the part I'd really feared.

"What do you want for the information?"

"Silly girl, you should have asked that first."

"Yes, I should. But I needed to know about the girls, so name your price."

She had a small, secret smile as she rocked forward onto her knees. She was on me before I could recoil. I'd seen her move that fast before and had no idea how she managed it.

One of her hands went on my thigh, entirely too high up for comfort. It felt warm. The other slid around the back of my neck and played with my hair. She leaned in very close to my ear so I could feel her breath on it.

She whispered. "You don't have to pay anything." Then she licked my ear.

Under much different circumstances that would have been an extremely arousing sensation, but the kind of involuntary shivers she sent down my body weren't at all sexual. I pulled back.

"Are you serious?"

"Of course. We're such *good* friends I couldn't *possibly* charge you for a tiny favour."

I tried to stop shivering. As soon as she left I was going to scrub the side of my head. "Um, thank you."

"*De nada, amiga.*"

She made little kiss noises and the horse came trotting back to her. She picked it up and cradled it in one hand, using the other forefinger to pet it under its chin. The little horse whinnied in an appropriately high voice.

There was a swirl of mist, and then nothing but the empty shower room, and my wet ear.

I got to my feet a little unsteadily after sitting on the cold floor, retrieved the file, and ran water into the sink. As I scrubbed I thought about what to do next.

I had a name and a place. All I had to do was figure out how to tell everybody without revealing anything about my source.

Because that would open me up all kinds of questions I really couldn't answer. Not and stay out of a psychiatric hospital.

Another thing bothered me. Beleth's lack of a price sounded entirely too much like a drug dealer saying "the first one's free."

～⌘～

I unlocked the door and made my way back to the command centre. There had to be some way to generate a new lead without actually *having* a new lead.

If only the guy who supplied the silver had gotten a name... and then I had it. I was about to do something that was exceedingly close to the dark side.

Lana looked up as I walked in. "Where were you?"

"Thinking about the case. Any developments?"

"None yet."

"I want to interview the guy who sold him the silver. They might not have gotten everything he knows."

"You'll need to run that by the Chief Inspector."

I called him and made my request.

"At the risk of sounding rude, what makes you think you can get any more information from him than my people already did?"

"Are your constables trained to conduct cognitive interviews?"

"No. I've heard of them at police conferences. Are you?"

"Yes. May I try?"

He considered for a minute. "I don't see why not. We already have his statement. If there is anything else you can discover it might be useful."

It wasn't quite a bald-faced lie, but it was close. I'd seen cognitive interviews done on TV several times, but I'd also done some research into the technique. It really did tend to get more information from witnesses than the standard police interrogation methods, and wasn't as difficult as it sounded. At least, that's what I hoped.

I found my Constable Trainee and told him to call the silver supplier, Fredrick Johansson. I was in luck—he was still at his shop.

Johansson had a small shop across the river from the Uppsala Cathedral. Also lucky for me he spoke English. I had my Constable Trainee assigned to me as my driver and guide. I'd have to get rid of him when it came time for the interview.

Johansson looked to be in his late sixties. When we arrived he was helping a young couple who were looking at rings. They left a few minutes later.

I started as soon as they left. "Fredrik Johansson? My name is Veronica Chandler. I'm working with the police on the kidnapping case. I was wondering if I could ask you some questions."

He seemed puzzled. "I already told a constable what I know."

"I realize that, but I was hoping that you would have the time to try a different approach. At this point, we can only save the girls' lives if you can remember more details."

I was deliberately putting pressure on him, setting him up want to help to the point where I could manipulate him. It wasn't ethical, and possibly illegal, and I wasn't at all happy about it. But it was the only way I could think of that would allow me to inject the demonic assistance into the investigation without the information being ignored until it was too late.

"How long with this take?"

"Not very long. We can do it here if you wish."

He hesitated, then called into the back. A woman about his age came out and they spoke in Swedish for a while.

"My wife will take over out here. We can go to the storeroom."

The room was jammed with shelves and boxes, which from my perspective was perfect. I spoke quietly to my driver.

"It's crowded back here. Why don't you go have supper? I'll phone you when we're done." He thought that was a great idea, as I suspected he would. None of us had been eating regularly.

We found two stools and I asked Fredrik to get comfortable.

"If you don't mind, please close your eyes. It will help."

"You aren't going to hypnotize me, are you?"

"No, nothing like that. I'll just lead you through your memories of what really happened."

He seemed dubious, but did as I asked. I led him through some quick breathing exercises so he'd loosen up a bit.

"What was the date on which Bjorklund came to your shop?"

"Excuse me, but who is that?"

"The man who bought the silver from you. Matteo Bjorklund."

"The third of March. Is that his name?"

"Don't people usually introduce themselves to you?"

"Sometimes."

"What was the weather like on that day? How did he enter your shop?"

He furrowed his brow, trying to remember.

"Cloudy. It was cold. There was a blast of wind that came in when he opened the door."

"What did he say?"

"He wanted to buy a piece of 1.6 millimetre silver sheet, a saw, some blades, and a graver. He was quite specific about it."

"Did you write a receipt for him?"

"I was going to, but he said not to bother."

"Was that before or after he mentioned his name?"

"I don't... I'm not sure when..."

"Think carefully. If you were going to write a receipt, you would have asked for his name and address, wouldn't you?"

"Yes."

"So did you ask before or after you started writing the receipt?"

"It must have been before, but then he told me not to bother with one."

"That's probably why you didn't remember the name before. You are used to writing them down."

He looked unhappy. "That makes sense. I'm sorry."

"Don't be. Just relax. We have the name now. Do you remember where he's from? Go back to the moment when you are about to write the receipt. You asked his name, yes?"

"Yes."

"And he told you his name before realizing he needed to hide it."

"Yes. Matteo Bjorklund."

"Then you asked where he was from?"

"Yes. I think so."

"You must have, it was the next logical question."

"Yes. Of course."

"It's very important that we know where he's from, so we can save those girls. Maybe you know but are having difficulty remembering. That sometimes happens to everyone, doesn't it?"

"Oh, yes."

"Was it Vänge?" I'd gotten the pronunciations of several villages west of Uppsala from the internet and hoped that I was close enough.

He shook his head. "No, I don't think so."

"Was it Hagby?"

"No."

"It was Testa?" I emphasized the name slightly. As expected, he subconsciously picked up on the added importance.

"I... it might be."

"Go back to that day in your mind. Can you picture yourself asking where he's from?"

"Yes."

"Good. Now picture him answering you. Focus on his lips as he says Testa. Can you see that?"

"Yes, I think it is. Yes. He said he was from Testa."

"Wonderful. You can open your eyes now. You should be proud of yourself. Without you we wouldn't have had a chance to save those girls."

He looked much happier now, as well he might. I'd just made him a hero. I thanked him again and called the constable to be picked up.

As I waited outside I felt like crap. Basically, I'd just installed false memories in a nice old man who just wanted to help. The nicest thing you could call what I'd done was witness tampering. That I'd done it for the best of reasons didn't make me feel much better about myself. I needed to establish some legitimate way that I could bring a name and location to the police, and now I had one.

Is it still wrong to alter a person's memories if they are happier afterward? Probably. Especially given that I sure as hell didn't ask his permission first.

Maybe I should have, but as a somewhat willing co-conspirator his story might have been broken in court. This way he'd defend the details he'd just "remembered," especially when they were justified by being used to rescue the girls. How could that have happened if what he'd remembered had been false?

My biggest worry was that Beleth was playing me for a fool. If the girls weren't in Testa then not only would I have wasted time and resources, but Johansson would eventually realize that I'd fed him the names and tell the police. At the very least they would want to know why I'd suddenly gone crazy. After all, I wasn't the consultant they'd originally wanted on this case. I was just a bonus player.

My only consolation was that Beleth didn't seem to like this demon Zepar that Matteo Bjorklund was summoning. I didn't trust her to care about the girls or me, but I did trust her to care about herself.

Before we left the shop I had my driver radio the Chief Inspector with the names and were told to stand by. A few moments later a picture of

Bjorklund, probably from his driver's license, was e-mailed to the phone so we could show it to Johansson for confirmation.

The jeweller confirmed that it was the same man, which made me feel much better about the accuracy of the information. By the time we arrived in the command centre only Lana and the lower ranking people were left. Everyone else from the range of Sergeant up had joined the operation. In Sweden ordinary Constables can't arrest anybody. You have to be at least a Sergeant.

For those of us who weren't invited along, the whole operation was a slightly frustrating radio play. I didn't really mind. There was likely to be a lot of people with guns running around and I was happy to listen in from a safe distance. One of the constables in the command centre translated for us more or less in real time.

The guest stars were a squad from the Piketen, the Swedish equivalent of our tactical or hostage rescue teams. They were based in Stockholm, so things got interesting about two hours after we called in Bjorklund's name. Somebody at the command centre had produced a hard copy of a map of Testa and stuck it on the wall for those of us playing along at home. The village was a kilometre off a secondary road and consisted of about half a dozen houses plus assorted other buildings nestled in a wooded area. Bjorklund's place was the first left immediately after turning into the village.

I could picture the scene all too well. A huddle of dark SUVs somewhere out of sight of the village. Dark clad people with helmets and MP-5s flitting through the trees like hunting cats. Teams reaching their assigned positions and squatting behind cover.

It was interesting to see that the same colour-coding of buildings that was used by the Calgary police was used here too: white and black for front and rear, green and red for right and left.

"All teams report." The voice on the radio was calm and authoritative. This wasn't their commander's first party.

"White team standing by."

"Red team standing by."

I couldn't resist. "Blue leader standing by."

Our translator looked confused. "There is no blue team. Blue would be on the roof of the house."

Lana snorted. "That will teach you not to make Star Wars jokes."

"Green team standing by."

"Black team standing by."

"Final briefing," said their commander. "Back-scatter x-ray shows one target moving. Front and back doors are reinforced steel. Breach will be through the green windows. Confirm."

"Green team confirm. Breach through our windows."

"There is no sign of the hostages in the house, so we need Bjorklund alive for questioning. Confirm."

All four teams confirmed. I knew the girls were in the cellar, but it wasn't something he would ever have told Johansson. As long as they were out of the line of fire, it didn't matter.

That the Piketen were using back-scatter x-rays to map the interior of the building before entry was impressive. It was the same technology used in some airport scanners. Basically, they could see through the walls. Who needs Superman?

"Command, we have eyes on the target. He's in the kitchen on green. He appears to be sitting at a table, possibly eating."

"Green team, copy."

"All teams, all teams. Execute on my order. Go, go, go!"

There was the sound of glass breaking, a muffled explosion that was probably a flash-bang, and men shouting in Swedish.

"Target is secure. No casualties. Commencing sweep."

"Command, green. The cellar door is locked and armoured. Target refuses to give us the key. Upper floors are clear. We'll need a breaching charge."

"Copy green. Demolition, go."

I knew a little about this from talking to the Calgary tactical team. One of their experts could put together a plastic frame that contained exactly enough C-4 (or Semtex here in Europe) in just the right pattern to buckle the door out of its frame without killing anybody leaning against the other side. That didn't guarantee that they might not be injured, though.

It only took a few minutes, but time dragged while the explosives were set. There was another muffled explosion.

The next fifteen seconds were the longest of my life.

"Command, we have secured all three hostages. Two are having trouble breathing. We need the paramedics."

The radio chatter remained professional. Where we were, people were cheering and hugging. My driver hugged me and I wasn't at all opposed. He was cute.

"Good job. Can you unlock the white door so the paramedics can enter, or will we have to breach?"

"Stand by." There was a pause. "We found his keys. Door unlocked. The hostages want us to bring them outside immediately. I don't blame them. You have to see this place. This guy was crazy."

I wiped the tears from my eyes. Everybody thought I was happy the girls had been found, but there was more. If they wanted to leave, Zepar hadn't had a chance to work on them yet.

I'd gambled and won. I might be the world's least ethical investigator but at least in this case Beleth had told me the truth and the ends justified the means.

I wondered how many bad guys throughout history had lulled themselves to sleep with that one.

⁓

For me, the aftermath was embarrassing. They'd brought in Lana because of her reputation as a criminologist, and then I got all the credit because I'd faked doing some stuff I'd seen on *Criminal Minds*. I just wanted it to end.

Fortunately, finding the girls tied up in his basement, lying on a ceremonial circle waiting for him to invoke a demon to make them his love slaves forever was pretty much a gimme as far as the prosecution went. Especially since he had told the girls exactly what his plan was, as well as confessing to the police. He seemed very proud of himself.

The case was so tight that Johansson was told that it was unlikely he'd ever have to testify. The facts were self-evident, and the ends justified the means.

The girls were in need of some good counselling, but physically they were barely even scratched. He'd captured them by simply walking out in front of their car at a stop sign and waving a pistol at them. Once he was in the car they didn't have much choice but to play along. It made me extremely glad that I'd been going to Krav Maga classes for the past—my god, was it really over ten years?

The case got us some serious reputation among the Swedish police. There was even talk of an award ceremony, but I absolutely refused. It was time go back to our own work.

Anything to get the taste of this case out of my mouth.

⁓

For two more days we waded through documents.

Dr. Lindberg was with us in the afternoon of day five. "I have found something."

Lana and I huddled around her microfiche reader while she translated aloud from the archbishop's journal.

"A plan has presented itself to me that, if successful, will not only put Johan the bastard far from the wrath of the Oxenstierna family, but also deliver a blow to Sigismund's activities in Poland. I must think more on the details, but tasking Johan with delivering Satan's Millstone to the Catholics as a gift might save many Swedish lives on the battlefield."

"Who's Sigismund?" Lana asked a fraction ahead of me.

"He was the Catholic king of Poland and Sweden until 1599, when he was deposed here by Charles IX. He spent the rest of his life trying to regain the Swedish crown."

"When did he die?"

"I'm not sure. Sometime in the 1630s, I think."

"So, whatever happened, the 'millstone' didn't seem to have much effect on him."

"It would appear not."

We went back to work with more enthusiasm. If Olof Mårtensson had sent Johan to Poland there had to be some record of it in his papers.

Dr. Lindberg split our efforts. Lana continued to look for references in the archbishop's papers. She gave me suggestions of where to look in the financial records. Fortunately for me, the ones I wanted had been digitized.

I hit pay dirt the next morning.

"It's a disbursement of 100 *thaler* to Ander Jorgenson. Isn't that the name of one of Johan's guards?"

"Yes. Let me see."

Dr. Lindberg examined the entry, and flipped back and forth between different documents a few times.

"Passage on a Danish ship to Gdańsk for three men, including a Brother Johan, and Pål—I can't read the last name. These are definitely the men we're looking for."

Lana looked thoughtful. "How much is 100 *thaler*? I'm wondering how far that would have gotten them."

"At the time that would have been about what a skilled craftsman would make in four years."

"So they were well funded. Now what?"

"I'd suggest the archbishop's papers. He would have mentioned it if they had come back."

We spent another two days staring at microfiche of old documents until I thought I'd go blind. Olof had several opinions about how words should be spelled, even within the same document, and 400 years had not been kind to some of the papers. There were tears, stains, and what, in a few cases, looked suspiciously like bite marks. Dr. Lindberg said they were from rats in the old archives.

There was no further mention of Johan.

"I don't think there's anything more to be found here."

I rubbed my eyes. "I don't think so either. We have them going to Gdańsk on their way to see Sigismund. The archbishop seems to have lost track of them after that. How do we follow them from there?"

"You'll have to try sources in Poland. From what little the Archbishop was willing to put in writing, they were pretending to be Swedish Catholics. There may be church records in Poland where they sought shelter on their travels. I can give you a letter of introduction that may open some doors for you."

"Thank you for everything you've done. We'll let you know what we find."

I turned to Lana. "Ready for another road trip?"

CHAPTER 7

The Confession (translated from Latin)

During the year I had been in Lappland I had attempted to stay warm by neither cutting my hair or shaving. My beard was massive, and my hair was as wild as any madman. If anybody was still looking for me in Sweden I had no fear that they would recognize me. The only exceptions would be my former companions in crime and Brita. They alone might discover me by my voice, though even that had coarsened somewhat by being exposed to the cold, salty air by the Murmans Sea.

After several months in Upsala the Archbishop called for me. He told me that it had been decided that the device, whatever its purpose, was of Demonic origin. No amount of praying for guidance had given them any hint as to its intended purpose. One priest had touched the lid while it was glowing and caused apparitions to dance above it, but after a time they went away and he could not remember exactly what he had done to cause it. Nothing that they had tried seemed to harm it in the least.

When not being examined, the device was kept wrapped in a consecrated altar cloth in a lead-lined chest covered with religious symbols and Biblical texts. So far this had kept our people safe, but the Church was growing increasingly nervous about the dire possibilities if we kept it in Sweden.

I was told that the king, Charles IX, had devised a plot whereby it would be gifted anonymously to his nephew Sigismund who had been king of Sweden and Poland until he was forced to abdicate the Swedish throne. Sigismund was Catholic, and was raising an army in Poland to reconquer the Swedish throne that he believed to be his by right.

I had doubts about the morality of gifting a diabolical device even to an enemy, but the Archbishop assured me that any stratagem was permissible against foes such as the Catholics.

As the man who had been given the device by the Sami, and in light of the skills I had obtained during my previous life as a highwayman, I was tasked with the mission.

Still, it was with considerable reservation that my companions and I set sail for Poland on a ship flying Danish colours. We were to make our way secretly to Sigismund's new capital, Warszawa, where we would contact a priest who was sympathetic to the Swedish cause.

Father Donat Bartosz of the Society of Jesus, since gone to the loving arms of our Father, had been placed in Warszawa by the Chancellor Jan Zamoyski who opposed Sigismund's bid to regain the Swedish throne. Father Donat would introduce us to Sigismund under the ruse that I was a Catholic priest who had survived in Sweden and, with my faithful companions, had smuggled this holy relic out of the country to aid the true king in his return to power. The plan was almost certain to succeed as Sigismund put great faith in the opinions of the Society of Jesus and would do almost nothing without consulting them. The endorsement of Father Donat was certain to sway him to our will.

All of this was very well, but gave me a great deal of unease that my companions and I would be required to lie in order to get a man to accept a demonic gift. Even if he was Catholic that didn't seem very Christian to me. King Charles and the Archbishop obviously disagreed with me on this matter. Being good soldiers, Ander and Pål expressed no opinions on this matter of policy.

Our ship landed at Gdańsk, a city with a large Lutheran population despite Sigismund's influence. Pål went ashore and arranged for four horses. It was fortunate that our finances for this trip were considerably greater than for my Lapland ministry.

Rather than try to find our way straight across country to Warszawa, my companions thought that we should follow the road along the Wisła River. Although this would take longer, it was a safer route. Catholic-paid mercenaries, especially the savage Croats, were roaming the countryside. We had no inclination to hurry and draw attention to ourselves. Traffic along the river met with more tolerance as it was the major trade route through the country.

It would take two weeks for us to arrive in the capital at the leisurely pace we set to spare both our horses and ourselves.

CHAPTER 8

History Sucks

We didn't leave immediately. Although I would have been happy to wander around Europe as a tourist, simply showing up in Poland and hoping for a lead wasn't smart. Instead, I spent more of my clients' money on a phone call to the University of Gdańsk. Dr. Lindberg let us use the phone in her office so we could put it on speaker.

It took a few moments to be transferred to someone who spoke English.

"We're researching the movements of a particular Swedish monk through Poland in 1607. Do you have somebody available who could help us?"

In the following pause I could imagine the person staring at the phone and wondering what kind of lunatic I was.

"Most of our faculty are on holiday, but perhaps Professor Kłonczyński can help you. Please wait."

There was the sound of a call being transferred.

"*Czeszcz.*"

"Hello, Professor Kłonczyński?" I hoped I hadn't mangled his name too much. I repeated it to myself: *Kwonchinski.*

"*Przepraszam. Nie rozumiem.*" Damn, he didn't speak English.

"*Guten tag Herr Professor. Sprechen sie Deutsch?*" Lana said.

"*Ja,*" he said. That was the last word I understood for a good twenty minutes. I *really* had to learn more languages.

At one point Lana scribbled something on a note pad. I had no idea what it said. Her penmanship was as bad as mine.

She finally pushed the button to terminate the call, and sat back with a sigh.

"Well?"

"He suggested that they likely followed the Vistula River rather than going cross-country. That's always been a major trade route so they'd have had no problem finding lodging and maintaining relative anonymity."

"Great."

"Unfortunately he can't help us much, but I did get a line on someone who can."

I gave her an impatient look while she consulted her notes.

"It's a graduate student named Pietr Debiak who is doing research on the Zebrzydowski Rebellion of 1607. The Professor thought that it's highly likely from the dates that Johan would have encountered some rebels on their way to Guzów."

"What or who is Guzów?"

"A town south of Warsaw where the decisive battle in the rebellion occurred."

"What about…"

"That's all he knew. We'll have to talk to Debiak for more details."

"Fine. Where's he?"

Lana gave me a wry smile. "Warsaw."

"Good. Let's go."

"There's one small problem."

I sighed. "Oh no, not again."

"He thought that our idea of consulting church records was a good one, but apparently a lot of them were destroyed or hidden at the start of the Second World War. After the war many of the people who had hidden them were dead, so some were never found."

"I guess we'll just have to hope the records we need aren't lost."

∞

I felt like I was getting to be a seasoned international traveller as I booked air tickets and a rental car in Poland. At least this leg of the journey promised to have a bit more sight-seeing in it. Due to a ticket sale it was actually cheaper for us to fly to Gdańsk and then drive to Warsaw.

Lech Wałesa Airport was eight kilometres outside the city. Its terminal building was impressive, with vast amounts of glass and a zigzaggy roof. The car we rented was a Fiat 500 Turbo: small and fast. I hoped Binky wouldn't be jealous.

After getting out of the parking lot we found ourselves on a two-lane service road. I expected it to be a nice, easy introduction to driving in Poland.

A car turned out of another parking lot in front of us. As in, maybe four metres in front of us. It was a good thing we were wearing our seat belts or Lana would have been a hood ornament. The moron continued along as if nothing had happened. The guy tailgating behind us stopped in time, but didn't seem to get upset. That either meant that he was a Zen master, or this kind of thing was common.

After that I paid more attention to side traffic, and left lots of room between us and the car in front. Inevitably, somebody would come up from behind and take that buffer zone to be an invitation to pass, regardless of what the centre line said.

Sometimes, there were cars or trucks coming the other way. That didn't seem to be a consideration either.

Of course, not all the drivers were trying to kill us. Most were driving more-or-less normally. But when you have steel projectiles flying at you from all directions there do seem to be a lot of them.

After that came Provincial Road 472, which was a divided highway with two lanes in each direction. The drivers seemed more sensible, or maybe it was because they had more room. I stayed in the slow lane and tried to do the speed limit.

The car had GPS, which he rental agent had set it up to speak English for us so we didn't have to rely on Lana's phone for navigation.

Gdańsk was National Geographic picturesque, if you stayed away from the industrial areas. Everything looked like I expected an old European city to look.

I decided to take the long way around because the roads looked better. The major Polish highways were in excellent shape, and on some the speed limits were higher than I was used to. We should be in Warsaw within three hours.

Lana was silent. When I glanced at her she was looking at the scenery. One thing that I found unusual was that there were frequent walls right beside the highway that I assumed were sound barriers. Every so often there was a perfectly normal glass door in the wall such as you'd see in the front of a shop. I wondered how long the glass would last in North America before somebody threw a rock through it.

We'd talked about small stuff on the plane from London, but there were still some things I wanted to know.

"How did a nice girl like you become a private investigator?"

She dragged herself out of her reverie. "I told you, my parents were investigators."

"Like mother, like daughter?"

"Something like that."

"What happened to them?"

"Has anyone ever suggested that you ask too many questions?"

"On occasion."

"Perhaps you should consider not doing so."

"We're working together. We're both members of the BSI. You said your parents were, too. That's great, but I've always worked my cases alone. You'll have to excuse me if it makes me nervous not to know how dedicated my partner is."

"Now we're partners?"

I smiled. "That's your fault, following me and generally making yourself useful."

She was silent for a while.

"My parents were investigating a particular Japanese businessman when they died. The circumstances were—suspicious. No charges were every laid."

"That must have been hard on you. At least when my sister's parents died it was a simple traffic accident. But it was still really hard not knowing exactly why the other driver lost control."

She looked at me sharply. "You said your parents are still alive."

"It's complicated. My parents are, but not my sister's. Our two families were very close. Kali and I have considered ourselves sisters since we met. When her parents were killed she moved in with us. She was never formally adopted, though."

Lana was quiet for several minutes.

"I also have a sister. Hikari was adopted by my parents almost 20 years ago. I was named her guardian after our parents died."

She looked out the side window. "She is the most important thing in my life."

There was another pause. "The businessman they were investigating was named Kagari Hikaru. He's Hikari's biological father."

"Oh my god, that's so screwed up."

"You have no idea. When he found out we had her, he wanted her back, and when my parents refused they died. He's been trying to pressure me into letting her go."

"I don't mean to pry, but what are the odds that he was the sniper in Spitalfields?"

Lana snorted. "You do nothing *but* pry. And yes, the thought occurred to me. It is extremely likely that it was either him or someone in his employ. It wouldn't surprise me if the Russian was his as well."

"You didn't think this was something I should know?"

"It was none of your business. He's after me, not you."

"It's my business if I'm standing beside you when a bomb goes off. Are there any more crazed people trying to kill you?"

"Not to my knowledge. You?"

"Well... There was somebody shooting arrows at me before I left Calgary, but they would have to be stupid to have followed me. It would be much easier and cheaper to wait until I get home."

"Unless they are also after the Sampo."

"That's really nuts. I hadn't even been hired yet."

"Unless they knew that you would be."

I signalled a right turn.

"What are you doing?"

"I don't know about you, but I'm hungry, and those golden arches are at least familiar."

We turned off the highway and found the fast food place. I wondered if there was any place in the world that didn't have them.

We got out of the car and stretched. Something caught my attention.

"What are you looking at?"

"That truck. The dark green one. It was behind us for a long time on the road. Now it turned in here after us."

"It's probably a coincidence. Maybe he's also going to Warsaw, and got hungry too."

"Yeah, you're probably right."

We had the usual burger and fries with coffee, although Lana had water instead. After hitting the washroom we got back on the road.

"So, are you seeing anybody at the moment?"

Lana sighed. "Why is everybody so fascinated by other people's romantic lives? No, I'm not seeing anyone at the moment. I find it difficult to find people who are interested in a romantic relationship without a sexual component."

"What? Are you telling me that you don't have sex at all?"

"Exactly. It doesn't interest me."

I was trying to figure this out. "Yet you have romantic encounters."

"Of course. I'm quite capable of falling in love if the person meets my standards—intelligence, of course; education; a compatible philosophy. And of course a distaste for Sherlock Holmes adaptations."

I knew that asexuals existed, but I'd never met one before. My overactive libido made the whole concept incomprehensible. I felt like somebody who was colour blind trying to understand what red meant. Or maybe somebody to whom red was all-important trying to describe it to a colour-blind person.

I had no idea what constituted an offensive question in this situation, so I just asked. "Have you always been that way?"

"I suspect that what you really want to know is if I was abused as a child or something like that, and as a result have repressed my normal libido. The answer to that is no."

"I'm sorry. I've never knowingly met someone like you and I'm trying to wrap my brain around the whole concept."

"I understand. That's why I'm answering your questions, even though

I don't *owe* you any kind of explanation."

"Thank you. I don't mean to pry, but the thing I can't understand is how somebody could do completely without it. Sex is such a huge part of who I am."

"I've had this conversation before. Most people find it confusing."

"It might be worse for me. I have a medical condition that gives me the libido from hell. If I wasn't taking medication I'd constantly have to be reminding myself not to pick up strangers. It might be peaceful to be like you occasionally."

"Would you really pick up strangers just for sex?"

"I prefer to be much more choosy, but it's very much like working in a restaurant when you haven't eaten for a week. The physical sensations of starvation for me are similar. After a while it's too exhausting not to sample from a random plate as it goes by."

"I'm intrigued, as I'm now the one who can't relate to your situation. Since we're being honest with each other, how often would you like have sex?"

"Under ideal conditions, I'm happy with several times a day. That assumes that I have the time, a partner who has that much stamina, and who is actually worth it."

"What about multiple partners?"

"Wow, we are being honest. I did have a friend-with-benefits once who was sleeping with several girls, but I've never had several lovers at once. It's never come up, as it were."

She looked blank. Obviously she wasn't big on innuendo either. "That would seem to be an ideal situation for you."

"Only if I could find several men who were worth sleeping with, and who were comfortable sharing me. I'd like to pretend that I'm above all that, but honestly I can see myself considering it."

"You are who you are. If you were diabetic you wouldn't apologize for taking insulin. Why pretend about your sexuality?"

"You're right, of course. Society is so screwed up about sex that it's hard not to absorb some of the slut-versus-saint attitudes. I try to accept myself and be happy, but it's difficult at times."

"From my own experience, finding even one person who is worth a romantic relationship is difficult."

"No kidding. I've kissed a fair number of toads and princes are still few and far between."

"How many toads?"

"Wow, we really are getting into personal details. Hmm..." I'd never kept a running tally, so I had to count on mental fingers. Twice. The totals agreed, which was embarrassing—another one of those societal expectations. "Nineteen in four years."

The whole conversation, not to mention this new personal insight, made me feel uncomfortable. Not because her lifestyle offended me, or because I thought of myself as a slut, but because once again it made me feel like I was a freak. For the first time in my life, I seriously wondered if there was some kind of surgery or something that I could get to turn my hormones down to a dull roar.

Damn it, I thought I'd figured out all this stuff. Society's opinions about whether my sex drive was acceptable were really beginning to irritate me.

We were approaching an overpass and a white cargo van was accelerating down the on ramp. I moved over to the left lane to give him room.

The crash was earsplitting. Our car slewed to the left, directly toward the concrete barriers guarding the overpass pillars.

Part of my brain fought to regain control of the car while the rest froze with the memory of the last time I had been in a car crash. It was a confusing sensation.

The white van was pushing against my right front wheel, forcing us into the Jersey barriers. It pulled away just before we hit.

The left wheel rode up on the flared section at the bottom of the barrier. We were saved from flipping by the van, which hadn't quite cleared us yet. The passenger-side roof caved in slightly as we struck, and the car bounced back down onto its wheels.

The van swerved after being hit, and then sped off. Our car slewed almost perpendicularly across the lanes and hit the guard rail.

That's when we flipped.

There was a slight ditch on the other side, and in the extra space the car managed a 180 and landed on its wheels again. I thought my spine had been shortened by half.

Most of that was in hindsight. All I knew was that we'd been in an accident, my face hurt, my ears were ringing, and there was a deflated balloon in front of me. Lana had blood on her face and was hunched over.

"Lana, are you all right?"

Her voice was weak. "No."

I undid my seat belt and tried the door. It protested, but it opened. I staggered out of the car. There didn't seem to be any smoke or flames, which was good.

The truck that had been behind us stopped on the highway. It was one of those military ones you see in movies with a canvas cover over the rear. The driver got out along with two men who jumped down from the back. All of them were carrying guns. They spread out to cover the area as if they were soldiers protecting an asset.

The man riding shotgun gracefully hopped the mangled traffic barrier.

"Are you injured?"

"I don't think so." I gently touched my nose and my hand came away with blood on it. Ow. "My nose might be broken from the air bag. I think Lana's hurt."

He went around to the other side and grabbed the door handle. It took a lot of pulling before the mangled door came open. He knelt beside Lana.

"Where are you injured?"

"My arm."

He ran his hands over her everywhere that he could reach except her obviously broken arm and a freely-bleeding cut on her head from broken glass. The whole examination took no more than fifteen seconds. It was a testament to how badly she was injured that she didn't protest. Then he went back and examined the cut. He found some paper napkins I'd brought back from our lunch stop.

"You will be fine. Press these against the cut to stop the bleeding. We have called for an ambulance."

Before I could ask him anything he gave a hand signal to the other men who all piled back in the truck. They roared off after the van before I even thought to look at their license plate.

From the first impact until they left couldn't have been more than ninety seconds.

What the hell was going on?

CHAPTER 9

The Confession (translated from Latin)

We estimated that we were about four days from Warszawa when a company of soldiers overtook us. They came at us from behind a bend in the road, and we were surrounded before we could do much to defend ourselves.

Their captain addressed us. "What is your business?"

"We are escorting this monk to Warszawa," Ander said.

The captain drew his sword. "Swedes!" It was apparent that Ander's Polish was not as unaccented as we could have wished.

The soldiers ignored our protestations, and searched our luggage. The captain gazed upon the device but fortunately he did not touch it.

"What is this?"

"A gift for king Sigismund."

A column of riders joined us. Several of them wore fine clothes and were obviously nobles.

"Now it's a gift for Mikołaj Zebrzydowski."

We were disarmed, and placed near the end of the column. The nobles were ahead of us, and the surrounding soldiers would not tell us anything.

Shortly after our capture we turned off the main road and headed almost directly south. One man galloped ahead, probably to report our capture to someone. I estimated our remaining number at about 30.

When we camped we were given food and water, but still no conversation. We speculated among the three of us as to who this Zebrzydowski was, but we had no clues other than he must be a noble himself, and he wasn't in our party.

After four days our guards were bored, and were willing to give us a little information. Our destination was the village of Guzów where a rebellion against King Sigismund was gathering. Zebrzydowski was the principal of the rebel leaders.

Ander thought that this was a stroke of luck for us. If the rebels were victorious then the Sigismund problem would be solved. We need only tell the rebels the truth about the device to save them from it. If the rebels were defeated, then Sigismund would have the device from the ruins, and we need say nothing.

The difficulty with this plan was that, either way, we would find ourselves in the middle of a battle. As Swedes it was unlikely that either side would be overly concerned with our welfare.

The next day we were saved from this consideration by a terrifying cry as our entire column was overrun by easily twice our number of cavalrymen. I heard a few soldiers cry "Croats!" before they were killed.

Although my knowledge of foreign lands was, at that time, severely limited, even I had heard of the Croats. They were renowned for their ferocity in battle, and their poor treatment of any survivors. It was said that mothers would terrify their children into obedience by telling them that if they did not obey then the Croats would come for them.

The hindmost of our captors galloped away at the first sign of trouble. I could not find it in my heart to name them cowards. By themselves they could have done nothing to change the outcome of the attack.

Pål managed to free himself from his bonds and gave as good an account of himself as anyone could wish, but in the end he was cut down with the rest. I resolved to say prayers for the soul of our brave companion.

When all was done, the captain of the cavalry had us brought before him. Ander's Polish was sufficient to thank him for saving us from the Protestant forces, for it was widely known that Sigismund had hired Catholic Croatian mercenaries through his sometime allies in the Kingdom of Hungary.

The captain, whose name we never did learn, laughed at us. We tried to explain the gift to Sigismund, but it came out that Sigismund's payment of his mercenaries had been lax of late, and this company was deserting. They decided to take our "gift" with them for their *ban* or viceroy.

The next two weeks were as close to Hell as I ever hope to get, and with God's grace this confession may help to keep me from it. The Croats rode much more quickly than our previous captors, and they were not constrained by Christian behaviour. We were tied to our horses by a rope around its belly, and fastened to our feet. If either of us had fallen from our saddles we would have been dragged upside down beneath the horse's feet. It was clear to both of us that our captors would have done nothing to help us save laughing as we were kicked and trampled.

We were given little to eat or drink, and as we rode south through what I later learned were the Carpathian or Tatra Mountains. The tracks we followed through the mountains were enough to terrify all but the bravest of men. At times my horse was barely able to make her way along a path with steep rock on one side and a river chasm on the other. Thus we left Poland.

In a moment of conscience, I tried to explain that the treasure they were taking to their *ban* was demonic in essence, but the only payment for my attempted good deed was more abuse. Sometimes they hit us with their hands, at other times we were kicked or struck with the hilt or flat of a sword. I'm convinced that the only thing that kept us alive was their desire to have us explain the device to their ruler, and perhaps to provide amusement when they tortured us afterward. Although I was trying not to judge them in accordance with God's will, I found it difficult to put any atrocity beyond them. I had seen too much of their treatment of the farmers whose holdings they razed after resupplying themselves on the road.

I began to believe that the Croats deserved to have Satan's Millstone.

CHAPTER 10

Treasure Hunt

An ambulance arrived a few minutes later along with a fire truck and several police cars. The circus began.

Neither of us were badly hurt apart from Lana's broken arm. Her scalp wound was small, but being a scalp wound it bled a lot. My nose turned out to be bloody but unbroken, although my face still hurt to touch. Our gallant Fiat 500 had given it's all for our safety, and had to be towed away. We'd need another car.

Just for a change, none of the rescue personnel spoke English, French, German, or Spanish. We had to speak to them through an interpreter over the police radio.

The paramedics wanted to take us to a hospital to make sure that we were okay. We protested, but given the language barrier they insisted. At least we got a free ride to Warsaw out of it.

The police were confused by our statement. So was I, to be honest. The skid marks backed up our story. Unless the white van driver was insane or blind the collision had to have been deliberate. That explained him zooming off afterward, but not why it happened in the first place.

Nor did the police have any idea who our paramilitary guardian angels were. I was really angry with myself for not getting a license plate number from either vehicle.

Poland, like most countries, has socialized medical coverage so the whole thing didn't cost us anything except time, inconvenience, and a lot of paperwork. I was released first, so I called the rental agency to replace our car with another Fiat 500. Another call got us hotel rooms near the university. Our car would be dropped off at the hospital for us.

It was all terribly efficient. It was also far more adult behaviour than I really wanted to engage in at that point. Once it was over I thought about the alleged accident.

The white van was waiting for us. That much was obvious. The easiest scenario was that they'd been watching for our approach and sped onto the highway just in time to ambush us. The big question is how they had known we'd be there. Somebody knew far too much about our movements and plans.

Karen Lindberg? I couldn't see it. She had no motive, unless somebody had bribed her. If she wanted to get in our way she could have refused to help us with the research.

Professor Nieminen? Again, no motive. He didn't have to give us his research.

I went through a list of the other people I'd encountered in this case. None of them made good suspects.

The only three real suspects were my unknown attempted murderer, my invisible stalker from the apartment lobby, and our mystery sniper. The first two were almost certainly demonic. A simple and obvious car crash didn't seem like their style.

That left the sniper. We had no more information about him than before, despite Lana's suspicions.

The men in the military truck that had come to our assistance also bothered me. Except for the man who examined Lana, none of them had spoken a word in my presence. They must have called the ambulance even before they stopped to help, and it must have been an extremely short call. That and their deployment at the scene indicated some serious military or police training. I had no idea what gun control was like in Poland, but the probability that everybody in a random truck would be carrying weapons seemed extremely small.

The man who played medic had an accent, but then everybody I'd met since leaving Calgary had an accent. I couldn't place it immediately, although it sounded familiar.

It wasn't English or Swedish. I didn't think it was Polish. That left Finnish. The more I thought about it, the more certain I was.

Why would a band of Finnish soldiers be following us through Poland? A better question might be, *which* Finns would be following us?

It had to be either the SIS or Karelian militants. I didn't see why it would be the SIS. If they still suspected us of terrorism enough to mount a cross-border operation they would have contacted their Polish counterparts. That was the whole point to Interpol, after all.

Okay, so the Karelian separatists we *weren't* involved with and had never knowingly met had followed us to Poland for some reason. Although they were content to follow us, it looked like they were also willing to step in if something tried to harm us. After this I doubted that we'd spot them again unless we got in trouble. They'd want to keep out of sight.

When I got back to the hospital Lana was sporting a snazzy blue cast and a set of butterfly strips on her head wound.

"How are you feeling?"

"Fine." She didn't look fine, but she wasn't about to admit that she was in pain.

"Did they give you anything for the pain?"

"Yes."

"I can help you with the bottle lid if you want."

"No, thanks."

That's what I thought. She wasn't about to take drugs even if they made her more comfortable.

I liked her even more. She was almost as stubborn as me.

After some chasing around the university, we found somebody who knew how to locate Pietr Debiak. We caught up with him at his apartment. His goatee matched his personality: neat and precise. I took an instant dislike to him for no identifiable reason.

"You are lucky to find me," he said. "I just get back from England."

Lana led the conversation. "We were told that you are an expert on the Zebrzydowski Rebellion. We're looking for information on the travels of a Swedish monk in 1607."

His eyes wandered over her. "Any monk, or maybe one in particular?"

"Johan Agnetason. He was in the company of two Swedish soldiers on his way to see King Sigismund just before the battle of Guzów."

"Is pronounced Goozof," he said with a smile.

Lana did not look impressed. "Regardless, we are hoping to trace his travels."

Pietr looked smug. "You have come to right man. Only I can tell you what you want to know. Maybe, you can help me too."

I was cautious. "What did you have in mind?"

"First I must tell you history. As you know, in 1939 Germans invade Poland. A Jew named Josef Berkowicz knows Germans only care about Germans, so he goes to many churches and gathered records. Some he hide with friends. Some of these we find after war. But many records disappear."

"We were warned that not all the records might have survived."

"Yes, and Berkowicz, he shipped to Oswiecim where he died. You probably know camp by the German name: Auschwitz. Of his family, only his son Abraham escapes the war through Romania."

He smiled as he leaned forward. "This is what you English call clever bit. Berkowicz buried documents with help of his son. This I know because I find diary of family member that says Abraham go to England. I find him, and get map from him."

"So you have the missing documents. That's wonderful."

He waved his hand. "No, no, I do not have them. This is supposed to be research thesis, not archaeology. I spend most of my own money to see Abraham, and spend much time with him. He is now very old and I have to make sure he remembers correct directions. It take a long time to get money from university. I have no money to go dig up documents."

"Unless," I said, "you happen to have some research partners who would be willing to help you to dig up the documents."

He smiled. "Is only fair. You help me, I help you."

Lana didn't look impressed. "What are we talking about here? Heavy equipment? Explosives? A team of archaeologists?"

"No, no. Abraham tell me that they put documents in steel boxes and bury them in small cave. He and his father alone piled rocks at entrance to keep it hidden, so two people can uncover them. We just need truck and tools."

I looked at Lana who nodded slightly. "All right, it looks like I'm renting a truck."

~

It took two days of phoning and arguing before we headed south. Not all car rental places have trucks. Pietr had no idea how many documents might be in the cave, but he agreed that a Mercedes Sprinter van was probably adequate. These were the most common commercial van in Europe, which would make us nicely inconspicuous if our Finnish friends were looking for us.

We returned the Fiat to our original rental agency, then went to the airport by taxi and picked up the van, as well as a stack of moving blankets in case we needed them to cushion the cargo. With Pietr's help we then did some shopping: mechanic's coveralls (which Lana called boiler suits), shovels, a largish crowbar, a hundred metres of rope, work gloves, and flashlights. Everything the well-dressed caver needs. We hoped.

One short-lived problem was that the van only had two seats. Pietr gallantly offered to ride shotgun and let Lana sit in his lap. I solved the issue by making him ride in the back. He wasn't happy, but finally agreed that Lana needed a proper seat and seat belt. Even with a broken arm Lana was sure she could take him in a fight, so we weren't concerned about him trying anything.

Once again I was the designated driver. There was no way I was letting someone we'd just met behind the wheel of a van I'd signed for. We headed south on highway E77 toward Krakow. Pietr estimated that it would take us four hours to get to the site, which would put us just in time for afternoon tea.

The highway kept changing size: three lanes superhighway, two-lanes divided, one lane either way with shoulders, and one lane either way. It was all called E77 or sometimes 7.

I managed the changing speed limits by following the average drivers. It must have worked; we were never pulled over.

Lana had a jacket draped over her. She awkwardly wadded it into a pillow with one hand and placed it against the door. "Wake me when we get there."

Everything was going well until the Pietr told me to turn off on the road to Czaple. There was no road number, or any other directions. The road itself was one of those "two lanes if you are feeling charitable" ones.

We kept going. Less than four kilometres later we came to a T-intersection in downtown Czaple Wielkie, which is to say that there was a house on each corner. Pietr said the name meant Great Egrets. There was no indication of which way to go, but left seemed better travelled. The only people in sight were two small children who were playing in the ditch.

I rolled down my window. "Excuse me. Do you speak English?"

They looked at me like I had two heads, then laughed and ran away.

I turned back to Pietr. "Any ideas?"

He studied a piece of paper. "Just keep on main road. We will be in Czaple Małe soon."

"And that means?"

"Little Egrets."

Of course. I rolled up the window and turned left. A hundred metres later I turned right because the road had more tire wear in that direction.

There was forest, farm land, and not much else. Eventually we got to Czaple Małe. I only knew because it had one of those cityscape-silhouette signs I'd seen in Finland.

"Turn left," Pietr said. Left was a wide driveway leading right to a building.

"There is no left," I said.

"No, *much left*."

Almost doubling back on itself was an even smaller road than the one we were on. I turned. It led through forest, with the occasional dirt track leading off to who knew where. There was no possibility of pulling off the pavement. Seriously, anything bigger than a bicycle would force us to back up to the last side track. I expected to see oncoming traffic around every curve.

We finally made it out into open farm land and relatively straight road. I let out a sigh of relief.

"Next we come to Wiktora."

Right, another small group of farm houses with no signs anywhere.

This insane journey seemed to last for hours, although the odometer said we'd only gone 16 kilometres. It reminded me of those stories you hear about city folk who ask a farmer for directions.

Yep, well, you go down this road until you see a corral, then you turn right, go until you see the old Foster place, and then turn left. You can't miss it. Of course, the corral has been rotting away for the past fifty years and is now just some logs on the ground, and it's been three generations since a Foster lived in the old Foster place, whose mail box now says Gomez.

We came to a stop sign. It was the first actual, official sign I'd seen since we left Highway 7. I felt like hugging it.

Pietr sounded proud. "Turn right. This is Nowa Wieś."

I didn't care what it was. There was an actual centre line on the road, and even something resembling shoulders. I felt like I was back in civilization.

A couple of kilometres later we entered the town of Skała. It was kind of picturesque in a run-down way. Maybe this was the bad part of town.

"How much further to the site?"

Pietr was fiddling with his piece of paper. "Little more than four kilometres I think."

I glanced across at Lana. She was still asleep. "Hey, Lana. Rise and shine."

Her eyes opened immediately. "I'm awake."

We navigated through Skała and were back on the highway. The land was getting more hilly, which boded well for finding a lost cave. I started laughing.

"What?" asked Lana.

"Ever since we got to this town I've been pronouncing it 'Skala' in my head. I just realized how it's really pronounced—Skawa." I waited.

"So?"

"Don't you ever read any Anthony Bidulka? *The Women of Skawa Island?* At the moment that would be us."

Dead silence from the other two.

"Does your friend ever make sense?" Pietr said to Lana.

"Wow, tough crowd. Read Canadian books some time."

"Turn left," Pietr said as we approached a side road. The sign pointed to Ojców.

The hilly terrain now sprouted actual rock faces. This was really looking promising. Of course, the road also dwindled to another barely-two-lanes-no-lines model.

A kilometre later we went through the village of Ojców. The only thing of interest to me was that they had a restaurant.

"Is this it?"

"No. Little further."

After the village we picked up a small creek on the left side of the road. As it passed by a rock buttress there was a tiny foot bridge leading to a round opening. A statue of the Virgin Mary stood in the opening, and there were offerings on the ground in front of it.

"Is *this* it?"

"Not yet. Soon."

We rounded the corner and there was a solid line of cars parked on the left next to a tiny chapel. There were rows of pews In front of the chapel doors for outdoor services. The chapel itself was built on concrete footings out over the creek which was weird. There was plenty of flat land available.

"We are here," Pietr said.

Lana looked at the church. "You're joking."

"No, cave is on hill behind chapel."

On the other side of the creek two rock buttresses poked out from the hillside. The upstream one had a small triangular hole near the base, which made a cave seem probable. The creek at that point was narrow enough to jump across. Maybe.

There was no place to park, even if we'd had a smaller vehicle.

"All right, now what do we do?"

"We must wait until tourists leave. Then we go dig. We can go eat now."

There was no hope of turning around on the road, so I kept driving. There were more tourists parked on the right side, narrowing the road to one lane if I drove carefully. A fork in the road finally gave me room to double back.

The restaurant in Ojców was called *Piwnica Pod Nietoperzem*, which Pietr translated as "Under the Bats." It was in a cellar, which sort of fit the whole Gothic motif of the name plus our caving expedition. I had the trout in herbs finished with butter, which was scrumptious. The Czech beer wasn't bad either.

Afterward we sat outside on a picnic bench. "What's the plan for finding the cave?" Lana asked.

"After dark we climb hill beside rock. Berkowicz say they carved star in rock so they can find it again. Probably Star of David. We find star. We dig. We take boxes. We go home."

"That sounds like a simple enough plan."

"You see? Nothing can go wrong."

Both Lana and I winced. We'd both heard that one before.

◦∞◦

The tourists began to thin out well before sunset, and by 8:30 it was nearly dark. There would be no moon until three in the morning, and even then it would be a waning crescent.

The meadow between the creek and the base of the hill was covered in tall plants. I thought some of them might be Queen Anne's Lace.

Pietr thought we should both change into our caving suits in the back of the van. I changed into my caving suit by myself, then Lana let him in to change. Lana would stay with the vehicle to keep watch. There was no way she could go caving while wearing a cast.

Pietr and I jumped the creek and waded through the meadow. The hill was really steep, but we were climbing beside the buttress so we could hang onto the rock as well as any trees or bushes that were close enough. The forest was a mixture of poplar, pine and maple. Old leaves on the ground made for occasional slippery footing.

It didn't help that we were carrying tools. I hung the crowbar inside the neck of my coveralls to free one hand. As long as I didn't gore myself it worked well.

The star had to be low enough for a man to use a hammer and chisel easily, but high enough to be above the undergrowth. We concentrated on the rock between one and two metres up. Pietr assured me that we would only be climbing for a few minutes, so we went slowly and examined the rock carefully.

He tended to shine his light directly on the rock, so I shone mine at an angle. I didn't know how much a carving might have weathered in 75 years, and the lower lighting angle showed up every little bump and crack.

We were about ten metres up the hill when a car came along the road. Immediately I snapped my light off. I had to cover Pietr's as he failed to react in time.

"People can see our lights from the road. The fewer questions we have to answer the better."

"Of course. You are as clever as you are beautiful."

Oh, brother. He was the mosquito of pick-up artists—persistent and annoying, but harmless.

After another ten metres there was a pine tree growing right against the rock. Pietr heaved himself up and around it and kept going.

"Wait."

My light picked out some unusually straight lines just above where the tree stood. My fingers made out three shallow lines in the shape of an asterisk.

"Josef, your crafty devil."

"What? You find something?"

"We thought a Jew would carve a six-pointed Star of David, but that's *exactly* what he wouldn't do in case the Nazis found it. Instead, he carved three lines to form six points. Much easier and not at all Jewish."

There was nothing unusual about the ground above the tree, except for a small rabbit or squirrel hole near the rock.

I got my head and light as close to the hole as I could. The hole seemed to be deeper than I would expect. I could smell a musty animal odour like a very old outhouse. It was probably from animal droppings. Great.

There was only room for one person to work, so I hooked the crowbar in the hole and pulled while Pietr watched from uphill. A few fist-sized stones came out from under the soil and leaf litter. I did it a few more times, moving some larger rocks, and enlarged the hole to the size of my head.

I poked my light in the hole. There was a lot of leaf litter and twigs inside. Beyond that I could just make out some regular shapes. I twisted the lens of the flashlight so it didn't reflect off the sides of the hole as much. There were definitely box shapes beyond the hole.

Pietr shifted position and almost stood on my head as his foot slipped. "Can you see anything?"

I remembered a line I'd read when I was a girl and fascinated by ancient Egypt. "Yes, it is wonderful."

I pulled my head back and grinned at him. "Holy shit, we found it."

It took remarkably little effort to pull the rest of the rocks away from the entrance, which was a narrow slot opening right against the buttress. I suspected that Josef had done most of the heavy lifting up the hill from the road, leaving his son Abraham to actually drag the boxes into the cave. There was an old scar on the tree near ground level that supported my theory.

Pietr tried to get through the opening, but he was too big. For once my A-cup chest was an advantage.

I squirmed through and crouched in the low space. The first metre of the tunnel was filled with old nesting material. It didn't appear to be occupied at present. The animal smell was strong, but too old to be disgusting.

Beyond the nest were two steel boxes with writing on their sides. The paint was flaking off and I doubted that even a native Pole would be able to read it. Each box was a bit less than a metre long, 20 centimetres thick, and about 40 centimetres wide with steel ring handles on either end. They'd easily fit through the opening if turned on their sides.

I carefully undid the latches on the top one. The hinge creaked as I opened it. Inside were stacks of old books and papers that looked like they were in decent condition. Jackpot.

I dragged the first one to the opening and pushed it through to Pietr. He called in. "How many are in there?"

"There are two boxes right here. The cave goes further in. Give me a minute and I'll let you know."

I slid the second box through, then turned my light further into the cave. There looked to be a drop-off just beyond where the boxes had been. The ceiling continued at the same level, which meant I'd be able to stand if I could get down there.

Fortunately, it was neither completely vertical nor deep. The bottom was probably only three metres away where the tunnel flattened out into something like a wide corridor. Both sides were lined with boxes just like the ones I'd already found. These were standing upright against the walls.

I did a rough count, and wished we'd brought a bigger vehicle.

I went back to the entrance. "There are about thirty in here. Go back to the van and get the rope."

While Pietr was gone I explored further. The cave dwindled to a small opening a few metres beyond the furthest box. I crawled part way in. The way was blocked by small stones that were fist-sized or less. I tried moving some, but there was a rattling sound from overhead as more stones fell from somewhere to replace them. If there were more boxes beyond the cave-in, I sure as hell wasn't going to risk being buried alive to get them.

Pietr called out, so I went back to the entrance.

"The other boxes are down a slope. I'll tie the rope to the handle on a box, then carry it as well as I can. You'll have to pull to take the weight as I climb up the slope. Wrap the rope around the pine tree once. That way if I slip there will be more friction on the line."

The next several hours were monotonous and exhausting. I tied the rope to one of the ring handles, then carried the box to the bottom of the drop-off. It wasn't a difficult climb as long as Pietr took most of the weight of the box. Once at the entrance I tipped the box on its side and he pulled it through. I estimated that each box weighed 60 kilograms.

Lather, rinse, repeat thirty six times—a total of just over two tonnes.

Seven hours later I crawled from the cave. I was muddy, exhausted, and there was blood in my hair from where I'd cracked my head on a protruding rock.

Pietr wasn't much better off. He wasn't in good physical shape to start with, and he'd been hauling the rope the whole time. At least he got to rest in between climbs.

I'd been wondering what he did with the boxes. There was no room for him to stack them outside. His solution was practical, if less than scholarly given that these were priceless historical documents. He'd just let the boxes slide down the hill.

There was a big, messy pile of them at the bottom. We had to climb over them to get to the meadow.

We picked one up and took it back to the van. We also got our feet wet in the creek. There was no way we could jump it while carrying a box.

We loaded the first one and told Lana what was happening.

"I can help."

"Not with a broken arm you can't."

"I can drag boxes closer with one hand so you don't have to carry them as far. They should slide easily on the grass."

It took the three of us another two hours to load our treasure. By then the sky was getting lighter, and we could easily make out details across the valley. We wanted to be out of there before the tourists started showing up again, which could happen at any moment. I peeled off my caving suit, put on my street clothes, and drove north. I didn't care if Pietr got an eyeful.

"I have some good news," Lana said as we passed through the village. "The highway that goes through Skała is Provincial Road 773. It joins up with E77 without all that fiddling about on back roads."

"Shit, you're kidding. Pietr!"

"I did not know! I use Google map! It say that way faster."

I was too tired to argue. "Lana, navigate us out of here."

There was no way I was making a four hour drive after a night of hard labour and no sleep.

The van wallowed, and I had a bad feeling that we'd exceeded its rated cargo capacity. The only way the boxes would fit was standing on end in the back. We'd padded them as well as possible with the blankets, but Pietr had to lie on top of them so he wouldn't be crushed. Almost every bump caused the suspension to bottom out. I just hoped there were no observant police officers on the road.

The boxes were banging on the van walls, so I stopped in a small parking area just before the turn to Skała. With Pietr's help inside, we adjusted the blankets so we wouldn't knock a hole in the side of the van.

There were two official-looking signs with maps on them beside where we'd stopped, and a third with pictures and a lot of text. I couldn't read the Polish, of course, but I recognized the style of the signs as well as a Polish word that was the same in English: *Park*.

"Pietr!" I yelled, "Get out here!"

He crawled out of the back and exited through the driver-side door. Lana shamelessly rolled down her window to listen.

I pointed at the signs. "What do they say?"

"Oh, is nothing. Just historical."

"Really? Then why is the east side of the road—the side we were digging on—a different colour on the maps?"

"Ah. Is national park."

"You didn't think it was worthwhile to mention that we were digging up historical artifacts in a *national park*? May I assumed that it's as illegal here as it would be in North America?"

He had the good grace to look guilty. "But nobody catch us. Nobody knows about cave or documents."

"Not yet. The only rental van in the whole area, last seen near a holy site where the meadow now looks like a herd of buffalo stampeded across it. Brilliant. Just brilliant."

"But we have documents."

"Get in the van. Now."

He climbed in the same way he got out. I slammed the door when I got in, and had to be careful not to break the key off when I started the engine.

There was no conversation for a long time.

Thirteen mostly straight kilometres beyond Nowa Wieś we got to E77. I'd have glared at Pietr again if I'd had the energy.

A sign on the highway announced *Zajazd Na Wesołej*, which Pietr translated as *The Merry Inn*. We stopped for breakfast.

Lana and I peeled down to our underwear in the washroom and scrubbed most of the dirt off. It was a relief to get into some relatively clean clothes. I didn't know or care what Pietr did in the men's room.

Breakfast was good solid peasant food—simple with lots of calories. I had three cups of coffee with it.

The caffeine helped, but an hour later I was fading fast. We were going through flat farm land and in the distance I could see houses on the left of the highway. When I saw the sign with a bed on it I signalled to turn off.

Lana woke up. "What's happening?"

"I can't drive any more. We're going to find a hotel." Pietr was snoring in the back.

Brzegi almost looked like a Calgary neighbourhood, except there were no sidewalks. The hotel was more of a bed and breakfast. It being the mid-morning, we had no trouble getting rooms. Lana and I elected to take a double to save some money. I made Pietr pay for his own.

It was late afternoon when I woke up starving. The owner directed us to a small restaurant. I don't even remember what I ate, but it was filling. Lana and I were still pissed at Pietr.

We rolled into Warsaw around supper time. My muscles were not happy. I was not looking forward to moving those damned boxes again.

Pietr had a key to a room at the university where we could store the boxes. Fortunately there was a big platform cart in the basement that we appropriated. It took six boxes at a time. Lana helped by holding doors open for us.

My arms were aching by the time we finished. "When do you want to start going through the documents?"

He looked at the pile of boxes. "Tomorrow morning? Nine o'clock?"

Bastard. "Good. We'll see you then."

The first thing we did was to return the van and get a more reasonable car. That took several hours, including a late supper. The Fiat was much easier to park at the university, and a lot less conspicuous.

The University of Warsaw was mostly shut down for the summer. They rented out the dormitory rooms like a hostel for next to nothing with no need for ID or questions. We had two rooms within easy walking distance of the document room.

Before crashing for the night I sent e-mails home. I was so tired I'm not sure whether they were in English or not.

∽

For the next week the only things we did were to go through the boxes, order in food, and sleep. There was far too little of the latter. Pietr kept his word to help us find any reference to Johan.

He insisted that we wear cotton examination gloves to handle anything inside the boxes. He was the expert; we did as he said.

Once we eliminated the records that were too old or too new, it didn't take as long as I'd feared.

Sigismund had hired Croatian mercenaries, that period's equivalent of stormtroopers, but occasionally he was lax about paying them. The philosophy of most monarchs was that mercenaries were being paid to die for the cause, so payment was made grudgingly. This led to a high desertion rate.

Among the papers dealing with the Rebellion we found a reference to a rider arriving in Guzów with news that a Swedish monk had been captured along with a holy relic. When the expected party didn't arrive a small force was sent out to find out why. They found almost the entire party massacred. From the brutality of the slaughter there was no doubt in anyone's mind that it was Croats. There was no sign of Johan or the

Sampo. It was assumed that the Croats had taken him with them. Nobody wanted to give chase.

A later document confirmed this from the testimony of the few men who had left the skirmish.

An account from Częstochowa (at the time a small town) mentioned a company of Croats who came through, looting and killing as they went. They had two prisoners with them. The dates matched.

It wasn't hard to see on a map that they were heading home, no doubt to turn the monk and his "relic" over to their leaders.

Of course we didn't tell Pietr about the Sampo. We managed to make it sound like we were only interested in Johan's fate.

He had even more for us. "At time when this happened, Slovakia is part of Hungary. Croatia and Hungary have personal union then—one king for two kingdoms. Once Croats are out of Poland they will stop at first safe place in Hungary to rest and get supplies."

"Any idea where they would be?"

He brought up an old map on the computer and studied it for a few minutes.

He stabbed the screen with one finger, leaving behind a grease spot. "There. In Hungarian it is Csejte. Now called Čachtice in Slovakian."

"Aren't there any closer places?"

"Not for Croats. They desert Sigismund and leave Poland, so no Polish castles. Czech Republic at time is part of Habsburg Empire. They pass through very quickly. Only when they reach Hungary are they safe."

Lana thoughtfully tapped her cast with her good hand. "Assuming that Johan and his remaining guard were not murdered and dumped by the road, that would be the best place to find mention of them."

"We can be almost certain they didn't make it to Croatia," I said. "I've been looking at Croatian history and there's no mention of anything like..." I realized I'd made a mistake and scrambled to fix it. "...Johan and his party."

Pietr looked interested. "How do we know that?"

"The point is that we have a possible point-last-seen, and a possible destination," Lana said to rescue me. "If we have to chase Johan to Croatia, we will. In the meantime, I think it's a good assumption that Johan would be kept alive as a prisoner of war. If they'd intended to kill him they'd have done it during the original massacre."

"True," Pietr said. He didn't sound convinced.

Again I had a feeling we needed to watch our step around him.

◦⁂◦

There was free Wi-Fi in the dorms. Every evening I e-mailed my family to keep them up to date (at least on what I could tell them), and kept an eye on the news. If something caught my attention I could ask my browser to translate it into English. The results were sometimes hilarious, but frequently they were good enough to read.

There was a minor news item from Krakow that somebody had been digging near the Chapel on the Water on the edge of *Ojcowski Park Narodowy*. Drag marks indicated that something had been removed from a previously unknown cave. The police were investigating.

If I'd known we were committing a crime, I'd have used some forensic countermeasures. Of course, if I'd known we were committing a crime, I wouldn't have done it in the first place. With first-hand testimony of where the historical records were buried, it might not have been hard to get an excavation permit. Pietr had put us all in trouble by cutting corners.

On the other hand, getting a permit might have involved government archaeologists who might not have released the documents to us for months or years. Maybe Pietr's way was better after all.

This whole good-bad thing is sometimes complex and confusing.

Now the trick would be to keep us out of police hands. I didn't know how Polish law worked, but it would likely be even money in Canada whether we got off as unknowing dupes or were charged with being accessories. Our word was two to one against Pietr, but we'd known what was happening for several days without contacting the authorities. That didn't make it look good for us.

At least I'd gotten rid of the van. The rental place knew who I was, of course, but not where we were staying now. The police would probably check regular hotels first. Master criminals don't tend to stay in cheap dormitories.

When we moved on, it would be in a small car that had nothing to do with the defilement of the park—unless they checked all the rental records. I just hoped that the offence was small enough that the police wouldn't try very hard.

I dumped our caving gear in various rubbish bins around the city after scrubbing the tools with alcohol to get rid of any finger prints. I wasn't paranoid enough to think that digging in a park was serious enough to warrant a DNA test. I hoped.

The day before we left, the police were looking for the driver of a white Sprinter van who may have been nearby when the crime happened. It wouldn't be long before they considered that it might be a rental, but rentals of those vans must be common. If they had a license plate they'd already have found it.

I made more purchases just in case. Fortunately, the Polish words for what I wanted were nearly the same as the English, so I didn't have to stand out by asking questions. I also picked up a small back pack for my kit.

Sadly, my preparations were needed. Lana and I arrived at 9 a.m., as usual. Pietr was already there, as usual.

"We must talk," he said. He sounded like he was trying to be tough, which he didn't carry off at all well.

Lana sat on a stool at one end of the big examination table. "About what?"

He tried for menacing. "What are you looking for?"

"We told you. Johan Agnetason."

"Yes, but *why*? Do not bother lying. I know he must have possession of some secret or treasure. You would not be going to such trouble otherwise."

I'd been afraid of this. I hoped I'd thought further ahead than he had.

"It isn't anything that is worth money," I said, moving toward the other end of the table.

"Stop moving."

I inched further away from Lana. Pietr reached behind his back and pulled out a pistol.

"I say stop moving."

I froze. I wasn't familiar with that model of pistol, but it used a button-type safety. The red band was showing, and he had his finger on the trigger. All he had to do was twitch and I'd have a new hole in me.

I raised my hands. "Pietr, be careful with that thing. Do you really want a dead body on your hands?"

He looked uncertain, and his hand dropped slightly. I carefully slid further to the side.

His hand came back up. "Don't move."

"All right, if that's what you want," I said very, very calmly. "But you need to think very carefully about what you are doing. If you use that there is no way to undo it."

As I was speaking there was a flash of movement and I dropped straight down to the floor. There was a sound like a brick hitting a side of beef followed by the clatter of the gun hitting the floor. It was a miracle that it didn't go off.

Lana might have a broken arm, but she was far from helpless. While he was busy looking at me she'd dropped down onto her good arm while doing one of her mule kicks to his head. Man, that girl was fast.

I gingerly picked up the gun, dropped the magazine and cleared the chamber. There was no round in it. He hadn't known enough about guns to chamber a round before threatening us with it.

Lana was checking Pietr's condition. "I think that he'll be out for a while. I didn't kick him very hard."

I took a deep breath and let it out. "Okay, here's what we're going to do. First, we're tying him up so he doesn't cause more trouble."

I lifted him into the office chair by the computer. I couldn't decide whether he'd weigh more or less if he worked out. Lana found some spare network cables that worked well as rope. I stuffed a few of the gloves in his mouth as a gag.

"Okay, does he know where we're staying?"

"I don't believe so. No. The subject never came up."

"Good. Does he know either of our last names?"

"Definitely not."

I picked up my pack and opened it. Inside were two, four-litre bottles of alcohol and some kitchen sponges.

"We're going to go over this whole place and wipe down any fingerprints. That means the outsides of all the boxes, the door, doorknob, work bench, and computer. Can you think of any other place we might have touched?"

"Light switch, search history, any computer files he's made."

"Excellent ideas. Let's get to it." We each put on a pair of cotton examination gloves and went to work.

It didn't take that long. By the end the place smelled like a hospital and Pietr was beginning to groan. I even cleaned the floor where Lana had put her hand for the kick.

"Welcome back," she said as Pietr opened his eyes. He struggled for a minute before realizing he wasn't going anywhere.

"Let me explain what's going to happen." She had his gun in her gloved hand. His eyes were very wide.

"This gun has your fingerprints on it. We're going to keep it in case the police want to talk to us. We'll be glad to tell them what you were doing with it."

I chimed in, forcing him to split his attention. "That won't happen unless you mention us to anyone, regardless of the circumstances. Just so you know, we've wiped all our fingerprints from this room. There's no evidence that we were ever here."

"We're going to leave now," Lana continued. "Thank you for your help. And remember, you'll be charged with attempted murder if you talk. You won't talk about us, will you?"

He vigorously shook his head.

I untied one of his hands so he could eventually free himself. We kept the gloves on, at least until we could dispose of them somewhere where they'd never be found.

Of course we had no intention of keeping the gun. For one thing, it had my fingerprints on it as well as his. I wiped it, disassembled it, and we went for a nice walk along the river. Every so often I'd pick up a stone and throw it in the water. About a quarter of the stones were gun parts, including the individual bullets.

~~~

The route to Csejte (or Čachtice) was relatively easy. South west through Poland to the Czech border, south through the Czech Republic, then south into Slovakia and west to the village. The GPS said it would take six and a half hours.

We'd both been short on sleep lately, so we decided to stop for the night in Częstochowa, a few hours south of Warsaw. I was craving Indian food, which amused Lana until the concierge gave us directions to the Diwa restaurant. The owner turned out to be Indian and he came out to ask us how we liked the food. He and I had a nice chat about Indian cooking techniques.

The next morning we continued on to the Czech border where I got a considerable surprise. I was expecting a line of booths, long lines of cars, people getting pulled out of line for detailed searches, uniformed guards with German Shepherds—all the things you see at border crossings in movies.

The only thing at the border was a small, blue, square sign with a wreath of gold stars on it surrounding the words *Czechá republika*. There wasn't even a line in the asphalt where one paving crew stopped and the other began.

Welcome to a world where paranoia wasn't the primary motivation for living.

I hadn't bothered to do any research about our route or destination other than programming the GPS. Frankly, after nearly two months of being shot at, threatened, stabbed, detained, and endless hours of staring at old documents, I was getting tired of it all.

Lana, on the other hand, was looking smug and waiting for me to ask why.

That lasted until part way through the Czech Republic. We'd been travelling through terrain that looked just like Poland: flat with occasional patches of flat. Now we were going through hills. It made me homesick for the Rockies.

"It's nice to have some up and down, but I wish we'd get some real mountains."

"Oh, these are real mountains. And real forests." Again with the smug look.

"All right, out with it."

"These are the western extent of the Carpathian Mountains."

"By Canadian standards they're hills. I want something with a tree line."

"They're also famous as the home of Dracula."

"I thought that was Transylvania."

Smug look.

No way. "Are you telling me that the village we're heading to..."

"Is considered by some to be the origin of the Dracula myth. The castle was owned by Countess Elizabeth Báthory, the most prolific female serial killer in history."

"And by prolific, you mean...?"

"The official count is 80, but one source claims she murdered 650 girls so she could bathe in their blood."

"Yuck. I thought Vlad the Impaler was the inspiration for Dracula."

"Perhaps you know the saying: If you steal from one source it's plagiarism. If you steal from several it's research."

The Czech Republic was a beautiful country, now that we were away from the lowlands. I felt quite at home zooming along the mountain roads, even if the peaks weren't that far above us.

We crossed into Slovakia with the same lack of fanfare. I did notice that the new, blue sign replaced an older white one that was faded. I wondered if that one was from the Soviet era.

The joy of travel was marred by the North American paranoia I'd brought with me, except that people really were trying to get us. I kept an eye on every van and truck behind us, sometimes abruptly pulling off at an interchange to see if they followed. None of them did.

Either that meant that we'd lost our pursuers, or they had better tradecraft than I did. I wasn't going to take bets either way.

It didn't take us long to reach the foothills where the highway was enveloped in forest. After that I could see a plain ahead with more hills—I mean, mountains—in the distance. We would follow the Váh River valley to Čachtice.

We turned off at Nové Mesto nad Váhom, and played tag with various roads until we found the 504 heading south through city and farmland mixed together.

There was a sense of accomplishment when I saw the small sign saying *Čachtice*. We'd successfully navigated our way through three countries to a small village that might have once been the creepiest place on Earth.

We passed a huge cemetery that spanned both sides of the highway. It seemed oversized for a village. Given the place's history, it made one wonder.

An onion-shaped steeple appeared, and it looked like the road went right through it. That was almost true. The road narrowed to one lane that dodged under a stone arch that was part of the wall of the church.

Lana was studying it as we passed. "I think we should check out the church."

"After lunch. There's probably a service going on now."

Not much further we found the Slovakian version of a strip mall, designed to strip tourists of their money.

There are some things that are just too horrible to pass up. We had lunch at the Pizzeria Báthory.

"You had to pick this one," Lana said as she looked over the menu.

"When in Rome, be a Roman candle."

The pizzeria was filled with mementos of the Mad Countess, including a portrait that really made her look like a serial killer and etchings of young girls being hauled away to their fates. All in all, it was a creepy place, but the pizza and service was good.

St. Ladislav Catholic Church was literally a fortress built on top of a solid-buttressed stone wall, although newer additions were less capable of repelling an invasion. There was no place to park closer than the strip mall.

The narrow, 500-year old stone steps from the road up to the actual church added a definite ambiance to our quest. All it needed was organ music.

We found a priest as soon as we entered. He was an old man who was puttering around tidying what looked like the community notice board.

"Good afternoon. Do you speak English?"

"Yes, but not so good."

I spoke more slowly. "We're looking for historical records from the early 1600s."

"If you want family records, all have been sent to archive in Bratislava."

"No, not family. We are trying to find a Swedish monk who might have been here around 1607."

He dropped a push pin. Lana picked it up for him. "You mean Father János? He is famous here because he is only Swedish priest."

Holy crap, was this the end of the quest? János would be the equivalent of Johan.

"Do you know his Swedish name?"

"Of course. János Agnetason." I tried not to let my excitement show.

"Are there any records of his life?"

"Only his confession. We keep it here because it is our history. Nobody ever come to ask before."

"May we see it?"

"It is very old. I cannot let you touch."

"May we take pictures?"

"Yes."

Walking slowly, he led us out to the stone arch I'd noticed while driving. There were stairs leading up and over the road to the parish house on the other side.

"By the way, my name is Veronica. This is my friend Lana."

"I am called Father Miklós."

The manuscript was a set of loose pages bound in a leather portfolio. Father Miklós used the familiar cotton gloves to handle them. Both Lana and I took pictures of them in case one camera failed. Of course, the confession was in Latin.

"Now all we need is someone who speaks Latin," I said.

Lana put her phone away. "I have a bit of Latin, but we'd better get someone who is fluent. I might miss a lot of the nuances."

"I can read. Many years ago Mass was said in Latin."

"That would save a lot of time."

I tried to give Father Miklós a pleading look. "Would it be too much trouble for you to translate it for us?"

"I have time, but early part is not good for young ladies to hear."

"Thank you. We only need the part after he was captured by Croatians."

We sat at the kitchen table while Miklós ran his gloved finger down the pages and muttered to himself. Finally, he decided where to begin.

CHAPTER 11

The Confession (translated from Latin)

After two terrible weeks we came out of the mountains onto a river plain. In the distance a castle stood upon a hill, and it was clear that was our destination. Now that we were on the plain, the Croats alternated between a gallop and a slow trot. You can imagine being in the saddle during such a ride with your hands tied before you, and your feet lashed to the horse's belly. The combination ate the distance to the castle and mercifully, within a few hours, we were at its gates.

The servants who tended us were much more charitable than our captors. They informed us that we in Csejte Castle, the home of Countess Ecsedi Báthory Erzsébet, or as we would say, Elizabeth Báthory of Ecsed.

The Countess herself greeted us, and appeared to be as gracious a Christian woman as one could imagine, despite being Catholic. She ordered that our bonds be removed, that we be bathed and dressed, and that we dine with her that evening.

The Croatian captain was not pleased with this change in our status, but it seemed that the Countess far outranked him and his men due to some ancient treaty between their countries. She also took the device from them, which would have led to much bloodshed if the Croats had been given the use of their horses. However, trapped as they were within the courtyard of the castle and surrounded by the Countess's men armed with muskets, there was nothing they could do. Rather than remain as her guests, they decided to press on for their own country. No doubt they would report the Countess's perceived treachery to their *ban*.

The dinner went well, and the Countess continued to be a gracious hostess. Our situation was delicate, and she assured us that she had saved us from the Croats because of our shared religious beliefs. This made it impossible for us to confess to being Lutherans, but as Sigismund had broken faith with his mercenaries, we told her for her protection that the device was demonic. We were vague in our description of where we were taking it. She was not Polish, and so Ander's accent did not cause her to question our origin. Our knowledge of the rebellion against him made her believe we were from Livonia as we said we were from "the north," and we were careful not to correct this impression.

She became more and more excited by our story of the finding of the device, and its certification as demonic. We carefully omitted any mention of things that might give away our origins, and I began to worry that her interest might have unhealthy elements.

Regardless, at the appropriate time we wished her a good night, and retired to our rooms.

The next day the Countess offered us positions. To Ander she offered a place in her guard. I was offered a position at the Church of Saint Ladislaus in the village of Čachtice at the base of the hill.

For the first time in my life I felt like I might have some peace. The priest at the church welcomed me, and I had not been sufficiently Lutheran in my beliefs to be bothered by my sudden conversion to Catholicism. Our mission to deliver the device to Sigismund had failed beyond reclamation and it was now time to live my life as I well as I could. That we were far from the retribution of either the Archbishop or the Oxenstierna family was a blessing as well.

The years have been kind to me. I have now passed my sixty-third year, and after the death of Father Laszlo 25 years ago, I have been the priest at this church.

There is one final thing to be told about the evil thing that was given to me so many years ago. The year after our arrival, the Countess began repairs and changes to the castle. During that time, she caused to have dug a secret well outside the castle walls at the foot of the mountain on the west side near the village of Višňové where Satan's Millstone could be buried for all time. The well's depth was ten feet into the rocky soil, and after the device was lowered into it the entire shaft was filled. The Countess had me say a benediction over the covered shaft to keep the evil influences at bay. So ended any possible temptation of men by the unholy object. What caused her to view the object with such horror and loathing after a year in her keeping I cannot say.

Three years later the Countess was sealed within her own rooms within her castle on charges too terrible to describe. Ander left Hungary to return to Sweden. I begged him to put the entire blame for our failure upon me to save himself any ill consequences. With the terrible wars that have spread throughout the countries in his path I pray that he makes it safely to the land of our birth.

In the intervening years I have tried to bury old Johan the thief and adulterer beneath my priestly cassock as thoroughly as we buried the Millstone.

This is the confession of Johan Agnetason, now known to my flock as Pap János, in the year of Our Lord 1641.

CHAPTER 12

Game On

We thanked Father Miklós for letting us see the confession. Before we left, he took us to Johan's grave.

We looked down at the modest stone. The inscription was faded, but we could still make out the years 1578-1642. He was 64 when he died.

Lana touched the stone. "I don't know why, but this makes me sad. It's not like I expected to find him alive."

"We've been chasing him for two months. Although he died almost four centuries ago, he's been part of our lives. I'm glad his story had a happy ending."

"That's all any of us can really hope for, isn't it?"

"It is surprising me that János has so many visitors after all these years," Father Miklós said.

Lana caught the implication. "What do you mean, many?"

"Two days ago, men came to ask same questions you do."

"What men?"

"They not give me their names, but I think they are foreigners."

"Were they driving one of those army trucks?"

He shrugged. "I not see."

"Did they say where they were going?"

"No."

We stayed silent until we left the church grounds.

"Do you think it's the Finns, or Pietr?"

"Either way, he's the only one who knew we were coming here. Some people don't get the hint."

I pulled out my phone and dialled. After a few rings a male voice answered in Polish.

"May I speak with Pietr Debiak?"

The man switched to English. "Who is this?"

There was something wrong. He should have been answering his own phone. I dodged the question. "I wanted to ask him a question about his thesis."

"I'm sorry to tell you that he is dead."

"What? Who is this?"

"Sergeant Stanisław Ostrowski of the Policja. We are investigating his murder. What is your name?"

I had a sudden inspiration. "Veronica Chandler. I was given his name by Professor Kłonczyński at the University of Gdańsk for a research project."

I had to spell my name for him. Lana looked concerned when I hung up.

"Pietr's dead. That was a police sergeant investigating his murder."

"Why would you give him your name?"

"He might have my number from call display, so I made it sound like this was the first time I'd contacted Pietr. With any luck, they won't follow up."

"I hope you're right."

We retrieved the car and followed the signs pointing to the castle. That led us to a one-lane side street with stone walls on either side. I doubt that the Sprinter would have fit.

This "widened" to a paved cow path that meandered among houses that in places touched the road. It finally led into a dense forest.

Leaves slapped either side of the Fiat. I went very slowly, because I had no idea if there would be oncoming traffic, or how we'd handle it. After a while there were the occasional dirt roads leading off. Every so often there were slightly wider spots on the road where two sports cars might pass each other if they were careful. As we passed each one I memorized where it was just in case we had to back up.

It was exactly what you'd expect driving up to Dracula's castle. I was really glad that it was daylight.

We did encounter traffic, but it was all on foot. We passed at a crawl as people got as far off the road as possible to let us pass. At least the road was paved.

The pavement gave out about 500 metres from the castle.

The castle wall loomed before us with a narrow arch through it. There was room for maybe half a dozen cars to park, but the only vehicle was a van that probably belonged to the woman sitting at a patio table complete with umbrella. She was selling snacks and souvenirs.

There was no obvious sign forbidding us from driving right into the castle, but we decided to be sensible and explore on foot.

I got to show off my Canadian woodcraft skills by using the sun to figure out which was the west side of the mountain. We could see a village and a small road at the bottom.

I contemplated the slope. "There's a whole lot of west side to this mountain. I wonder where the Sampo is buried?"

Lana was frowning. "We're looking at years of work to cover the area, assuming that the Sampo really is buried here."

"How about using a metal detector?"

"That probably won't help. For one thing we don't know if the Sampo is metallic, and if it is buried ten feet down that's beyond the range of all the usual detectors. If we could get ground-penetrating radar that might work."

As we looked over the extremely scenic valley, I noticed a faint buzzing sound. At first I ignored it, but it became obvious that it wasn't natural. It came and went, and sounded like it was coming from the whole valley.

"Do you hear...?"

Lana cocked her head. "It sounds like..."

I spotted it as the sun reflected off some part of it.

"A drone."

It was flying parallel to the mountain near the northern end of the valley floor.

"A big drone," Lana said. She took a picture, then enlarged it as much as possible.

I squinted at the fuzzy image. "A big drone carrying something?"

Lana sounded bitter. "Years of work to cover the area. Unless you use a remote sensing platform. If Professor Nieminen is right and the Sampo is a technological device, what are the chances that it emits enough of an electro-magnetic signature to be found by sensitive instruments?"

"Wouldn't somebody else have found it before this? Oil company surveyors or something?"

"Probably not. Even if the survey was made in this area the Sampo would likely show up as a tiny anomaly. Oil and gas deposits are huge in comparison."

I looked at the drone as it occasionally sparkled in the sun, and flew in an obvious search pattern.

"Oh, fuck."

❦

We drove back down the hill as fast as we could without killing anybody. Once back in the village we turned left just before the church to get onto highway 1229. It was very picturesque, if you didn't mind scraping your side mirrors off on houses or rock outcrops.

Although we were in motion and heading in the right direction, I had no idea what the plan was. "What do we do when we get there?"

"I'm not sure. I'm beginning to wish we'd kept Pietr's gun."

"That would be worse than useless. There are at least four of them to our one and a half. It would be assault rifles versus one pistol."

"You didn't mention assault rifles."

"I didn't?"

"What kind are they?"

"I have no idea. Wooden stock and pistol grip, curved magazine."

"It sounds like an AK-47. Wonderful. The preferred weapon of terrorists worldwide. Fully automatic and they can put a round completely through this car. All right, forget the gun. How do we stop them from finding the Sampo?"

Another inspiration hit. Wow, two in one day. "Maybe we don't."

"I'm not willing to give up yet."

"Neither am I. But they have an aerial sensor platform and we have two people with eyes. We let them find it and then we take it away from them."

"I seem to remember a discussion about AK-47s a moment ago."

"I'm not suggesting a frontal assault. I'm wondering if there's a way we can steal it without them knowing."

There was silence for a few minutes. The road continued to snake its way around the mountain. The speed limit was 40. I was doing 30 just in case we met traffic.

"You are insane, but it might work."

"Okay, we have to put on our SAS and JTF-2 game faces. What do we need?"

"That depends on what we find when we get there. At the moment we are in reconnaissance mode."

"Recon it is."

Three and a half kilometres from Čachtice we turned south. We were now officially on the west side of the mountain. I'd noticed that a creek had paralleled the road ever since we left town.

"You know, in some traditions running water is a barrier to evil forces. Maybe the Sampo was buried in or near this creek."

"That makes sense. Where did you hear that?"

"Research for an old case."

As we went south the valley got wider. There was now a strip of ground several hundred metres wide to search. The Sampo was still a needle in a haystack.

We came around a corner. Ahead, on the right, a canvas-topped truck was pulled off onto what looked like a single-lane dirt side road leading down to the creek.

"Get down out of sight! It's them!"

Lana unfastened her seat belt and scrunched down into the foot well as much as she could. I hoped it was enough.

The truck was facing away from the road. Most of the men must have been inside. I caught a glimpse of one by the creek with something in his hands. I'd bet that he was the pilot.

Two hundred metres later we turned another corner and were out of sight.

"You can get up now."

She wriggled for a while. "No, I can't. I'm stuck."

I stopped for a moment to give her a hand.

"I'll be glad when I can use both arms again."

"I think I saw the man piloting the drone. That's them."

Lana flipped her sun visor down, then slapped mine down as well.

"What are you...?"

The drone zoomed overhead. At close range it was *huge*. At least a metre and a half across with eight propellers. Some kind of equipment was attached underneath the platform.

The visors weren't great protection, but they should help to hide our faces from a flying camera.

The road turned right into the village of Višňové. There was a parking area on the outside of the curve.

"Stop here."

Lana rolled down her window and looked out, which seemed foolish. "Don't get spotted by the drone."

"It's all right. It flew up the valley. I can see the castle directly above us. If any place counts as the western side of the mountain, it's right here."

"Then why are the Finns scanning the other end of the valley?"

"Maybe they want to eliminate it before concentrating on a place where there are a lot of witnesses."

"Maybe. That makes sense. It also means that they are just starting their survey, so we have time to gather the information we need."

She smiled. "It's a good thing we know some investigators."

⸻

First we needed to be able to keep our targets under surveillance. It was still mid-afternoon, so we drove back to Nové Mesto nad Váhom. Unbelievably, the city was only five kilometres north of the church. I kept getting confused by how *small* Europe was. We kept asking directions until we found shops where we could find what we needed.

There was a farm right beside the road to Višňové. We got back there around supper time. Perhaps not the best time to ask for a favour.

A middle-aged man and woman were working on the fence by the road when we pulled up.

"Excuse me, do you speak English?"

The man said something. It wasn't English.

Lana tried. "*Sprechen sie Deutsch?*" Nothing. "*Parlez vous français?*"

I was about to try Spanish when the woman cupped her hands to her mouth and used her Mother Voice. "ŜTEFAN!"

A younger man came out of the house. Lana tried again.

"Do you speak English?"

"Yes, can I help you?"

She held up her credentials. I did the same, although mine looked different. "We are investigating suspected terrorists in this area and we need your help. Can we talk inside?"

A pitch like that was nothing if not intriguing. They invited us inside. I parked the Fiat as far out of sight from the road as possible. Lana seemed to have a plan so I let her do all the talking.

She made our introduction to Jozef and Mária Horváth via their son Ŝtefan. The differences between our credentials somehow led them to get the impression that we were from Interpol, although Lana never said so directly.

"Have you seen the drone flying overhead?"

"Yes. It's very annoying."

"We have been pursuing a group of men from Poland where we believe they have been responsible for at least one death. Now they are here looking for buried treasure to finance their activities."

I caught Jozef staring at Lana's cast.

"Please tell your father that my colleague was injured when they tried to kill us near Warsaw." That was close enough to the truth. When the message was relayed Jozef nodded as if he suspected that was the case.

"What kind of treasure would be buried here?"

"We have documentation that it was buried by the Mad Countess. We don't know exactly what it is."

"What do you want us to do?"

"We need a hidden place to stay while we are watching them. At the moment we can't prove that they have done anything wrong. Once they have the treasure we can take them into custody."

Jozef spoke, and his son nodded. "My father does not want us put in danger."

"All we need is a place to stay, and to hide our car. We have camping equipment so we don't need to trouble you. Your family will not be involved."

The three of them spoke among themselves for some time. Ŝtefan turned to Lana and me to give us their decision.

"We have all heard the news of terrorists in other countries. There have not yet been any attacks in our country, and we would like to keep it that way. If you can promise that our family will be safe I'll show you where you can put your car. You may sleep in your tent if you wish, but my mother insists that you eat with us."

We promised, and thanked them for their hospitality. Fortunately, they had a long shed row barn so I could carefully back the car straight into an unused stall. It couldn't be seen with the door closed, especially after he'd found a tarp that we could throw over it.

We set up the tent in the stall beside the car, got the sleeping bags ready, and went in for supper.

CHAPTER 13

I Spy

Keeping an eye on the Finns was tedious but not difficult. The hillside above the valley was easy to climb, even for Lana, so each morning we got up and one of us would position herself in the woods with binoculars and sit for four hours. Then we traded places.

Lana insisted on taking the first shift. From the farm to the observation point was less than 500 metres, and Ŝtefan drew us a map that showed an intimate knowledge of the game trails and how to move in these woods without being seen.

When I went to relieve her, I realized how badly we'd have done without that map. The bush was incredibly thick in places. The last fifteen metres or so there was a possibility of being seen from the road so I crawled. That must have been difficult for Lana.

I found her sitting on a foam pad looking down through the binoculars. Her BSI phone was on the pad beside her. We were using them to record our observations since she couldn't write with a broken arm.

"How's it going?" I whispered. We had no idea how well sound would carry.

"There are definitely four men. They fly the drone for exactly 20 minutes at a time, then they land and change batteries. I counted six battery chargers in the back of the truck. I got a look at their weapons—definitely AK-47s, some kind of pistols, as well as several ammunition crates. Most of the time they all just sit in the truck except the drone pilot. I believe that the drone has an on-board camera, but I haven't been able to see the control unit clearly."

"Got it. I'll see you in four hours."

"Two more things. They have a place down the hill to the left they use as a toilet. I moved to get a better look before I realized what they were doing."

"Good. I'll avoid that. What's the other thing?"

"Have you noticed the little blue signs with a shield on them by the road?"

"Yeah, I was going to ask Ŝtefan what they are."

"You won't like it. This entire mountain side is a national nature preserve. Nobody is allowed to go through the woods except on the official hiking path up to the castle."

I sighed. "You mean we're breaking the law in yet another national park. Great. Maybe we can defile all the parks in Europe before this is over."

"I couldn't tell him that this might be a problem. He still thinks we're sanctioned by Interpol."

"So we could be arrested in at least two countries if the terrorists with enough weapons to take a small town don't get to us first. Gotcha. I'll keep my head down."

She crawled away, surprisingly adept at doing so with one hand. I settled in.

Tedious.

The highlight was just after a battery change. The men got out along with several spare battery packs. Two of them got in the front and drove away toward Čachtice. Apart from the drone pilot, the other disappeared from my sight below the embankment. He wasn't using their communal toilet.

That made me nervous as hell, until the truck came back an hour later and he re-appeared from where he'd vanished. The two in the truck unloaded pizza boxes and beer. They'd gone on a food run.

I decided that we'd both take the third shift. Unless it had an infrared camera, the drone couldn't fly at night, and we needed to know where they were staying. It would be ridiculous for them to sleep in the back of the truck along with all their equipment, especially as it was parked on a considerable tilt. I didn't want Lana trailing them on her own.

Great minds think alike. When Lana came for her shift she said she'd pulled some of the car's fuses. The regular head lights still worked, but the marker lights and high beams were inoperative. As long as there was enough light to be able to stay on the road, we could follow the truck at night without being seen. She'd also arranged for our hosts to bring the car to us if we called. Given the speed limit on the road, it wasn't like they could get far before we caught up with them. With all that illegal gear on board, speeding was not something they could afford to do, even if the road conditions had allowed it.

We waited. Around sunset the drone landed for the last time. Their search grid started about halfway up the mountain and moved back and forth until they got to the other side of the valley. In other words, covering every bit of ground that might reasonably be described as "at the foot of the mountain on the west side." The search was steadily moving south toward the village.

While they loaded the drone into the truck Lana called Ŝtefan. I packed up our gear, and we sneaked down the hill for our rendezvous.

The truck headed south toward the village. Our car arrived two minutes later. Ŝtefan was grinning as we piled in, but he didn't move from the driver's seat.

I opened the door. "We need to move!"

"I know where they are going."

"What? Where?"

"They passed me as I was leaving our farm and went up the road to the castle."

"*What* road to the castle?" The only one I knew was back in Čachtice.

"There is a dirt road just south of our farm that goes up the mountain. They will not get very far with their truck, so they must be camping there."

"That makes sense," Lana said. "Close to their area of operations but away from prying eyes. They must know about the nature preserve."

"Nobody uses that road unless they are from the government," Ŝtefan confirmed. "Maybe once a year."

I could feel a plan coming together in my brain. "All right, let's go back to your place."

⁂

We didn't bother surveilling the truck the next day. Instead, we took a hike up the hill road, keeping to the edge so we wouldn't leave obvious tracks.

Their camping spot was easy to find in the soft soil. They'd drive up the road about 60 metres so they were invisible from the highway, then do a many-point turn so the truck was pointing down hill for a fast getaway. Flat areas in the grass showed where four sleeping bags had been laid out on the uphill side of the truck. They hadn't made a fire that we could find.

This was both good and bad. It looked like they all went to sleep at night instead of setting a watch. After all, what kind of threat were a few villagers? That was the good news. The bad news was that they'd all be dark adapted and armed if something disturbed their sleep.

The plan I'd had earlier really was taking shape, complete with details. It sounded completely reasonable if I didn't think about it too hard.

The next day the drone broke its search pattern in mid-afternoon. We watched from the shelter of our stall as it circled the area near the final turn into the village. It then flew much lower, spiralling in on some particular spot. After a minute it disappeared into the trees by the road.

The truck drove by a while later.

I put down the binoculars. "I think they've found it."

"Or at least they think they have. They must have landed the drone on the spot to mark it."

"The big question is what they'll do now. I wish we could see what they are up to."

"We could always ask one of the Horváth's to drive past."

"Not a hope. For all we know they're in the village threatening to shoot anybody who doesn't dig for them."

"Don't be so melodramatic. There have to be 200 people there. Four of them can't control that many people, and they'd have to kill all of them afterward in order to get away. Not to mention any other people who came along while it was happening."

"Fine. Be logical. So what's their next step?"

"They'll have to dig it up themselves. Machinery would lead to questions. They'll have to dig by hand at night and hope that nobody catches them."

"I have been working on an idea about that."

We didn't have to look far for Štefan. He was tending horses in the other stalls.

"I have a very important question to ask you: Are there any people in Višňové who would put themselves in harm's way to try to stop the terrorists by themselves?"

He looked thoughtful as he patted a horse's neck.

"No. I think everybody is sensible, especially when it might involve their families."

"Good. I hate to ask this of you, but can you and your parents to speak with every person in the area? The men we are hunting will probably be digging near the village tonight, and we want to let them do it. If everybody stays completely out of their way then no harm should come to them or their families. If the men think they have been caught, people could die."

"Yes, we can do that."

"Once they have found their treasure, we will turn them over to the police. One neat package."

"Why not arrest them now, and then send archaeologists to dig up the treasure?"

"That's certainly a possibility, but we don't know what they know that we don't. Even now they might be looking in the wrong place. It's easier if we let them locate it for us."

Štefan, unfortunately for us, was not stupid. Our story was beginning to sound a bit thin. If we could just keep things together until tonight, everything should work out.

Yeah, Veronica. You just keep telling yourself that.

⌬

There were exactly two people in Višňové who weren't obeying the curfew from Interpol.

"How much longer do you think it will be?"

Lana looked at her phone. It was nearly midnight. We were sitting in our car, which was parked in the village behind a building by the bridge over the creek. I never did find out the creek's name.

"Not too much longer. They'd wait until everybody is in bed."

I saw a spark of light showed on the mountain side for a moment.

"Houston, we have lift off."

Headlights showed as the truck made its way down to the main road, then stopped at the bend before the bridge. Although we were over 200 metres away and there was no reason that they would come any closer, I still felt nervous. Especially when I considered my fool-proof plan.

Up against the side of the far side of the creek was the village soccer pitch. In the useless triangle of land between the far edge of the pitch and the curving road was a belt of virgin forest. The drone had come down in that belt, so to they were partially shielded from both the road and from us. With the binoculars we could see just well enough to tell that two men were standing guard while the other two began digging. There was no way they could see us at all.

Some time later the pairs swapped jobs. This went on for about two hours. The ground should be fairly easy to dig unless the Countess had ordered rocks to be put on top of the Sampo.

My nerves gave way to excitement as the complete weirdness of the situation struck me. Were we really about to watch a mythical Finnish artifact created by their blacksmith god be unearthed in a Transylvanian village below the castle that served as partial inspiration for Dracula?

Holy crap, would I ever be able to take a normal case again?

Johan said they buried it ten feet deep. The Finns were using as little light as possible, but from what we could see of the mound of dirt it looked like they were getting close.

The two guards suddenly went to the excavation. One climbed into the hole along with the two diggers. The one on top got something from the ground and took a stance near the excavation.

"Something's happening."

Lana held her good hand out for the binoculars. "Let me see."

She said nothing for a good thirty seconds. I was about to poke her when she said, "The man on top is hauling something up with a rope."

The suspense was killing me. "What is it? Did they find it?"

"It's about the right size. I wish he'd move his light—it's a white disc, about as wide as his chest."

She put the binoculars down. "They found it."

Holy shit. Now all we had to do was steal it from four heavily armed political fanatics who considered the Sampo a sacred relic, and get away alive.

Piece of cake.

CHAPTER 14

Ninja Attack

It took them another half hour for everybody to climb out of the hole, collect all their gear, and wrap everything up.

This was the first of many critical parts of the plan. If they left immediately we'd have no choice but to follow them and hope that we got another chance to grab the Sampo. My guess is that they'd rather go back to their camp and leave after some sleep. After all, digging a ten foot hole couldn't have been *that* easy.

We both let out held breaths when they got back to their truck and went up the mountain. They were going to camp.

We weren't taking any chances. I waited an hour for them to settle in before making sure that the headlights were set to the inoperative high beams before starting the car. There was no moon. I drove very slowly, literally by starlight and the dim reflections of the village streetlights, to the beginning of the mountain road.

I tried not to think about the covert operation I'd done during the Blakeway case. If there was ever a cautionary tale, that was it.

At least the operation would be stylish. I'd borrowed Lana's dress for my commando raid, as it was the only black outfit we had between us. She wasn't wildly happy about it, but saw the necessity.

I also got some cooking oil from Mariá and charcoal from their fire place. Ground together, they made a fairly decent blackout paint for my face, hands and lower legs.

I opened the door as carefully as possible to avoid making a sound.

"Are you sure you want to do this?"

"Not in the least. If I'm not back in half an hour get back to the farm and call in the army. Or if you hear gunfire. Or me screaming for my life."

She completely surprised me by leaning over and giving me a kiss on my cheek. "Good hunting."

I felt myself blushing. "Keep the engine running."

I eased out the door, and closed it by pushing it with my hip until the latch engaged. There was just barely enough light from the village for me to see the lighter dirt road where it led upward through the undergrowth.

Things got better as my eyes adapted to the darkness. I knew where their camp was, and I hoped that they hadn't changed their routine. A girl wearing a black dress with black makeup sneaking up on them probably wouldn't be able to talk her way out of the trouble she'd be in. Assuming she lived long enough to speak.

The truck almost came into sight. By walking to one side I could see the faintest of silhouettes. The men should be sleeping on the far side.

I put my feet down very, very carefully, testing each step to make sure I wasn't going to snap a twig or something. It felt like it took forever for me to reach the truck.

There was a sense of accomplishment as my fingers touched canvas. I listened as hard as I could. There was no sound but the light wind, and an occasional sound from insects. Most animals larger than a mouse would be scared off by the human presence.

The obvious place for the Sampo was in the truck. They'd want it loaded in case they had to leave in a hurry. I found a foothold by touch, and slowly put my weight on it. I was expecting a creak, but the truck made no sound as I did so.

The canvas flap wasn't tied down, so I just slid underneath and oozed over the tail gate. I was prepared to use my phone as a flashlight in the Stygian interior, but there was no need.

The Sampo glowed slightly in the darkness. At first I thought it was an illusion, but when I put my hand on it I could see the outline of my fingers.

Slowly, I took the empty pack off my back. The Sampo was heavier than I'd expected—maybe 30 kilos. I wouldn't want to hike all day with it, but getting back to the car should be doable.

The Sampo fit into the pack, which was another worry I'd had. Once it was secure on my back, I listened carefully. There were no sounds outside.

I climbed out of the truck just as slowly. I had almost another half my weight on my back, and falling would be a really bad idea.

Something occurred to me as my toe touched the ground. I felt my way forward to the cab, paranoid about twigs or hitting something sticking out. It took a while for me to figure out the footholds by touch. It didn't help that I was a lot shorter than your average soldier. I wondered if I could get in without making a noise. I wasn't stupid enough to think I could open and close the door soundlessly.

Somebody was looking out for me. The driver had left the window open. I climbed part way in, balancing on the window sill on my stomach, and felt around. After a while it was getting painful, but I found what I was looking for.

I had just started to wiggle my way out of the truck when something grabbed my legs and pulled me out.

The keys in my hand flew out into the night, which was what I'd intended anyway. I hoped they flew far enough.

The man who'd grabbed me said something loud, angry, and Finnish. I'm sure he intended just to warn his friends that there was an intruder, but in the pitch darkness I'd landed on him back first. The Sampo gave me extra heft and was a lot harder than the rest of me.

By pure luck I'd been breathing out when I fell, so I didn't get the wind knocked out of me. In the blackness I could feel the Finn trying to figure out what to grab to keep me from getting away.

If I wasn't out of there in the next few seconds I wouldn't be going anywhere ever again. I flipped over and my own hands tried to find a useful target.

I found his throat first, and hit him as hard as I could. His movements became a lot less coordinated and I heard gurgling, rasping breaths.

I staggered to all fours, then got my feet under me. The weight of the Sampo threw my balance off as I ran in the direction of the village lights. I didn't care what sounds I made at this point.

There was more shouting from behind me, and the beam from a flashlight damned near gouged my eyes out even with my back to it. I expected the shooting to start at any second and I could feel my back uselessly tightening up to stop the bullets.

My eyes hadn't adjusted to the light and I ran into a bush. I fell head over heels and rolled down the hill just as there was the sound of a shot. The Sampo protected my back but I still felt like I'd found every stick and stone on the mountain.

The ground dropped away one more time and I fell hard on the paved road. In hindsight that one shot was a fluke. They couldn't afford to shoot at me while I had the Sampo. None of us had any idea what it would take to damage it.

The armed men were advancing down the hill. I had no time to get myself together.

A car stopped beside me and Lana yelled for me to get in. She helped open the passenger door as much as possible, but it was on her bad side. I clawed my way up the door and fell into the seat as she accelerated.

The pack was in our way, and I couldn't easily take it off in the car.

We wove up the road with the headlights on. It was that or run off the road almost immediately. There was almost no starlight and we were well away from the village lights.

The flashlights disappeared behind us as we rounded a corner.

"Stop for a moment while I get this thing off."

She slammed on the brakes and opened her door. I got mine open, got the pack off, threw it in the back, and traded seats with her.

I drove away at a more sedate speed. Without their truck keys they wouldn't be following us any time soon, and this road was a death trap at anything above the posted 40 kph. "I didn't know you could drive."

"Of course I can drive. I just don't like to. Shouldn't we be going faster?"

"It's okay, I stole the keys to their truck."

"Then what's following us?"

There was a single light behind us. It was gaining rapidly.

"What the hell? You didn't see a motorcycle in their truck did you?"

"No. It's above the road. They've sent the drone."

Bastards. Some bright boy had removed the instrument package and jammed a flashlight in its place so they could fly the drone at night.

"What did you do with their keys?"

"I dropped them when one of them attacked me. They could be anywhere."

"So they could be right behind the drone."

"Shit. Shit, shit, shit, shit."

It would take us six minutes to get to Čachtice. Whichever way we went after that, they'd know about it. The drone could fly much faster than we could drive on these roads. We were so screwed.

"I have an idea. When we get to the village head south."

"We don't know what's in that direction. It could be a dead end."

"It shouldn't matter. Trust me."

I drove while our aerial tormentor kept pace. Lana was working her phone at a frantic speed.

"We're good. Just keep on the main road."

A kilometre later we were out of town. Two kilometres after that, we were in another one. I could speed up occasionally on straight sections, forcing the drone to fall behind. It caught up with us again on curves. I could see headlights behind us in brief flashes.

"Not yet," Lana said. I didn't know if she was talking to herself.

Another two kilometres, another village.

The drone dipped, and hit the road, flipping over into the ditch. It must have run out of power. It didn't matter. Those headlights were just around the corner and gaining.

"Now! Take the next road to the left!"

I almost hit a concrete wall as I left the highway far faster than was safe or sane. We were on another one of those one lane streets. It went down a slight dip and turned a corner.

"Kill the lights."

I went to high beams, and we were mostly in darkness. There was the glow of a street light ahead, around a corner.

"There!" Lana said. She was pointing at a gap between a building and a tree. It was a lawn, but the Fiat would fit in between them.

Once at the back of the building, I cut the engine. The silence was made even louder by the beating of our hearts. Lana whispered, even though nobody could possible hear us.

"I reasoned that they probably wouldn't have changed batteries after their last flight, so it was only a matter of keeping out of their way until the drone gave out before they expected it to."

I wasn't going to question that assumption. "I'm glad you were right."

"We should be safe here. They can't know where we turned off, and it will be some time before they do. Even then, they'll have to search the whole town. In the meantime, I have an escape route planned."

All we had to do was go to the end of this street, and turn left. That would put us on highway 1222. We'd follow that east until we were back on the highway we'd been on since Poland. From there it was about an hour to Bratislava where we could get flights home.

In the meantime I fished through my bag until I found the card given to me by Detective-Sergeant Laakso. I left him a message describing the terrorists, their vehicle, and their weapons. I even gave him a fairly accurate description of what they'd been doing in Čachtice and why they were following us. I did leave out the minor detail that I'd stolen the Sampo from them. After all, nobody had seen my face.

After an hour we agreed that it was as safe to move as it ever would be. In a few hours it would be light, and then they'd be able to see us at a distance.

I made one change to Lana's plan. I turned north on the D1 to take us back to Nové Mesto nad Váhom. It was in the opposite direction to the one we'd been going, which should confuse our pursuers, and it was big enough to have hotels. And after all that running around, it was only 12 kilometres away. I still wasn't used to the scale of Europe

We needed to be rested before we made our dash for home in case something else went wrong.

CHAPTER 15

The Elephant on the Settee

We were getting cunning in our old age, and I hoped it wasn't too little too late. We found an ATM by the simple method of driving around until we saw one, then both Lana and I got credit card advances. That would leave a trail, but it couldn't be helped. It wasn't likely that they had spies in the Slovakian banking system.

Cash in hand, we picked a hotel at random. I was about to open my door to get out of the car.

"You might want me to register alone." She looked at me like my mother telling me something obvious.

I looked at my hands. They were still black, just like the rest of me. I must have looked like a refugee from a nineteenth century American minstrel show.

"I'll stay here."

Fifteen minutes later Lana let me in the back entrance. As agreed, she'd paid for a double. If somebody did come calling, we didn't want to be picked off one at a time in separate rooms. Unless somebody contacted every hotel in the area directly, nobody should know where we were until we'd moved on.

My first order of business was a long shower. The dress was relatively clean except around the collar and cuffs. There wasn't anything we could do about that until we found a dry cleaner.

Morning came late. Neither of us wanted to address the big pink elephant waving flags in the room, so instead we had lunch. It gives you some idea of my mental state that I have no idea what I ate. I don't even remember ordering.

We returned to our room. I pulled the Sampo out of its pack and put it on the bed so we could stare at it. Even though it had been dug out of the mud, it was clean and white. Whether that was because the Finns had scrubbed it, or that was part of its magic, I had no idea.

My clever-opening-statement generator wasn't working very well. "Well, there it is."

"It certainly is."

"Now what do we do with it?"

"I was asked to locate it."

"So was I. Technically, we've fulfilled our contracts. We could just leave it here and go home."

"I don't think that's acceptable."

"Neither do I."

We stared at the pristine, white, object on the bed.

"I'm curious as to what all the fuss is about," she said.

I sat beside the Sampo. The seam between the lid and the body was extremely thin. It looked like it would be difficult to get a hair in there, let alone something to pry it open. Even though it was at least 400 years old and had spent most of that time buried in wet soil, there wasn't a mark on it anywhere. No chips, stains, scratches, or anything else.

I put my hand on the side and tried to move the lid with my thumb. It rotated easily enough with just enough resistance that it stopped when I stopped pushing. I turned it through several full revolutions in both directions. The crack didn't change size. The lid wasn't any looser or tighter than it had been before.

Lana intently watched me without saying anything. I took that to mean that she approved of my experiments so far.

I put my palm on the lid.

Immediately it lit up on top with a variety of symbols. Although some of them looked alphabetic, they were in no language I'd ever seen before. The symbols were in groups, with different groups having different colours. The rows across one side looked a bit like keyboard.

"Do the symbols look familiar?"

She shook her head.

Other symbols looked like icons. One looked like two open hands beside each other. On a whim I touched it.

Two things happened. The icon changed to two hands together as if they were praying, or maybe closed. The other was that some symbols rotated up off the lid and stood in midair above it along with what appeared to be readouts. The keyboard-like array of buttons stayed on the lid. I remembered two lines from the Kalevala.

> Sees the magic Sampo rising,
> Sees the lid in many colours.

I licked my dry lips. Lana reached out and turned the lid by its rim.

The mid-air display moved with it.

I touched the praying hands icon. The whole thing shut off.

It was once again a featureless, squat cylinder. It occurred to me that it had about the same dimensions as a really big, white hockey puck.

Lana let out a long breath. "We need to make notes."

I went downstairs and got some notepads and pencils from the desk clerk.

I did the writing. "Touching it turns on the surface display. The hands icon turns on a holographic display, or turns the whole thing off. The lid spins to orient the display so the user doesn't have to move the whole thing."

"I wonder what the power source is?"

"I'm not sure we'd understand it if we knew. I read somewhere that nuclear reactors are refuelled every 25 to 50 years."

"Nowhere near enough."

"No."

I turned it on again and studied the display. A major part of it had relatively simple shapes contained within circles. Assuming that the operator was meant to be in front of the display with the icons ready to hand, the array of symbols across the front was a keyboard. I put my hands on them as if I was going to type something. The reverse curve made it much more comfortable than one of those ergonomic keyboards people occasionally tried to sell me on.

Beyond that were colour-coded groups of buttons. Farthest away were a cluster of three teal buttons inside a border. One of those icons looked a bit like the Egyptian hieroglyph for a mouth, except that the lips were more lip-shaped rather than just two curved lines. I touched it.

Immediately things started happening on the vertical display. We couldn't read any of it, of course, but it certainly looked busy.

There was a brief swirl of mist, and a pile of off-white powder appeared across from me on the bed. It looked like there was enough to fill a two-litre milk carton.

The display went back to being static.

Neither of us moved for a while, and the Sampo turned off.

I made notes while Lana examined the powder.

"It looks like flour. It's not wheat, though. Maybe barley."

"Would that be consistent with ancient Finnish agriculture?"

"I don't know, but it wouldn't surprise me."

I looked up the poem on my phone.

"According to the Kalevala, one side produces flour, another salt, and the third money."

We removed the sheet from the bed and dumped the powder in the bath tub. Once we'd cleaned the sheet as well as possible we tossed it back on the bed. On a whim I added some water to the bathtub. The powder formed an acceptable dough. Definitely flour.

For the next test we moved the Sampo to the bathroom, and arranged the bath mat to catch anything it produced.

I pressed the button with an icon that reminded me of waves with a cube below them.

Flashing display, swirling mist, and a mound of small crystals.

I touched my finger to some and licked it. Pure salt.

Neither of us could figure out what the third icon was supposed to represent, but then I'd seen international money icons that showed a bunch of currency symbols. If you didn't know what a dollar, pound, or yen was, you'd have no idea about that either. I pushed the button.

We got a pile of metal nuggets. I estimated that there was enough to fill a two-litre milk container.

"Silver?"

Lana scratched a nugget with the car key.

"Probably. It's soft enough to be pure silver."

I went into the bedroom, got my BSI phone, and sent a text. *Need a lab in western Slovakia immediately able to do isotopic analysis of silver.*

"What are you doing?"

"Testing an hypothesis."

The answer wasn't long in coming. *Comenius University, Bratislava. Faculty of Mathematics, Physics and Informatics. See Dr. Alexander Bazovský.*

I texted back. *Tell him we'll be there in a few hours.*

"We were going to Bratislava anyway to get flights home. This will just be a side trip."

"But why?"

"An old case of mine. If the isotope ratio of this silver is abnormal it means we have bigger problems than arm wrestling for who gets to take the Sampo home."

"Are you going to explain that?"

"Not yet. Believe me, if the silver is normal then it's not something you will want to know. If it isn't I'll tell you everything."

"You're infuriating."

"Aren't we all, on occasion?"

༺༻

We got a hotel room in Bratislava in case we needed it. The Faculty of Mathematics, Physics, and Informatics was located in the northwest corner of the city. Our biggest problem was finding somebody who could direct us to the physics department.

At least this faculty receptionist spoke English.

"Can you direct us to Dr. Bazovský's lab? He's expecting us."

She gave us the lab number as well as directions that would at least get us in the right area. The door was open when we got there.

Dr. Bazovský was short and ugly with hair like Albert Einstein. When he spoke he would often smile, and then all you could see was a charming and acutely intelligent man.

We introduced ourselves and I gave him the silver nugget. He did various science-y things to a piece of it, put the results in a vial which then went into a science-y machine. Then he pushed buttons.

"Come, we will have coffee while the sample is analyzed."

He led us to a small office down the hall that was the communal coffee room for the labs on that floor. The coffee machine they had was almost as technical as the machine that was working on our sample.

"Tell me why you want this analysis."

"We're private investigators, and that lump of silver came up during an investigation. I submitted another piece of silver to a BSI lab several years ago and it turned out to have an abnormal isotope ratio. I wanted to confirm whether this one does as well."

"Hmm, most mysterious. You must know then that all silver has roughly equal amounts of isotopes 107 and 109."

"It's been a while, but yes, those sound familiar."

"The only way you could have silver with abnormal isotope ratios is if it was produced artificially from two isotopically pure samples. That would be expensive."

"How expensive?" Lana asked.

Dr. Bazovský shrugged. "I don't know, but it would have to be done by a similar process to purifying uranium-235 from natural uranium, then recombining the products. Hundreds of millions of Euros, perhaps?"

"So only governments or large corporations would be capable of doing so?"

"Yes, but *why*? That is the important question. How far outside of normal do you suspect this sample might be?"

"Again, I don't remember the exact figures. Something like 40/60," I said.

He stared at me with surprise giving way to annoyance. "That would be ridiculous."

"I quite agree. How long will the sample take to analyze?"

"Oh, the mass spectrometer should be done by now. Let's see whether you have made scientific history or are wasting time."

We went back to the lab, where he brought up software on his computer.

He muttered to himself. "This cannot be right."

"What does the analysis say?"

"Thirty-eight percent Ag-107. Sixty-two percent Ag-109. I'll have to run this again."

"Don't bother. That's what happened last time. The lab kept re-running the sample hoping for a different answer. Thank you for your time—and coffee."

"Please, you can't leave yet. This is incredible. Where did you get the silver?"

"I'm sorry, but I can't tell you. You could call the head of the BSI if you wish. She may be able to give you more information."

He protested all the way out the corridor to the elevator.

"Now what?" Lana said as we rode down to the ground floor.

"Now, we have the most bizarre conversation of your life."

⁓

I refused to tell my story until we were back at the hotel room. It was something that I thought would require an unmoving reality. When I finished my recitation Lana was quiet and logical.

"You are trying to tell me that the Sampo was made by literal demons?"

"Yes."

"And that you have personally met two of these demons face-to-face?"

"Yes."

"And the silver is unusual because it comes from hell?"

"As far as I know. That's the gist of it."

"And you solved the Blomgren kidnapping by conjuring one of those demons to tell you who the kidnapper was?"

"Yes. I know how that sounds."

"I thought you were sane. Or that you could come up with a more believable lie than that."

I sighed. "The Sampo is at least four centuries old. Do you agree?"

"Not necessarily. It could have been buried last week for all we know. The clues could have been manufactured and left for us to find."

"All right, I'll grant that it's possible. How likely is it?"

"Not terribly, I'll admit. Just forging the documents would cost a fortune. It's still more likely than your story."

"Right. What powers the Sampo?"

"If it was built in modern times it could be a regular battery."

"But how did it create the items we saw?"

"Did we? Maybe it emits an hallucinogenic gas or something."

"I've been down that road before. Okay, let's do an experiment. Take a video of it with your phone."

I ran the Sampo through another salt batch. I dumped the salt into the bath tub. The video showed exactly what we expected from what our eyes had just seen.

"Maybe the hallucinogen makes us think we're seeing a confirmatory video."

"That would have to be one hell of a specialized drug. The other problem with your hypothesis is that a complete stranger saw and handled the silver nugget that your theory says is an hallucination. He found exactly what I hoped we wouldn't, although I didn't tell him about the isotope ratios until the sample was in the machine and we were all out of the lab. Unless you think that co-conspirators sneaked in and fiddled with the report before we got back to his lab."

"No, I'm willing to concede that the silver is almost impossibly abnormal."

"Good. Now you have to ask yourself, what would I or anybody else have to gain by spending hundreds of millions to fake you out? Or us, actually. You'll have to trust me that if there's a hoax, I'm not in on it."

"All right, it's demonic. Now what do we do with it?"

"That's the big question. How much silver do you think it produces in one batch?"

"I'd say about 20 kilos."

"And how much is silver worth?"

She looked it up on her phone. "Around $15 US per ounce."

"An ounce is around 30 grams, so that's..."

"Over ten thousand dollars per batch."

"It would be easy to build a simple mechanical device to push the button over and over again. Each button press is worth $10,000."

"I see where you're going with this. We need to know how fast can it cycle."

"Good question." I looked at the bedroom clock and quickly tapped my finger on the bathroom counter. "Thirty three in five seconds. About six per second."

I tapped the salt button twice as fast as I could. I got one pile of salt.

"That's too fast for it to keep up with."

I tried counting single seconds, and pressed the button twice. I got two piles of salt.

"More than one press per second, fewer than six."

"One day is 86400 seconds. That would be a minimum of 864 million dollars per day. Good god." She called up a calculator on her phone. "That's over 1700 tonnes of silver."

"Exactly. Whoever has the Sampo can be however rich they choose. They don't even have to avoid taxes; they just make more silver. That's if they only press the one button. I suspect that the keyboard can be used to program the Sampo to produce other things. Otherwise, why is it there? Gold, maybe. Or diamonds. Or weapon-grade uranium. Who knows? And who knows what the other buttons do!"

"What about the three buttons we know about?"

"I think they're function test buttons. Silver is an element. Salt is a compound. Flour is a mixture of many organic compounds. It's a progression from simple to complex."

"You are making a compelling argument for never letting anybody get their hands on this device. At the very least it would destroy the world economy."

"Yes. I am. The demons I've met are crazy, and they are up to their eyes in hidden agendas. If this thing was made by them I wouldn't be surprised if there are booby-traps of some kind built in. Apart from the lure of endless wealth, that is."

Lana sat on the toilet, which was the only seat available. "Endless wealth doesn't sound bad if the owner is a philanthropist. Imagine the good that could be done."

"Or imagine it in the hands of the politicians or corporate executives in either of our countries. Or any others, for that matter."

"There's one thing about the Sampo that bothers me."

"Just one?"

"The display looks like something from a science fiction film. If it's magical the iconography doesn't belong to any occult tradition I've ever encountered. There's nothing demonic-seeming about it. It's more like an alien artifact."

I'd thought of that. "In some ways that makes it worse. If it's a purely technological device, it could be reverse engineered. If somebody learns how it works, it could jump our technology forward a century or more in one shot. That's sounds fine until you look at what's happened to societies that weren't ready for large technological advances. There's another question: Where do the products come from? Is the Sampo somehow manufacturing them? Or is it transporting them from elsewhere? Either way the technology is easily adapted to both criminal and military uses."

Lana tapped her fingers on the sink. "All of these are valid points, but think of the good it could do. If it pulls items from somewhere else, could it be adapted to remove otherwise inoperable tumours? If it can make flour can it make replacement organs? Cure world hunger?"

"So, what are we going to do with it?"

"We already know that some people are willing to kill for it. Despite my counter-arguments, I vote for getting rid of it."

"I'm tempted to agree. I just have one little question."

"How," Lana said. It wasn't really a question.

"Yeah. We know it's harder than diamond and has survived 400 years underground without even getting dirty. If the Kalevala is accurate, it was originally damaged in a battle between gods, or at least sorcerers. If Johan's account is accurate..."

"Which is likely given that it got us here."

"...which is likely, then it survived an unknown amount of time at the bottom of the sea, repaired itself, and somehow made its way back toward land."

"You're suggesting that it has some sort of artificial intelligence and won't allow itself to be destroyed."

I eyed the Sampo. "Not really. It may have a lot of fancy software, but I don't think it's really intelligent. We aren't talking about an evil magic ring here."

Lana smiled. "Out of the mouths of babes."

"What?"

"Everything has physical limits. A truly indestructible object cannot exist. If you took an immortal creature and threw it into the Sun, the ionized atoms would eventually be spread throughout the star's volume. Every time two of them tried to get back together they'd be torn apart again. After several billion years the Sun would become a white dwarf with a surface gravity three hundred thousand times that of Earth. The immortal would be squashed to a thin paste and unable to move if its body did reassemble. End of immortal."

"You know too much. Are you honestly suggesting we throw this into the Sun?"

"That would be best, but I admit that there would be practical issues. Your literary reference gave me a more reasonable idea. What if we tossed the Sampo into a volcano?"

"I'm not sure that's much easier than throwing it into the Sun. How do we get close enough to an active volcano to toss it in without being roasted?"

"I can think of several ways, but none are easy or foolproof. What we need is a lava lake. We just stand above it, toss the Sampo in, and watch it sink. If anybody can retrieve it from the bottom of a lava lake, they can have it as far as I'm concerned."

"Are you sure it would sink?"

"That's a fair question. We need to test that assumption."

"What's the density of lava?"

"It probably depends on the type. We'll have to pick a location first."

The next couple of hours were taken up with research and trying to remember grade twelve math. Don't ever let anyone tell you that algebra is useless in real life. Some day your life may depend on being able to calculate the density of an ancient alien artifact. All we needed was the exact dimensions of the Sampo and its weight.

We loaded the Sampo into its pack and I lugged it down to the hotel's gym. They had tape measures so people could see how huge various parts of their bodies were. It also had weigh scales like those in a doctor's office.

Do you know what kind of looks two young women get when they are in a gym full of sweaty men weighing a big hockey puck?

I could feel my libido perking up at the sight of certain shirtless men pumping iron. I told her to shut up and go back to sleep. I'd deal with her later. She was not happy about it.

The Sampo weighed a trifle over 32 kilograms. My original estimate of 30 was almost right.

I worked out the density while Lana looked up lava lakes.

"The density of the Sampo is 1.71. Do you have our lake yet?"

"Guess how many active lava lakes there are in the world?"

"I don't know. Dozens? There must be a lot in Iceland."

"Five. Worldwide. None in Iceland."

"Ouch. Any we can get to?"

"I assume you don't want to go to Antarctica."

"Not so much. Any others?"

"The easiest to get to is in Hawaii."

"Okay, let's go with that one. Besides: Hawaii."

While she worked on the lava problem. I looked for ways to get us from Bratislava to our chosen lava lake. The answer was amusing and surprising.

She put down her phone. "Okay, the Hawaiian lava has a density of 1.4. The Sampo should sink like the proverbial stone."

"Great, now we just have to switch countries and we're all set. If we fly from here we have to bounce over to the U.S. and then fly to Hawaii. I suggest we fly from Vienna just in case somebody's waiting for us here. It's only something like half an hour away."

"We may have a problem. What about the police?"

"The...? Oh."

Well, crap. I'd temporarily forgotten about the Finns. Our path through Europe was physically quite simple, but at each stage we'd made decisions that, by themselves, seemed very sensible. The total, however, was a potential legal nightmare if various people started comparing notes.

Normally, I'd have been happy to cooperate with a police investigation. But the Sampo had a date with a volcano in Hawaii, and once its existence became known to officials it would be treated as an Important Historical Artifact. In other words, it would be taken away from us and studied by anybody who could get the accreditation. At least, until somebody's military stepped in and classified it top secret.

In other words, we were completely and totally screwed. In theory, rich people tend to get away with crimes much more easily than most folk. I had a credit card on me that in theory was good for any conceivable amount of money, but the problem was application. Rich people get off because they have a huge number of people who know the right people. Money by itself does no good. It's a tool and you have to know how to apply it.

Besides, this was a complete mess that would take a long time to sort out, and I had one month left on my contract. It was a fair assumption that after that the credit card would go poof.

"I don't suppose we could just sneak out of the country?"

"No. So far the countries we've visited have had open borders. That's not true of Austria. The moment we get to the border we could be arrested."

"You could have mentioned this before."

"Sorry. I thought you knew."

"We might as well have supper. It's going to take a while to figure this out."

꿈

I began making a list of who wanted us and why. It was a depressingly long and complicated list.

It started with the sniper in London, whoever they were. If they were caught there would be questions about why we didn't file a report. Of course, due to that lack of a report nobody was looking for him. He could thank us later.

The Russian in Finland was another person who could rat us out if he was connected with the sniper. Or if he *was* the sniper. And if he ever regained his ability to communicate.

Pietr had caused us to commit a crime, although we could argue that we have no idea that the cave was in a national park or that permits were required, or whatever else they threw at us. On the other hand, we'd concealed his attempt to blackmail us and our part in the excavation of the document boxes. We'd also disposed of the gun. He'd later been murdered by the Finns, although I put that down as supposition. It was the only way they could have gotten ahead of us at the castle, though.

Once we were in Višňové things really became confused. Interpol might want to have a word with us about the confusion over the scope of our credentials. Although we'd tried to keep our hosts out of the line of fire, there might be some issues of reckless endangerment. Not to mention another count of trespassing on a national preserve.

Since we suspected the Finns of murder, it was our duty to turn them in immediately. Especially since they were armed to the teeth and were illegally camping in the aforementioned national preserve.

We did nothing to stop them from digging up an Important Historical Artifact. Our warning to the villagers showed that we knew what they were doing and provided a clear field for them to operate. We also didn't turn them in although we considered them a threat to the villagers.

Then we stole the IHA from the terrorists and didn't turn them in until we'd gotten away. The unreasonable part of that was that I'd turned them in to the Finnish counter-terrorist Detective-Sergeant who'd been investigating us earlier instead of local authorities. I'm sure he'd have more questions for us after this.

We needed a team of lawyers to advise us.

I showed my list to Lana. She didn't disagree with any of it. Nor with my assessment as to what we needed.

"We may be able to hire the legal help we need locally. There was a lot of legal confusion after Communism was ended. There should be some very sharp people if they'll take our case."

Lana rummaged in her luggage for her red phone. "Here's a thought. Rather than pick a name out of the phone directory, let's ask the BSI for a recommendation."

"That's a brilliant idea, Holmes."

She typed a text message. *Need emergency criminal legal advice.*

"I wonder how long it will..."

Stand by for call.

"That answers that question."

The phone rang. The SECURE CALL bar appeared on the screen. Lana put it on speaker.

"Lana Reviere? My name is Sakineh Pagliari. I understand you need some legal advice." The speaker was a woman.

"Yes. I also have Veronica Chandler here with me."

"Hello, Veronica. Just so you know, although this consultation is *pro bono*, you are both considered my clients and as such full lawyer-client privilege applies."

"Good," Lana said, "because we're in some difficulty. There have been some awkward aspects to a case we're working on, and we're going to have to clear them up before we try to leave Europe."

"Tell me exactly what happened."

It took a while for us to go through the whole story. Then Sakineh had us go through it again to clarify certain points.

"Let's start at the beginning. There is no way to prove that you knew you were being shot at in London unless you admit it. Did either of you actually see a gunman?"

"No, although I did see a muzzle flash." I said.

"A flash in the twilight could have been anything. The stone veneer on the building could have shattered for any number of reasons. Lana ran away and you followed her. It's that simple."

"So, if somebody asks about being shot at in London, neither of us know anything about it."

"Precisely. That also takes care of your Russian friend. Whatever his motive, if he mentions a shooter you simply know nothing about it."

"What about Pietr?"

"That's more complex. Excavation in a national park requires a permit, which he failed to apply for. However, the fact that neither of you speak or read Polish means that you have an excellent defence. You were simply unaware that a completely reasonable act you performed was illegal under those circumstances. It helps that you saw no signs that might be construed as park boundary markers. The BSI has some connections in Poland who can have that charge dropped. You are just two foreign girls who were led astray while trying to do a favour for somebody who promised to help you with your case. Sadly, it helps that Mr. Debiak is now unable to contradict anything you say."

Lana let out a long breath. "I admit that I'm starting to feel better about the situation."

"I've had an associate checking records while we talk. It seems that Mr. Debiak didn't have any gun permits. He must have obtained the pistol illegally, which means we can pretend that officially it never existed. Unless somebody saw you disposing of it?"

"That's highly unlikely. I disassembled it down to individual parts, and then threw them in the river one at a time in between throwing small stones. The gun is scattered along at least a kilometre of river bottom."

"Very clever. Even if somebody suspects, they would have to get divers to comb a large area to find small parts. They are unlikely to be able to show probable cause to conduct such a search."

"Now we come to the first potential problem. Are you certain that you wiped all your fingerprints from the areas you visited?"

Lana answered. "Yes, quite. We were extremely thorough. It helped a great deal that we were always wearing cotton examination gloves from the time we entered the room until we left except for the first time when we carried the boxes in. Pietr was extremely strict about protocol to protect the more fragile documents."

"Are you quite certain that these Finnish terrorists could only have learned of your destination through him?"

"It's the only explanation we can think of. The only other real possibility is for them to have planted listening devices in our rooms as well as the specimen room."

"Were you there when he was murdered?"

"Of course not. We were probably in Slovakia. I'm not sure of the exact time line."

"Yes, you mentioned that you found out about it when you spoke with one of the investigators. The Finns might have found the link to Čachtice somewhere else. After all, you learned of it through searching historical records. They might have done the same."

"The timing doesn't work for that."

"Only if we suppose that the records you searched were unknown before you got there. If you didn't unearth them, then who knows when Debiak did?"

"I see your point."

"Now we get to the mess at Višňové. Are you absolutely certain that you did not represent yourselves as agents for Interpol?"

"No," Lana said. "That was an assumption originally made by Jozef and Mária Horváth because we are from different countries and were after nationals of a third country. We simply didn't correct them."

"You can't be held responsible for other people's mistakes. At worst someone from Interpol might contact you and try to—I think the correct expression is 'put the fear of God into you.' They are, after all, an international police force liaison organization. They don't actually have field operatives, so the Horváths were mistaken in their understanding of what Interpol is, as well as your potential involvement."

"That brings us to your final difficulty. As I understand it, the Finns dug up an artifact that is not native to Slovakia, and indeed is one that almost all scholars would agree is fictional, yes?"

"That's correct," I said.

"It was not your place to stop criminals from digging an unsanctioned hole on another person's property. It speaks highly of your character that you warned the villagers to prevent unnecessary loss of life. However, you should have called the police at that point."

"Isn't that a big problem?" Lana asked.

"Not necessarily. Not speaking the local language, and being in a village with no police presence, you might have been tempted to watch and wait. That seems even more likely given that you called your one European police contact in Finland rather than attempting to waste time trying to determine which Slovakian authorities to notify. It could be argued that you were guilty of poor judgement, but nothing more."

I looked at my notes. "That only leaves one thing. The artifact."

"Yes, that's a problem. You say this item is of mythological interest to the Finns?"

"Yes. It's mentioned as being created by the gods in their national poem. If they actually believed that it exists the whole country would want it back."

"But you have reason to believe that would be a poor idea."

"Definitely. Not only would it serve as a rallying point for the Karelian nationalists, but it would have grave consequences for the world."

"That's a difficult premise to accept since you say you can't tell me why."

Lana and I exchanged a look. "It's better for you that you not know."

"Very well. Is there any chance that they would be able to recognize you as the thief?"

"I don't see how. It was so dark that I had to find a five ton truck by touch. The one man who tried to stop me didn't have a light. We couldn't even find places to hit or grab each other except by feel. I'm lucky I found his throat before he found mine. As I ran away all they could see was my back."

"What about the drone?"

"All it ever saw was the back of our car."

"So they have your license plate number."

"We'll have to assume so. But it was rented in Warsaw. They'd have to have someone on the inside of the rental agency who could tell them who rented it. Wouldn't they?"

"Probably. But since we suspect them of murder and know that they are thieves, they might just break into the rental office and steal the records. Or they may have a computer hacker on their side who could get the information remotely. Or they might bribe someone to look up the records. We must assume they know who you are. If they are caught they might name you rather than risk you taking the artifact beyond their reach. Is this object obviously ancient?"

"Not at all. If anything it looks like a plain, white, disk."

"That's very strange. What you are saying is that, to the naked eye, it looks ordinary and unremarkable."

"Pretty much, yes."

"What about x-rays or microwaves? Both technologies are used at airports for scanning luggage."

"We have no idea. We can probably find someone with an x-ray machine tomorrow."

"The machines at airports are low-power so they don't kill the passengers, so you don't have to find an industrial machine. A diagnostic x-ray will be fine. As I see it there are several possibilities."

"I think I see where you are going with this," Lana said. "If it is opaque to x-rays they'll want us to open it. If it shows some kind of harmless internal structure we may be able to pass it off as something else."

"And of course if it shows a suspicious internal structure they'll want to examine it more closely. You'll have to see what the tests reveal before you come up with a story to fit the artifact."

"What about the Finns telling everybody it's a sacred object from the dawn of time?"

"Depending on what the x-rays tell you, it may be possible to just tell the police that they are lying as revenge for you turning them in. As long as you have a decent explanation for what it is, you should be safe."

"I'm sure we can think of something."

"One last thing. I'd suggest you confuse your trail as much as possible. Until these men are caught you are in danger."

"I had the same thought. I think that's about as much help as you can give us at the moment. I hope we haven't kept you up or anything."

"Not at all. In fact I'm only a few hundred kilometres south of you in Italy."

"Your first name doesn't sound Italian."

"I'm originally from Iran. My husband is Italian."

"Cool. Thanks for your help."

"Any time. And I'd like to know what this mysterious object is, if you ever feel you can tell me."

"Believe me, it really is a matter of global security, but once we deal with it we may be able to tell you part of the story."

"Thank you. Good evening."

Lana turned her phone off. Given what we'd been discussing, I was really glad that BSI phones encrypted all communications.

Just to spread the joy, I used my phone to locate a nearby BSI facility to do the testing. When the reply came back I snorted.

"What's wrong?"

"Nothing. This is going to be so much fun." I showed her the text.

Comenius University, Bratislava. Faculty of Mathematics, Physics and Informatics. See Dr. Alexander Bazovský.

CHAPTER 16

It's a What?

The esteemed Dr. Bazovský was not as happy to see us as he had been last time.

"What do you have for me this time? Fairy dust? Unicorn horn? The Ark of the Covenant?"

"I wish we did," Lana said. I was busy trying to pretend that I didn't have a 32 kilo pack on my back. "We just need an interior scan of an object."

I heaved the pack onto the lab bench.

"What is *that*?"

I could see her trying to think of a clever reply, and giving up. "That's an excellent question."

He looked at the Sampo and sighed deeply. "Let's get it into the x-ray machine."

Apart from ones at the dentist, I've never had to have an x-ray. I was a bit surprised that they have gone digital like any other camera. The image immediately came up on the monitor.

It was almost blank. As in, the x-rays went right through it without leaving more than a ghost of a shadow.

"Hmm." He rummaged in a drawer, and pulled out a steel box with some magnets in it. They must have been good magnets—it took him a lot of effort to pry one off the inside of the box. He placed it on the Sampo in various spots. It didn't stick.

The doctor made a call and spoke for several minutes. Then he grabbed a lab cart and we put the Sampo on it.

"Come." We followed him to the freight elevator. We went down a floor, then followed a maze-like route along some corridors. The room we entered had several warning signs on the door.

A woman in a lab coat met us and between them they put the Sampo on a sliding platform in front of a big metal tunnel. We all went into a control room while the platform slid into the machine.

The machine was loud and made various clunking and buzzing noises for ten minutes. At the end we were left with a blank image. The Sampo didn't show up on an MRI at all.

I could tell that this was getting personal for Dr. Bazovský. We wheeled it to another lab where it was bombarded with microwaves. It neither absorbed nor reflected them. No image.

Another colleague had a small selection of chemicals. Bazovský tried various things that should have caused most materials to scream "I'm melting!" while turning into a pile of evil goo. The chemicals mostly just ran off and ate holes in the pad underneath. Some of them left an etched trail down the side.

However, when we looked again a few minutes later, the surface was as smooth as ever.

As a grand finale, he took it to a lab in the basement where they had a high-powered laser. High-powered as in gigawatt pulses. The laser made some small pits in the side. A few minutes later they were gone.

We went back to his laboratory, where he got several graduate students to help him cobble together an x-ray crystallography rig. One of the students explained to us that normally this kind of thing is done on a thin section of crystal and it's a very precise apparatus. Dr. Bazovský was just trying to get some indication that the Sampo had any kind of internal structure at all.

The x-rays were scattered, which made them all happy. After a lot of analysis and argument, during which Lana and I went for lunch, they decided that there were extremely fine filaments and nodes inside the object on a very small scale. They had no idea what they represented. I thought it looked like some kind of circuitry, but in three dimensions. For the sake of Bazovský's sanity I kept my opinion to myself.

The only thing he tried that got any kind of response was a magnetometer. Apparently the Sampo generated a weak electromagnetic field. That must have been how the drone detected it. How it could have a magnetic field but not be magnetic, he couldn't say.

We finally thanked him for his help and took the Sampo away before he began pulling his hair out. Now it was our turn to rack our brains.

What could we say the Sampo was that fit its physical properties and would make the people at airport security happy?

∽

We were back at the hotel, staring at the Sampo. I made suggestions. Lana shot them down.

"How about a sample of stealth coating for airplanes?"

"Good, but we don't have the credentials, and why would we be carrying a piece of top secret technology on a commercial flight?"

"Never mind. Game console? That would explain the display."

"We don't *want* to explain the display. It's beyond current technology. It would be better if it never comes up, if you'll pardon the expression."

"Yes, but how do we hide it if somebody touches the lid?"

"I wonder..."

She pulled down her sleeve to cover her hand, and poked the lid. Nothing happened.

I tore off a sheet of hotel stationery. As long as the paper was between my hand and the lid, nothing happened.

I really felt relieved about this. "All we have to do is wrap it."

"What if they want to unwrap it?"

"We use that plastic film stuff they use for cafeteria sandwiches. That way they can see through it."

"We can also wrap it in gift paper. Call it a wedding present."

I was getting excited. "*Now* we're talking. We can slip it through right under their noses. It won't show up as a bomb on their scanners, so they shouldn't care what it *actually* is. We'll have to come up with something to tell customs in Hawaii, though."

"We're flying through Korea. Tell them it's some geeky device the groom wants. A home entertainment controller, perhaps."

"Brilliant."

"Now we just have one more problem. Can we bring it on the plane?"

I opened my mouth, then closed it. My carry-on suitcase was my mother's, chosen based on her own travels. I had never thought about any size limitations.

I checked several airline web sites. The Sampo was almost the right size for carry-on, but it was far too heavy. We'd have to check it.

"That makes me nervous. What if they lose it?"

Lana had been busy with her own phone. "That's another reason for flying through Korea from Vienna. Incheon airport has the lowest misplaced luggage rate in the world."

"I guess we don't have much choice. We'll need another suitcase. Fill the voids with packing peanuts so it doesn't rattle around."

"No, we'll just use the ruck sack it's in now so it can be carried easily. We can fill the voids with bubble wrap so it can't shed. Let's go shopping."

That was a good idea anyway. Both of us had wardrobe issues due to our recent active lifestyle. Issues such as gaping hole and tears. The only intact piece of outwear was Lana's dress, which was filthy.

We found a dry cleaner and the favourite dress was restored to its condition before the commando raid. At least my underwear was still in good repair. I got new jeans, a shirt, and a jacket that should serve under adverse conditions. I also bought slightly bigger luggage so I could fit everything into one case while still conforming to my new understanding of carry-on restrictions. Mum shouldn't mind the change. Lana did the same.

The staff in the hotel restaurant were happy to wrap the Sampo, although I could see they were itching to know why. The gift shop wrapped it in paper for us. It was a pain trying to handle something that heavy without tearing the wrapping. A stationery store provided us with bubble wrap.

Once in the car we headed south to the A6, also known as E58. European road names confused me. We practised our cover story, which was designed to be simple and boring to a border agent.

Less than a kilometre after we turned west we joined the lineups at the Austrian border. It didn't take long before we were talking to a middle-aged, grumpy guard.

I was driving, of course, but I let Lana do the talking.

I presented our passports, and he asked questions in German. Lana answered. He glared at me and said something.

"I'm sorry, I don't speak German."

"Why are you visiting Austria?"

"My cousin and I are flying from Vienna to Hawaii for a wedding."

"Why not fly from Bratislava?"

"We've heard that Vienna is really beautiful. If we are this close we wanted to see it."

"You are right, it is a beautiful city. Have a good trip."

He handed back our passports and waved for us to proceed. I tried not to react until at least a count of sixty. Then a let out a big breath.

"I don't believe it. We made it."

"The first hurdle, at least."

"Gee thanks. I needed to be reminded of that."

The A4 is an *Autobahn*, which in Austria means a speed limit of 130 kilometres per hour. The Vienna airport was less than half an hour away. Sadly, it was on the east side of the city, so we wouldn't actually get to see any of Vienna.

As we were approaching the city my phone rang. Lana answered it.

"Hello?"

"I'm afraid she's driving at the moment."

"Yes, I was there."

"You were the only police officer we know in Europe. Veronica and I assumed you'd be interested, and would know who to contact."

Ah, it must be Laakso.

"Oh dear, that's troubling news."

What is? We so don't need this.

"All right, I'll tell her. Thank you." She hung up.

"How's our favourite anti-terrorist?"

"They haven't caught the Finns yet. The truck was found abandoned and burned with a lot of their equipment inside. No weapons, though. He warned us that they could have split up and may be still after us."

"Unless they are psychic, it shouldn't matter soon."

It didn't take long for us to find the car rental area and turn in our trusty Fiat. From there we found seats in the terminal so we could execute the next part of our plan.

I sat there working modern magic with my phone.

"Okay, the first non-stop flight to Incheon leaves in about seven hours at 6:40 this evening."

"Shall we do some sight-seeing?"

"I'm not sure we should. The more we wander around the more likely it is that one of the Finns will see us."

"On the other hand, if we stay in the airport then it is certain they will find us if they check here."

"Crap. Damned if we do and damned if we don't."

"On the third hand, a moving target is more difficult to hit. We should probably see some of Vienna. I know I've always wanted to visit Austria."

I stood and held out my hand as I affected my best bad Austrian accent. "Come with me if you want to live."

I bought our tickets to Incheon, as well as the ones to Hawaii. The total trip time was brutal, so I booked us first class seats. It wasn't like it was my money, after all.

That bothered me. The client's credit card was for case expenses, and I'd completed my contract. It was quite clear that I was not required to retrieve the Sampo, merely locate it. At this point the only expenses I should be charging would be involved with returning home as quickly and economically as possible.

I felt like a thief, because I was. The rationale I constructed for myself was that nobody had said that I had to locate an intact Sampo. Nor had they mentioned that people would be trying to kill me at each turn. I could go home afterward and tell them exactly where it was. If they were really put out, I'd be happy to pay back the later costs from what they owed me.

We managed to check our single piece of luggage. It was overweight, but the extra fee didn't worry me much. It still made me nervous to watch it disappear into the bowels of the conveyor system.

We took a taxi into Vienna. Lana asked the driver to drop us somewhere picturesque. He decided that meant the Schönbrunn Palace.

I'd seen pictures of Versailles in books, and wondered at the incredibly ornate Baroque architecture. Schönbrunn left it in the dust, particularly since we were there in person.

We paid for the grand tour, which took us through 40 rooms in about an hour. We had to be back at the airport around 3:30, so that still left us with several hours. Lana decided that the garden labyrinth was worth a look. We split up when we got to the entrance.

It reminded me of that Harry Potter movie. Fortunately, not so much of The Shining. At least I didn't have to worry about magical perils.

It was fun wandering the labyrinth. Occasionally couples wandered by, hand-in-hand, children ran by laughing. There were also individuals who looked anywhere from smug to confused.

Lana and I were going to meet at the centre where there was an observation platform. I took my time and got there in about 45 minutes.

There were several tourists on the platform taking pictures of the labyrinth and the gardens beyond. In the distance I could see the Gloriette, a massive stone structure built on a hill at the end of the garden. Baroque residences didn't bother with small. There was a breeze that provided some welcome coolness after the still air of the hedge maze.

A Japanese tourist a few people away fell. I assumed that he'd passed out or was having some kind of seizure until I saw blood on his chest. The sound of a rifle shot came a few seconds later.

By then the people around me had figured out that something was wrong, and I was surrounded by screaming and running tourists. I saw Lana at the base of the stairs leading to the platform, so I jumped over the railing to get to her. I wasn't the only person jumping.

"Run!"

She didn't argue. We dodged back into the maze, where at least we couldn't be seen from the hill.

"What's going on?"

"There's a sniper somewhere near the Gloriette."

"Finnish?"

I was feeling panicked. "How should I know? If he was after me he didn't compensate for windage properly. At least this time."

Lana, of course, had memorized the route out of the labyrinth. The exit wasn't in the line of fire, and people were starting to run in all directions as the news spread. As targets, we were two among many.

There had to be hundreds of people in Schönbrunn. News of the shooting hadn't made it to the taxi stands at the front of the grounds yet, so we got away without having to answer any questions or drawing more fire.

"How the *fuck* did they know we'd be here?" I said once we were underway. Lana told the driver to take us to a good restaurant.

"I have no idea. Perhaps the other driver?"

"This is ridiculous. How did they know which taxi we... oh, shit."

She just raised her eyebrow.

"They must have had somebody covering the airport. They just noted which taxi we took and followed us."

"Going after us at the palace feels like an act of desperation," she said. "What would they gain?"

I checked the inside pocket of my jacket. Our plane tickets were still there.

"They must have had somebody on the ground who could grab the tickets once I was down. That would let them retrieve the luggage by cancelling the reservations."

"Assuming they didn't bring in more people, we'll have to be on the look out for familiar faces from now on."

The taxi pulled over at the restaurant. Lana handed the driver a pile of money, and spoke to him in German. He seemed to agree with whatever she'd said.

"I told him that an ex-boyfriend is stalking us. He promised to forget he'd ever seen us, or where we might be."

"That won't last long if they put a gun to his head."

"It's the best we can do."

We didn't begin walking until after our taxi left. A few blocks later Lana hailed another cab.

This time she told him to take us to the airport.

"Is that wise? Maybe we should take another random trip."

"Mathematics. They know we have to go back to the airport for our flight. Another diversion would just waste time and money. Our advantage at this moment is that there's still time before we have to be at the gate. They probably won't be expecting an early arrival. Once we're through security they can't get at us as easily."

"Okay, I'll buy that."

"Actually, I've changed my mind." She spoke to the driver.

He changed directions and took us to a shopping district.

"Now what?"

"Now we disappear."

This was more like it. We found a wig shop and bought the first two that fit. I was now a long-haired blonde. Lana was a short-haired red head.

A few more shops and we had new coats, and completely unsuitable, huge purses.

Shoes were next. I wobbled even though the heels weren't as high as Lana's. Our boots went into the purses.

She bought slacks. I bought a short skirt. In a public washroom we changed so her dress didn't show below her coat. My jeans went into my purse. I then rolled the skirt up even more.

"What are you doing?"

"Female Countermeasures. If they are looking at my legs hard enough they might miss my face."

I couldn't imagine her using sex as a weapon, but I could see the wheels turning behind her eyes.

Dark glasses completed our lovely ensembles. We looked like stereotypical tourists rather than desperate investigators fleeing from assassins.

We took another taxi to the airport. Checking through security wasn't a problem, although our belongings raised some eyebrows. Lana explained to a female agent that our ex-boyfriends were after us and we were trying to get away. Our passports hadn't raised any flags, so she was sympathetic and explained our weird purse contents to her colleagues.

Once on the air side of security, we found another washroom and dumped all our new purchases in the garbage. Once again just Lana and Veronica, we went to our boarding gate. We were two hours early.

"We forgot something," I said after we'd been sitting a while.

Again, I got an eyebrow.

"I'm starving."

"You're always starving. Just as long as it isn't hamburgers and chips again."

The best we could find was a Burger King. Lana sighed deeply.

My reaction to this whole adventure really concerned me. I was getting used to people trying to kill me on an almost daily basis. I thought back to my reaction to the shooter in Calgary a few weeks before I'd left. If that happened now, I doubted that I would cry in my mother's arms. It would be just another—what the heck day was it anyway? I looked at my phone—Friday.

Maybe it was true that familiarity bred contempt. Or maybe Lana's tendency to get upset only long after the event had been resolved was reenforcing my own leaning the same way.

I hoped that the man who took a bullet for me today recovered, but his life wasn't high on my priorities right now. I certainly wasn't going to visit him in the hospital or send him flowers. Given the ability of these guys to find us and keep trying to get the Sampo, that would be stupid.

Did that make me a monster, or a professional?

Or just a scared girl who was in over her head?

CHAPTER 17

Girding of Loins

No potentially Scandinavian men showed up in the boarding area before our flight. Boarding itself went smoothly, and this time I let Lana have the window seat. We were both ready to throw ourselves out into the aisle at the first sign that somebody outside was armed.

Once again, in unison: It's not paranoia if people really are trying to kill you. Repeatedly.

The whole question of our partnership had come to a head shortly before boarding.

"You know, there's no reason for you to come to Hawaii. You could change your flight and go home."

"Trying to get rid of me?"

"No. Not really. I just figured you'd rather go home than climb a volcano."

"Seriously? And miss the end of the story? Besides, climbing a volcano might be fun."

"With a broken arm?"

"It doesn't get in my way as much as you'd think. And I can still walk. What's this really about?"

"I just don't want to get hurt."

She wiggled the cast at me. "It's a bit late for that. Besides, somebody has to look after you."

That annoyed me. "I don't need looking after."

"No, of course not. You're tough as nails."

"Damned right."

"And you've nearly died several times on this case."

"So have you."

"You know, I was going to suggest the same thing to you."

Now I was confused. "What?"

"I was going to suggest that you go home and I complete the mission. From the photos I've seen, all I have to do is drop the pack off the edge of the caldera and it'll bounce straight into the lake. I don't need two arms for that."

"Now who's being ridiculous. What if somebody shows up to stop you?"

"Now you're beginning to understand. I didn't make the suggestion because this really is a two-person job, and neither of us is used to working with a partner."

I thought about it.

I was getting comfortable having Lana around. It was nice to have a friend along on this adventure. She was deadly in a fight, which she'd shown several times by saving my life. Also, it was good to be able to bounce ideas off someone competent. Kali was still my sister and best friend, but when the bullets started flying I wanted someone with experience I could trust to do exactly the right thing.

This whole partnership thing, though, was just weird. I'd always worked alone, and the thought of worrying about a partner felt like it would cramp my style. I also worried about delegating.

Lana was competent. I didn't have to worry about her, and she had proven herself to be reliable.

Maybe I was growing up. Learning to trust others to carry out a plan. Trusting them to have the getaway vehicle in position when I needed it. Trusting them to kick the crap out of a stupid graduate student while I distracted him.

Or maybe I was relying too heavily on her. Was having her around damaging my ability to work alone? That would not be good.

By my own argument, this was a two-person job. I needed somebody to watch my back while I was tossing the Sampo into the lake of doom. She needed to see this through to the end. *That* I could relate to. Part of my anger at her suggesting I should let her do it was that I wouldn't be on the mountain, watching the Sampo go up in smoke. I'd never *really* know if it had happened. The event would forever be hearsay.

Damn it, this was almost worse that trying to figure out my sex life. There were too many pros and cons floating around in my brain.

At least society wouldn't call me names for working with a partner.

⁂

I wish we'd have been able to wait for a day flight. It would have been cool to see the Himalayas from above.

"Unfortunately, it doesn't work that way." She brought up an atlas app on her phone. Measuring the distance between Vienna and Seoul also showed that the straight line between the two went nowhere near the mountains. Instead, it arced over Russia almost as far north as the Arctic Circle. *Welcome to the reality of living on a sphere instead of a plate, Veronica.* I felt stupid, and decided that I needed to know more about everything.

One thing that had been pushed aside by everyday life was a first aid course. I'd promised myself I'd take one over a year ago.

"Have you ever taken a first aid course?"

Lana smiled. "That's an odd change of topic after navigation."

"I was just thinking that I need more skills. I was going to take a course a while ago, but I never got around to it. If cases are going to be as dangerous as this one I'll need it."

"Definitely. Rather than taking the usual urban first aid course, I contacted a paramedic who works in rural areas. He taught a course that went far beyond the usual 'stabilize and wait for an ambulance.' It's comforting to be able to keep someone from dying of trauma as well as some common and uncommon medical conditions. We also learned how to transport a patient when medical help is days away. It wasn't that expensive and well worth it."

"I know what I'll be doing when I get home."

"Have you ever wished you'd had taken a course? Before now, that is."

I swallowed to get rid of a sudden lump in my throat. "Yes. Last year my sister was knifed by an ex-client. She would have died if someone else hadn't helped her."

"I can't imagine how horrible that must have been for you. My sister hasn't been in danger of dying, but I took the course for similar reasons. I wanted to be prepared for anything. In our line of work, that's the only sensible thing to do."

༺༻

We landed at Incheon International Airport right on time: ten minutes to noon. Too bad we only had 45 minutes before our next flight. I'd have liked to have seen more of Korea.

It was a good thing that Incheon has lightning-fast customs people.

We raced for our next gate and made it with 10 minutes to spare. I'd booked us flights with short layovers to lessen the possibility of being seen, but that one was maybe a bit close. As far as we could tell, nobody was watching or following us.

Our next leg was a hop to Tokyo-Narita. We had a four hour stop there, which wasn't really enough time to sight-see, even though it was practically certain that nobody following could have beaten us there.

Lana as usual was wearing her neutral expression as we landed. I suggested we check out the Kaizosha book store while we waited for our flight. She looked more and more unhappy the longer we were there.

"What's wrong?"

"Nothing."

"I don't believe you."

"Believe what you want," she snapped.

It wasn't too hard to put two and two together. Especially with the evidence right in front of me.

"You said your mother was Japanese."

"Yes."

"Have you been here before?"

"Not for years."

"Don't you have any family here."

"Not any more."

It was obvious that the bookstore was just making her more depressed. I suggested the cafe next door.

We sat there like a scene from an art movie. I was staring at my cup of coffee. She was staring at her glass of water. Neither of us were speaking.

"*Gomen nasai.*"

Her eyes snapped up to mine.

"Don't expect much more. I know how to say 'thank you' and count to ten in Japanese. Oh, and how to say I'm sorry."

She relaxed a little. "You have nothing to be sorry for. Before my parents died we came here every year. My mother expected me to go to the University of Tokyo as she did. I disappointed her by going to an English university instead."

"That's harsh."

"Not really. Her connections could have gotten me into *Tōdai* and it's the most prestigious university in Japan. I was being a stubborn teen."

We went back to not speaking.

"There is also my grandparents' grave. There has been nobody to tend it for years. That is my duty, and I've neglected it."

"Surely nobody expects you to fly halfway around the world to tend a grave?"

"You don't understand Japanese culture."

She drained her glass. "We should find our gate."

"We have another two hours until our flight."

Lana got up and left the cafe. It was clear that I could follow or not as I chose.

That was the last she would say on the subject. It made me sad to see her unhappy, but you can't do anything for a person who won't let you in.

It was almost 7 p.m. when we boarded our flight to Honolulu. Our final destination was on the Big Island, but to get us here quickly we had to accept a two hour layover in Honolulu. Again we were in first class, which didn't suck. That let Lana spend most of the time with headphones on watching some Japanese movie. The rest of the flight she was buried in her phone. She didn't say a word, and as far as I know she never slept. That did suck.

Our flight took over seven hours, yet we landed at just after 7 a.m. The magic of changing time zones. We'd also crossed the International Date Line, so it was the next day. Or the same one. I just didn't care any more.

If I was in a mood for omens, I might notice a lot of sevens popping up lately. I wondered what they could mean, if anything.

∞

Honolulu was less weird than I'd feared. I had visions of hula dancers draping *leis* over our heads as we deplaned. Apparently that only happened if somebody arranged it. I think Lana might have done somebody grievous bodily harm if it had happened to us.

With only a two hour stopover, so we just sat there and waited. After about half an hour Lana spoke.

"*Gomen nasai.*"

"About what?"

"Visiting Tokyo without being able to go anywhere affected me more than I thought it would. It's nothing to do with you."

"*De nada.*"

"That's one of the few Spanish phrases that *I* know."

"Now we're even. Let's go save the world."

She laughed. "Pretentious much?"

"At this point, not really."

At 9:30 a.m. we boarded our flight to Hilo. Compared with the rest of our travels this was ludicrously short. Fifty-four minutes from wheels up to landing. We didn't even cross a border.

I was beginning to lose track of the number of airports I'd been through. Ten?

We went through the airport formalities without any problems. The car rental agencies that were our next stop were all across the street from the terminal.

The clerk seemed reluctant to believe that I knew what I wanted.

"We have some nice sporty convertibles," he said. "Just right for two beautiful young ladies like you cruising to the beach."

We stared at him silently just long enough for his sexist grin to fade.

Lana enunciated very, very clearly. "There are no beautiful young ladies like us. Anywhere. You'd be wise to remember that."

"My apologies," he said with barely hidden insincerity. "I'm sure you know what you want."

"Damned right we do," I muttered under my breath as he started the paperwork for the four-wheel drive vehicle Lana and I had decided was best. Who knew what kinds of weird off-road things we might have to do to get to the lake? An unlimited budget certainly gives one a sense of freedom.

I mopped the sweat off my face twice on our way to the Jeep. It had to be nearly 30 degrees Celsius outside. Research had assured us that it got down to something like 20 degrees at night. After the nice spring and early summer weather in Europe, this was too much like being in a fire pit for me.

If we didn't go shopping for more appropriate clothes I was going to die. Lana didn't look very well either, especially wearing black.

Driving around an American state was really confusing for the first while. I'd gotten used to European traffic signs and the American ones just looked weird.

We hadn't made any hotel reservations to make it more difficult for anyone to find us. Unfortunately, we were just entering the summer busy season for tourists when families came to the Islands with kids who were off school. There weren't a lot of empty rooms available.

Except for the Warsaw dormitories, we'd been staying in fairly upscale hotels. This time we booked a hostel on the theory that any break in our pattern would make us harder to find.

At this point I'd been through so many time zones that my body had no idea what time or day it was supposed to be. Ditto with my stomach. Balanced against this was the gut feeling that we might have some really annoying people catching up with us at any moment. I wanted to get this over with and go home.

In fantasy stories the heroes never seem to know exactly where they are going, and run into all kinds of problems that solid information would have let them avoid. Either that or they just happen to find somebody who has the critical fact that they need. That wander-aimlessly-through-the-waste-lands thing was not our style.

We'd both been doing research on our destination, and could quote relatively useless facts about Kilauea, its lava lake, and its history. Useless to our mission, that is. Example: The caldera of Kilauea bears a striking resemblance to the caldera of Olympus Mons on Mars, which is also a shield volcano. There's no lava lake, though.

Once we'd reserved our bed for the night we went shopping for new clothes. Not only was I hot and sweaty, but our European clothing stuck out almost as badly as if we'd been wearing parkas. Being in a black dress, Lana might as well have been wearing a parka. Sometimes she reminded me of Kali.

We got light-coloured t-shirts and shorts to go with new sandals. My body temperature immediately went down to something livable. Our next stop was an outdoor/surplus shop. We got lucky—there was parking right outside the warehouse-like building so we could keep an eye on the Sampo.

At first, the man behind the counter just looked up and gave us a smile. He was probably used to people browsing.

I picked up a rope suitable for climbing, a combination axe and hammer, another pack, two military flashlights with red filters, and some really long, steel tent pegs. They looked like they'd hold in a hurricane, which is what we wanted if we needed an artificial anchor. We also got leather work gloves and Army Combat Uniforms—the ones that have a grey camouflage pattern that would be great on a mountain.

I put our purchases on the counter.

"Did you find everything you need?"

"Not quite. Do you have any gas masks?"

His fingers paused on the cash register.

"Sure. Is this for a costume?"

"No. We need functional ones."

He looked at Lana, who have him her deadly serious look, then he went back to me. "Do you have a model in mind?"

"No, as long as they cover the eyes, nose, and mouth."

He went into the back and came out with a black rubber mask.

"Try this."

I put it on. The straps needed adjusting, which was more difficult with my thick hair that it was meant to be. There was a mirror on the wall that showed me exactly how creepy I looked with the bug eyes and gaping mouth where the missing filter canister should be. The mask also gave me a slight feeling of claustrophobia. At least neither of us needed to worry about beards spoiling the seal.

I looked at Lana. "Are you my mummy?" I said in a childish voice.

I swear, she rolled her eyes like a teenager. Call the news services.

I pulled the mask off and took a deep breath, even though it hadn't hampered my breathing at all. I put it on the counter.

"Two of these should do."

"Do you need the filters?"

"Yes."

"That's a problem. I don't have any working ones at the moment. I'd have to special order them."

"How long will it take them to get here?"

"If you are lucky they have some in Honolulu. They could be here this afternoon. If I have to go to the mainland, maybe a week."

"Can you check Honolulu please?"

He crossed his arms. "First, I have to ask what you want them for."

Lana and I had discussed this. There aren't a lot of uses for a gas mask on the Big Island except the one we wanted them for—keeping out volcanic gases.

"An independent movie," I said with a completely straight face.

"Doesn't that count as a costume?"

"That's what the uniforms are for. The masks are props."

He was stubborn. "I thought movies had wardrobe people who bought costumes."

"Not on our budget. Besides, this way we get ones that actually fit."

"What's the movie about?"

"It's a horror thing. I can't tell you much more than that or the producer will have my head."

"You wouldn't be planning to go out of bounds in the volcano park, would you?"

I looked as shocked as possible given that he'd nailed it exactly. "Good heavens, no. We're not crazy. Although there are scenes that will look like we're in clouds of volcanic gas. But that's just smoke generators."

He didn't look completely convinced. "I do have some non-functional filters you can have. Your prop guy can just punch out the old filter elements so you can breathe easily."

I pretended to consider it. "That won't work for our director. He wants everything to be authentic."

"In an indie horror movie?"

"It's the way he is," Lana said. "Besides, we're going to be wearing these things for who knows how many takes running through the clouds of smoke. It's not as bad as real smoke, but I have asthma and I'd really like a working mask."

"How are you going to shoot a movie with your arm in a cast?" He looked like he'd just found the hole in our story.

She lifted her arm in its sling. "Oh, this is coming off in the next day or two. We aren't shooting until the rest of the crew gets here next week."

"Your arm will be pretty weak for a while, you know."

"It's not like I have to fight monsters or anything. My character is the one that does most of the screaming."

I'm glad he wasn't looking at me when she said that. I had to choke back a laugh at the thought of Lana being cast in the role of the helpless screamer. I might as well follow up.

"Yeah, I'm the fighter," I said. He looked at the difference in our heights, and was about to open his mouth. "I know. That's why it works. Everybody will expect the tall, exotic beauty to be the one who gets them out of trouble. Instead, it's the short, feisty honey badger on crack."

He gave up. "All right, I'll see about those filters."

"Tall, exotic beauty?" Lana whispered while he was on the phone.

"You're taller than I am."

"Honey badger on crack?"

"There's a story behind that. I'll tell you later."

He hung up. "You're in luck. There's a flight this morning, so they should be here before closing time today. It'll be expensive."

"No problem. We have a company card."

"One other thing, those filters are good for about eight hours, depending on how much crap is in the air. If there's a lot of particles like smoke it may clog up fairly suddenly. If you need more, try to give me 24 hours notice so I can get them in."

He rang up our purchases. We had to pay for the filters in advance since they were special order. I was glad I hadn't gotten us a small car. We'd have to go back for the filters that afternoon.

"Can you think of anything else we need?" I asked Lana as we headed to a sushi place we'd noticed on the way there.

"Not at the moment. I think we're ready to go."

After lunch we headed back to the hostel for a few hours sleep. This was going to be a busy night.

CHAPTER 18

Party Time

The Big Island is quite small. We left Hilo around 3 p.m. after picking up the filters. It would take us less than an hour on Highway 11 to get to Kilauea.

Most of the trip was through dense rainforest with frequent roads leading off to various towns.

When we were close to the Hawaii Volcanoes National Park there was a sign beside one such road that read Volcano Solid Waste Transfer Station.

"Maybe we should just throw the Sampo in there." Anything to break the tension.

Lana didn't laugh. For that matter, neither did I.

We entered the park and cruised past the turnoff to Crater Rim Drive. That was the road that circled the Kilauea caldera. It went right past the point overlooking the lava lake, which would have been convenient. Of course the section we needed was closed, even to foot traffic.

Part of the reason was that rockfalls into the lake triggered eruptions that had showered the visitor parking lot with fist-sized pieces of hot lava. Another reason was the billowing clouds of toxic gases from a new vent in the crater floor that had opened in 2008. You weren't allowed to go past the Jaggar Museum, which was four and a half kilometres short of where we needed to be.

Instead, we stayed on the highway for another couple of kilometres. There was a mostly anonymous turnoff on our left, toward the volcano. A discrete sign indicated that the Department of Defence would be highly displeased with any uninvited guests.

"I hope the troops don't get called out to stop us." I wasn't really kidding.

We were losing the rainforest on the left side of the road. It was being replaced by the occasional short tree, some bushes, and low-lying scrub. It didn't look too horrible to climb, but there was no way we were taking the Jeep up there.

A sign announced END FAULT ZONE.

"I wonder whose fault is it," Lana said while looking out the side window. I smiled. That was as good as the humour was getting.

We found the turn off to our destination, which was Nāmakanipaio Park. I turned into the camp ground and wound along the single lane park road until we got to the self-registration station. Camping was $15 a night, plus the $10 park fee. I did the paperwork, then put the Jeep in the parking lot with the ticket in the window.

I loaded our supplies into the secondary pack, which Lana would carry. We changed into our boots, grabbed the packs and walking sticks, and started off.

Our BSI phones included a compass app. Once we were out on the highway again I took a sighting on a unique tree that was due south, and we started up the mountain.

It was now 5 p.m. We'd eaten in the Jeep on the way down, having stopped at a fast food place on our way out of Hilo. Twilight was in about two hours. We had that long to make it up to Crater Rim Drive. At that point we'd be at least a kilometre past the Museum. With any luck at all nobody would notice us.

The Sampo felt like a tonne of bricks on my back. The scrub was mostly dead and scratched our legs as we walked. With all the equipment, Lana's pack wasn't that much lighter than mine.

"We can change here," she panted. I dropped my pack and looked back. Sure enough, we were out of sight of the highway below.

She pulled the uniforms out of her pack and we changed from our tourist clothes. I made sure that the gas masks were on top of her pack when we closed it. I also put one of the water bottles in a uniform pockets, and helped her on with her pack.

There was one minor detail we'd forgotten. I grew up in Calgary, at something like 1150 metres above sea level. Lana had lived her entire life *at* sea level. The Kilauea overlook was at 1280 metres. To me this was home. To her it probably felt like she was at the top of Everest.

Lana was breathing hard and concentrating on putting one foot in front of the other. I had to keep slowing down so I wouldn't leave her behind.

"Are you going to make it," I said after a few hundred metres.

"Yes."

"Are you sure? I can take it the rest of the way."

"I'm. Sure."

Stubborn didn't begin to describe Lana. She'd get to the top if she had to crawl up the sharp lava naked. My kind of girl.

The going wasn't difficult, but it did require concentration. The lava was anything but smooth. After a while we had to go under a single wire fence that defined the out-of-bounds area. The sun hit the horizon just after we hit the Crater Rim Drive. At least the road was smooth and clear so far.

Twilight wasn't that much longer. We used our flashlights sparingly, and always in front of us so our bodies would shield the light from the Volcano Observatory that was right beside the Museum. The Observatory also maintained a bunch of cameras circling the caldera. The less light we used the less likely it was that one of them would pick us up. The closed road was still used by the Observatory staff and park rangers to service equipment. It would take them a few minutes to catch up with us and arrest us. We were trespassing in another damned national park.

In 90 minutes it would be fully dark, at least as far as the sky was concerned. Before the sun set we could see a huge plume of white rising above what we assumed was the crater just beyond our local horizon on the road. As the sun got lower there was also a red tinge to that horizon, where occasional rocks were high enough to be visible to us as well as illuminated by the glow of the lava.

"Stay here. I'm just going to check how far we have to go."

I helped Lana take off her pack, shed mine, and cautiously moved toward the caldera lip.

I could say that it was a scene from hell, but that would be trite, and meaningless. Who knows what hell really looks like? Apart from the demons I'd met, that is.

The Kilauea caldera was like nothing else but itself. All I could try to do was to grasp it a piece at a time.

The first thing was the scale. Start with the small details.

The lake was the bottom of Halema'uma'u crater, which was easily a kilometre across. The lava glowed a dull red except for a network of brighter cracks spread across its surface. I could only see part of it from there—it was 50 or more metres below the surface of the caldera. A bright spot on the near side was hidden from me by the lip of the crater.

That didn't prevent the light from spreading out, illuminating the rising column of gases so they looked like boiling blood rising into the night sky. In the distance I could see the walls of the caldera, flickering in the orange light, up to five kilometres away.

In human terms it was shockingly huge. I stood there in the red glow, a little human woman leaning on a stick to support me and keep me from losing my balance in the face of immensity.

No wonder the Hawaiians considered this the home of the goddess of volcanoes. Nothing less than a god could comprehend the full scope of what I was seeing.

Halema'uma'u looked to be a kilometre or so away, more or less in the same direction we were going, which probably meant not much more than that distance by road. We were almost there.

As I returned to Lana I saw a flash of light down slope by the highway. A vehicle with a bar of driving lights was coming up the winding road to the Museum fast. Way too fast for anybody with any sense.

Oh, fuck. We were in trouble. I could feel it in my guts.

When I got back to the road, Lana was half carrying, half dragging the Sampo pack. She'd seen the vehicle and come to the same conclusion.

"The Finns!" she gasped. I grabbed the pack from her and slung the shoulder straps to my back.

"Run!"

I did my best to get up more speed than a jog, but the pack weighed over half of what I did by myself. Lana had forgotten her pack, probably because of the lack of oxygen to her brain.

"We need the equipment!" She went back to get it.

As I ran I estimated that it would take me seven minutes to get to the drop-off point. The Finns were about five kilometres behind me, which probably meant five minutes until they overtook us. Our advantage was that the closed parking lot was covered with lumps of rock ejected by the lake, and beyond that was nothing but a jagged lava field. At the least they'd have to slow down to cross the parking lot. Then it would be a pure foot race, even if they had a 4x4.

Damn it, I needed to make time to take up running. I could already feel my throat burning from sucking in the thin air.

It took me a minute to realize that the burning wasn't me being out of shape when I suddenly began coughing. We were well into the danger zone from the sulphur dioxide and who knew what else being spewed by the lake.

I stopped running and let Lana catch up. She was doing pretty well considering.

"Masks!" I took the pack from her and pulled the masks out. It took us only a few seconds to put them on. In the distance the lights were bouncing around. Too fast.

We were at the edge of the old parking lot. Our feet crunched on pieces of tephra. We had our lights on continuously now. Being seen by the Observatory staff was the least of our worries. Some pieces of the tephra were the size of basketballs.

We could now see that it was a truck, and it was on Crater Rim Drive.

Within a minute or so it would be on us.

The old trail from the other side of the lot was still marked. We stumbled along it as well as we could. Below us, the light was much stronger and flickered like a god-sized bonfire.

Even over the sound of my own breathing, I could hear the volcano below us. A slow, soupy, bubbling sound overlaid with sharp cracks like individual firecrackers going off at random intervals.

There was a safety fence some distance back from the rim to keep tourists from dropping the 150 metres to the caldera below. The actual rim was composed of old lava that could crumble away into the lake at any moment. I'd seen a video of what happened when it did, and it was terrifying.

The truck hit something and its front end bounced into the air. When it came down the truck was sideways. I could hear the engine race for a moment. The driver hadn't seen something on the road and they were high centred on one of the lava boulders. It was now a foot race. The good news was that Finland isn't mountainous. They wouldn't like the thin air any more than Lana did.

We kept going until we got to the end of the old trail. Lana dropped her pack and desperately tried to get some oxygen into her lungs while getting the equipment ready.

I wasn't in much better shape, but I got the rope and tied one end around my waist. I pushed on the fence. It seemed solid, so I passed the other end around it several times, then handed the free rope to Lana.

"We don't need the spikes. Don't let me fall."

I wasn't thinking of anything but throwing the Sampo over the cliff. If I'd stopped to consider what I was doing I probably would have curled up in a ball.

Lana looped the rope around her own waist and braced her feet against a large boulder.

When I got close enough I could see most of the lake below me. I was staring into infinity.

The lava formed a dark crust shot through with cracks except in that one bright place near the edge, where the magma was streaming to the surface. The bright red lava bubbled, splashing the surrounding crust and the edge of the crater. If I fell here I probably wouldn't even feel the landing as my body simultaneously flashed into super-heated steam and burned.

I would never see pictures of volcanoes the same way again.

The pack was easy to get off. Not so easy to lift again.

"I see you found it. Splendid."

There was the dark silhouette of a man standing on the edge of the cliff. He seemed unconcerned by the danger.

He strolled toward me, stopping when he was beside me. Despite the location, he was wearing a three-piece suit and polished shoes. I'd never seen him before.

Whoever he was, I was trapped and he knew it. I would never be able to throw the Sampo far enough to hit the lake from here. I needed to be closer to the edge. I'd also need to wind up to make the toss. Unless he was exactly what he appeared to be, he'd have the Sampo for himself before I could move. That didn't mean I wasn't trying to think of a way out.

Above the roar and popping of the lake I heard the crack of rifle shots. The Finns had caught up with us. Either they were ignoring Lana or they couldn't see her, camouflaged by the uncertain shadows.

I dropped to the ground. The man just stood there, smiling.

I saw holes appear in his suit where bullets struck him. He didn't seem concerned. He raised his arms above his head, forming a Y-shape, then took a few steps and gracefully dove off the cliff.

A moment later he rose again into sight, his arms transformed into vast, membranous wings to support his many-times-larger body. Back-lit by the crater below, he had three heads. Two were animals. The middle one appeared human.

He wheeled in the sky, and shot back toward the men. They laid down a barrage without apparent effect. As he passed above me the human head vomited fire toward the men still firing up at him.

Two of them were on the back of the truck. Something in it exploded as the stream of fire hit it. I heard them scream as they burned. The other two men dove out of the way. I lost track of them.

I yanked on my safety rope, hoping that Lana would understand. I doubted that she could hear me over the volcano if I said anything inside my mask. I felt some slack in the line, and crawled closer to the edge while dragging the pack containing the Sampo. It caught on a sharp edge and I worked my way back to free it.

As I looked back to pull on the rope there was a swirl of mist and a miniature horse appeared.

"Give it to me," it said in a croaking voice. Another demon.

"Come and get it, horse face."

It dashed forward, attempting to grab the pack strap in its teeth before I could react. It didn't know me very well. As its head reached forward, I pulled the pack toward me.

It was nice to see that physics sometimes applied to demons as well as humans. The hoofs failed to get enough grip to stop its forward momentum and it pitched over the edge. I doubted that was the end of it, but at least it was out of my hair for a moment.

While I was playing dodge ball with the horse-demon, the dragon wheeled again and slowly glided back toward me.

I could see his plan. If I threw the Sampo now, he'd just pluck it from mid-air before it could be destroyed.

The seething below became louder, and I could feel the ground vibrating. I tried scrambling back toward Lana in case that section of the caldera wall was crumbling.

There was something wrong with the vapour column above the crater. The billows became less random and looked like they were forming a human face. One that must have been 50 metres high.

As the definition improved, it was the face of a beautiful woman.

Her full lips opened and sound rolled over me. I think that there were words, but the sound was so vast that I couldn't make them out. The ground shook delicately in time with them.

The dragon roared his defiance and spat fire at the image. That was stupid. Fire was her servant, her weapon, and her being.

The goddess had come to defend her dwelling. What would she think of a mortal littering her home?

A blast of air caught the dragon in mid-flight and he tumbled. As he lost altitude a shaft of lava shot up from the lake and engulfed him.

Almost blind with terror, I inched toward the edge again, and saw the dragon crash onto the floor of the caldera below. The echo boomed from the facing cliffs in all directions. Another shaft of lava shot into the sky and gracefully arched to land directly on his back. The demon was buried under tonnes of molten rock.

As the thunder died away, there was a sound behind me. The horse was back, trying to sneak up on me and grab the Sampo. I kicked and actually got him in the face.

Screw this. I grabbed the pack and made for the edge. If the rock crumbled the rope would save me. Maybe.

I was almost there. Almost close enough to see the steep slope below me so I could judge the throw. The horse-demon tried to grab the pack again. Then he looked up, whinnied in fear, and disappeared in a swirl of mist, red in the fire light.

I glanced up to see if She was paying any attention to us. The clouds of fumes had roiled back into normal shapes.

"Stop." The voice was loud enough to be heard over the maelstrom below. It was the voice of a goddess.

She was standing on the rim a dozen metres away, difficult to see between the flickering light of the burning truck and the dazzling glare of Her crater, but I think Her clothes were red or orange. Her skin was dark, like a native Hawaiian, and Her face was exquisitely beautiful. She was literally radiant, a soft glow coming from Her entire body as if a fluorescent gas was escaping from it. She carried a wooden staff. Her long, flowing hair was the colour of dark honey and shone exactly like metallic gold.

"You have brought demons to my home. Why would you do this?" Her English was flawless.

I tried to think of something to say, but my brain was on strike. There had been too much, too fast.

"Great Lady," Lana said as she hobbled forward, "we have stolen an object that the demons greatly treasure. We came to Your mountain, intending to offer it to you, and did not expect them to dare to follow us to Your sacred place. For this we are deeply sorry. Please accept Our offering."

I managed to understand that this was my cue. I dumped the Sampo out of the pack.

She came forward, crouched to touch it, then stood.

"Very well. I shall accept your offering. Cast it into the fire."

Lana turned toward the fence. "Give me a moment to belay you." I picked up the Sampo, ready to roll it off the edge of the cliff. It should bounce straight into the lake.

"There is no need."

The rope disappeared as if it had simply evaporated, and my feet left the ground. I floated outward.

Have you ever played a video game where you are flying over a cliff? You know that moment of fear you feel as the pretend-ground disappears from beneath your pretend-body? Then you laugh at your self and keep playing.

This was nothing like that. I was carrying a heavy object in my arms and the ground fell away from me. I drifted over the edge and I clasped the Sampo even harder to my chest as the ground was suddenly two hundred metres below. If I fell I would barely make a splash in the molten rock below.

What would happen when I dropped the Sampo? Would I shoot upward into the toxic gas cloud? She had no reason to spare me. Maybe I would follow the Sampo down, screaming the whole way.

I had a bad few moments before Veronica the Honey Badger remembered who she was.

Fuck that. With a goddess watching me, I would be damned if I would act like that mortal that I was. I think my previous experience with demons might have helped me to cope.

At this altitude the gas plume wasn't in my way. I waited until I was over the centre of the lake, and then dropped the Sampo.

Less than an eye blink later I was back on solid ground, almost exactly where I'd been before. My brain was thinking it was time to pass out.

"You have done well. Just remember that actions have consequences," She said before vanishing in a swirl of mist and laughter.

The Sampo hit the mostly solid surface of the lake. I think that I expected it to lie on the crust and slowly burn.

Instead, it broke through and disappeared. The lava seethed in the new opening, and cracks spread outward. The roiling of the new opening broke off more of the crust, which in turn spread the cracks further.

The reaction became more violent, the surface boiling with geysers of lava spewing into the air. The slope below me, disturbed by all the activity taking place, dumped a small avalanche into the lake, spreading the disruption even further. The geysers threw lava almost as high as the rim where I was standing.

Something under the surface surged upward, forming a dome covering the entire lake's surface. I did not want to be there when the bubble burst.

I raced back to the fence as fast as I could, collecting Lana on the way, and we ran down the slope, sliding as we went. A fiery column of lava roared upward, far above the rim of the caldera, and swamped the area. The noise was deafening.

Our packs, the truck, and whatever remained of the men was buried under a thick layer of orange-hot, molten rock.

CHAPTER 19

Aloha

We stopped running when we couldn't run any further. Not having paid attention to direction other than "away from the scary lady and her lava," we had no idea where we were.

"That..." Lana gasped through her mask, "was... intense."

I lifted my mask and tried to sniff. I couldn't smell anything bad.

"You can remove your mask. I think we're outside the poisonous gas zone."

Lana gratefully removed her mask and lay on her back on the rocks, just breathing.

We could still hear the eruption above us. Fortunately, there wasn't enough lava on the slope to flow. It just hardened in place.

"By the way, that was very clever of you offering the Sampo as a sacrifice."

She was starting to breathe more easily now. "From what you told me, these beings don't need the old ritual elements, but they do seem to enjoy them. It was the obvious ploy. Any idea who the demons were?"

I was glad I'd put my phone in my pocket.

Ever since the Blakeway case, I'd carried a copy of the Lesser Key of Solomon with me in my phone, just in case of emergencies. It took a few minutes to go through the entries, but there they were.

"The horse was probably Gamigin. The dragon must have been Asmoday. Both of them are involved with the sciences. I wonder if they made the Sampo, or whether they wanted to steal the technology?"

"We may never know. I'm just glad it's over. It is over, isn't it?"

"I think so."

"Good. How do we get out of here?"

The good news is that, being a shield volcano, Kilauea's slope is extremely gentle. I'd figured it out before we got here as about six percent—considerably less than a wheelchair access ramp. There were no sudden drops. All we had to do was to walk in the right direction. Fortunately we had technology on our side. I got my phone out of its pocket.

"According to the GPS, we should head west for a kilometre or so. Then we can head for the highway."

"Any chance our clothes survived?"

I looked up slope. The eruption had subsided to a smaller series of explosions, but there was still a dull red glow where the overlook had been.

"I don't think so."

The walk wasn't difficult as long as we watched our footing. There weren't that many loose rocks this far down the mountain. We had our phones, flashlights, gas masks, and keys.

Without the flashlights we'd have been completely screwed. When they were turned off we couldn't see each other at more than arm's length. There was no moon. The stars were outrageously bright, but that didn't do us much good.

After an hour we turned north. We could see the occasional headlights on the highway below, which was comforting.

Putting a foot on horizontal asphalt was a wonderful feeling. So was the accuracy of our path finding. From the occasional vehicle we knew where the road was in the darkness. A small collection of lights showed us where the camp was. Between that and the GPS, we just walked toward it.

The campground had water. I think we drank most of it. Lana's bottle was on top of the mountain and mine had been in the pack with the Sampo.

There was a sense of luxury when we got in the Jeep and were able to sit without rocks punching holes in our butts.

"Now what?"

"I vote for sleep."

"Seconded."

The front seats in a Jeep don't recline. We didn't care.

―⁂―

In the morning we cared. Between my neck, various complaining muscles, and a few lava burns I hadn't noticed the night before, I was ready to call this adventure done. It didn't help that we were out of food too.

On the way back to Hilo I saw the sign for a modest place called Verna's Food. We were almost past it. I didn't quite do a sideways drift into the parking area, but it was close.

The server was a nice Hawaiian woman. "Hi there. What can I get for you?"

I was about ready to bite her arm. "How big is your ham and cheese omelet?"

The server made a fairly big circle with her hands.

"Double it. And coffee. Lots of coffee."

"I'll have the same, but just water," Lana said.

It must have been the feral look of starvation that we gave her. I think our food came within five minutes. It lasted maybe three. That, and three cups of coffee, and I was mostly ready to meet the day. My chiropractor was going to have to do serious things to my back and neck before I was fully recovered.

It didn't take us long to get back on the road. One advantage to being in the U.S. was that we could understand the news broadcasts. One in particular was interesting.

"Scientists at the Hawaiian Volcano Observatory today are scrambling to recover after a freak power surge knocked out all of their instruments last night."

Another voice came on. *"At about nine p.m. the observatory lost all power. The outage lasted approximately an hour, and coincided with a massive eruption in the Halema'uma'u crater. At this time we don't know if or how the two events may be related. The instruments at the observatory itself sustained some damage, and all of our remote cameras were destroyed."*

"That was Dr. Robert Karlin of the Hawaiian Volcano Observatory. In other news..."

Lana turned off the radio. "That was lucky for us."

"If it *was* luck. I don't trust any coincidences that happen when demons are involved."

"Or gods. Assuming that the woman we saw isn't just another demon."

"You seem to be taking this well. I was a wreck for days after I found out that my world was a lie."

"I'm sure I'll have a reaction later when I have the time. For now, we have to determine what to do next."

I was suddenly reluctant to say the words. "I suppose we go home."

"It's curious, isn't it? When I took on this case I couldn't wait to get back to my flat and see what new devilry the police had for me to solve. Perhaps a clever robbery, or a bizarre murder. Something to occupy my mind."

"Adventure has a way of being addictive, doesn't it?"

"It does."

"As does friendship."

"I will miss you. Even if you are an uncivilized colonial."

"I love you too."

∽

When we arrived in Hilo we stopped by the surplus store.

"Aloha. What can I get for you today?"

"Actually, we're returning the gas masks. We decided not to use them after all."

"Okay, I can give you a credit for the masks. But the filters were special order. They're non-refundable."

"You don't understand. We're giving them back to you. Sell them again if you can. The filters are slightly used."

"You're just giving them back?"

"Yeah. It's not like we have a use for gas masks at home."

I think he was still confused when we left, but it didn't seem right to either of us to just throw them out.

We both had evening flights. My flight was scheduled to leave at 7:54 —Hilo to Honolulu to Vancouver to Calgary. Hers left at 8:40—Hilo to Los Angeles to Chicago to London. When we said goodbye at the terminal, that would be it.

If I was going to stick it to my clients I might as well do a good job of it. I tried paying for our airline tickets with the demonic credit card. I half expected it to have vanished from my wallet, but not only was it there, it was accepted.

At first Lana wasn't happy about me paying her way home, but it wasn't like I was paying her way myself. Besides, she wouldn't have *had* to fly home from Hawaii if it wasn't for my clients.

By now our luggage consisted of the clothes we were wearing, toothbrushes and such, and, in my case, a statue of Isis and two deerstalker hats.

Hell, we were in Hawaii and there were almost six hours to kill until we had to be at the airport. We decided to relax a little.

Our first stop was a book store where I bought something for Dad.

After that we bought actual bathing suits and spent most of the day on the beach, slathered with sun block and dozing in the sun. We even did a bit of swimming.

Two relatively hunky guys tried to pick us up, but of course Lana wasn't interested and I used loyalty to her as an excuse for not taking one of them aside and relieving three months of celibacy. Or both of them, for that matter. Three months was a *very* long time for me to do without and I was getting a little edgy.

"It's time," Lana said. We had waited until the last minute before leaving the beach.

I stood by the check-in counter with my boarding pass in hand and a lump in my throat.

"Well, I guess this is it."

"Yes, I expect so. I have a present for you."

She handed me a memory card.

"I've been taking pictures throughout our travels. I thought you'd like copies."

Lana, bless her pointy little head, extended her hand for an off-handed shake. Screw that.

I put my arms around her. After a few seconds I felt her left arm return the hug.

I was still trying to swallow the lump in my throat when she spoke. "Thank you, Veronica. This has easily been the most—interesting—case I've ever been involved with. And the most interesting partner."

"I'm going to miss you. We *are* going to see each other again."

"Undoubtedly."

I felt something wet on my cheek, but I wasn't sure whose tear it was. I was seriously going to start bawling if I didn't get going.

I cupped her face in my hands, and gave her a quick kiss on each cheek. Then I picked up my carry-on bag and headed for security.

"Hey, Veronica."

I turned. She mimed adjusting the brim of a fedora, then put two fingers to her brow and gave me an informal salute.

"See you around, sweetheart." She did a rather good Humphrey Bogart imitation.

She turned and left before I could think of anything else to say.

∞

Go through security; find my gate; sit for entirely too long; get called to board. By now it was such a familiar ritual that I did it without thinking.

Instead, I spent the time thinking about the past two months.

My first thought was about my promised fee. I might as well find out if this had been a job or a paid vacation.

I accessed my bank account from my phone. I'd had about five thousand in there for emergencies and up-front expenses. I called up the balance.

Three hundred twenty-nine thousand, one hundred twenty dollars and forty-two cents. My clients had kept their word and paid me. Maybe this was one of those stories you hear about where the Devil makes a deal and the person gets out of it by exploiting a loophole in the contract.

My first reaction was *I'm rich!* My second reaction was that I'd have to call my financial adviser and ask about what to do with it so I didn't get taxed to death. I sent her a text giving her the situation and asking her to call me in a few days if she didn't hear from me.

The next thing I did was to text Mum, Dad, and Kali to tell them I'd be home the next day at noon. It was after midnight in Calgary so I wasn't surprised by the lack of an immediate reply.

Having done several practical things to successfully keep from thinking about the case, I forced myself to look at what I'd done.

My first resolution was that I wasn't going to second guess clients. For some reason demons seemed to like me, and I'd been suckered into finding a lost item for a pair of them. That didn't mean that the next hundred, or thousand, clients wouldn't be legitimate. I'd thought the deal was too good to be true when I took it. All right, in future I'd stay away from golden-egg laying geese unless I was damned sure that the eggs were not only 24-carat, but also had the right isotope ratio.

At least some good had come out of the Sampo. When it dumped a pile of silver on the bed we switched over to having it produce salt, which was easily washed down the drain. That still left us with 20 kilos of silver that we couldn't afford to lug around with us.

I found a charity in Bratislava that not only got children out of orphanages and into adoptive families, but also provided support for those families. A call to the hotel concierge got us a sturdy cardboard box and a packing tape dispenser. I boxed the silver, wrote the address of the charity on it, and got the concierge to find someone to deliver it. Inside I included a note that said "For the families." It shouldn't be hard for them to find somebody to translate. That was the end of the silver problem. I did keep one nugget, though.

The rest of the case wasn't quite so pristine. We'd promised Professor Nieminen that we'd complete his research. We had, but I wasn't looking forward to writing him to tell him we'd destroyed the Sampo.

We still had no idea who was in the white van that tried to kill us. That would bother me.

To hell with it all. I had a long time to think about this case. Right now I was going home.

My first stop on this flight would be Honolulu, so at least I was flying off into the sunset at the end of my adventure.

CHAPTER 20

Did You Miss Me?

The airline for the flight from Honolulu was WestJet. It made me unreasonably pleased that I was in the hands of a Canadian carrier. Almost like I was already home.

About half an hour into the flight an attendant came back and leaned over my row.

"Veronica Chandler?"

Red alert! Adrenaline to maximum! There was no good reason why I would be singled out at this point. "Yes."

"You've been upgraded to economy plus. If you would come this way?"

How the hell could I be upgraded in the middle of a flight? Lana would be on her own way home by now. Mum and Dad? Unlikely in the extreme. If I'd had my baton it would have been in my hand and extended.

I grabbed my carry-on and went forward with the nice man.

I was shown my new seat. The one beside it was occupied.

"Veronica! So nice for you to join me."

It was Jack Hoag. That did not make me feel better.

"I should have known."

He looked amused. "Known what?"

"That you'd show up. You know that I met our mutual clients."

"Oh yes. They spoke highly of you."

"Really? Last time I saw them they weren't doing very well."

He shrugged. "These things happen."

"What are you doing here?"

"I couldn't stand to see you crammed into that tiny seat. Isn't this more comfortable?"

"Yes, but you'll forgive me if I'm leery of accepting gifts from people who associate with strange horses."

He laughed. That's when the light bulb went on.

"Oh, for god's sake. Jonathan Hoag."

"I wondered if you'd get it."

"I didn't think about it until I knew you weren't a normal person."

"I'll try not to be offended at that." Then he was wreathed in mist and...

Oh, fuck no. This was not fair.

I gave a deep sigh. "Hello, Beleth. So you were Hoag."

She almost came up to my shoulder, even when we were seated. Her long dark hair was in a pony tail over one shoulder. This time she was wearing a business suit.

"It's been a long time since we've just chatted. Did you miss me? How are things?"

"They've been better. And considering that we're probably the shortest two people on this flight, we hardly need extra leg room."

"Nonsense. Just because we're short doesn't mean we don't deserve the best. So, you've had quite the adventure lately."

"Been watching?"

"Oh, yes. It's been quite exciting. You must be very pleased."

"Not really. I made a promise that I can't keep."

"That doesn't sound like you. What promise?"

"To complete someone's research."

"Is that all? You have all the information. It's just a matter of delivering it. I can help you with that."

"No! I don't need any—"

She touched my arm, and in a split second, the universe disappeared and returned. I was not sitting in an airplane seat. I was in a chair by a hospital bed. From the light streaming in the window, it was morning. My ears popped.

The past two months had not been kind to Professor Nieminen. His arms, lying on the covers by his sides, were terribly thin. His eyes and cheeks were sunken. His head turned toward me. He seemed to have trouble focusing on the fact that somebody had come to see him.

Lana had speculated that the Sampo could remove tumours. I wondered, not for the first or last time, if we'd done the right thing when we destroyed it.

His voice was hoarse. "Hello, Ms. Chandler. I've been waiting for you." He paused as if the effort exhausted him.

"Hello, Professor. How are you feeling?"

Stupid, Veronica. How do you think he's feeling? And I bet that counts as a personal question. Stupid and rude.

He ignored my gaff. "Where is Ms. Reviere?"

"She went home. I came to see you."

"Did you find it?"

I could have said no, and left. If I said yes he'd want to see it, to know the details, to have his life's work vindicated. By destroying the Sampo I'd made that impossible. Really, there was only one possible answer.

"Yes. We did."

"Where is it?"

"I'll have to tell you the whole story, Professor. I'm afraid it doesn't have a happy ending."

I must have spent at least two hours telling him the whole story, including all the details. If I wanted to be callous, it didn't matter because he probably wouldn't live long enough to tell anyone. Even if he did, who would believe a drugged and dying man?

He was remarkably calm as I told him about the demons, and about the goddess. I suspected that his personal philosophy included the possibility of more supernatural beings than his academic friends might have been comfortable with.

By the end of the story I was crying. I felt like we'd betrayed him. I was so ashamed that I buried my face in the sheets beside him. I felt a light touch on my hair.

"Did you really see Her? In person?"

"Yes," I said into the bed.

"Don't be upset. You did the right thing."

I looked at him. "I did?"

"Of course. The tools of the gods are not for mortals. I was chasing a myth for so long. Even when I knew it was real the implications didn't really occur to me. At least you have saved other foolish people from seeking the Sampo as I did."

He paused for a while with his eyes closed, and I wondered if he'd gone to sleep.

"I would like to ask you to do something for me, if you will."

"Name it."

"You are young, and have a long life ahead of you. It would please me if, someday, you wrote a book about your adventures, including your quest for the Sampo. Even if nobody believes you now, perhaps some day they might."

"I promise."

"Maybe you could even acknowledge my research. I have no children, and it would comfort me to know that I have at least that much of a legacy."

"I will. People will know you as a great scholar."

"Please, such praise from a young woman will turn my head."

He chuckled, which quickly turned into a wet coughing fit. A nurse came in and helped him onto his side until the fit passed. She said something stern to me in Finnish before she left.

"She wants you to stop being funny." He held out the hand closest to me. I gently clasped it, afraid of hurting him. "Thank you, Ms. Chandler. You've made me happy. I think I'll rest now."

I got up and kissed his forehead. "Goodbye, Professor."

I left his room without really paying attention to where I was going. I supposed I'd have to find the exit unless Beleth suddenly plucked me from the hospital. It would be like her to let me find my own way home.

A short announcement came over the public address system.

Several people hurried toward me. As they passed I looked back. They were going into Professor Nieminen's room. More people were coming from the other end of the hall. Two of them was handling a cart loaded with medical equipment.

I went back to his room. One of them closed the door just as I got there.

I needed to know the end of the story, so I waited, squatting by the opposite wall of the corridor. Everybody who walked by ignored me, except the doctors and nurses. They gave me a brief glance, assessing whether I was in need of help, before passing by.

Time passed.

The door opened, and the doctors and nurses filed out. They all looked sombre. I stood as the last one came out, and I saw into the room before she quietly closed the door behind her.

The figure in the bed was still, and there was a sheet pulled up over his face.

Damn it. "Goodbye, Professor."

I turned to walk down the hall. The universe jumped, and I was sitting in an airplane seat. Beleth had her hand on my arm, but it was in a different spot.

For several minutes we sat in silence. I was thankful for the quiet, but eventually I had to say it.

"Thank you."

"I know that your promises mean a great deal to you."

"That's very human of you."

"Don't be insulting."

There was another silence. Finally, I wiped my eyes, took a deep breath, and let it out slowly. I looked around. Nobody seemed to be in hysterics.

"I take it that I didn't cause any panic by disappearing and reappearing."

"I used an image of you sleeping. Nobody knew you were gone."

"I don't know whether that's clever or creepy."

She shrugged. "I imagine you have some questions."

"You could say that."

"I just did." Right. I'd forgotten how literal demons could be. "Who was the sniper in London?"

"More of a sport shooter than a sniper. Kagari Hikaru."

"Isn't that the biological father of Lana's sister?"

"The same. He also hired Grigor Lubikov, and the driver of the van in Poland that tried to run you off the road. That wasn't well done. He was supposed to crush the passenger side of the car instead of just pushing you into the barrier. Incompetent."

"Shit, So all of those were his attempts to kill Lana."

"Not everything is about you."

"Gee, thanks."

"You're welcome."

"What about Pietr?"

"You already know the answer. The Finns tortured him to find out where you were going, then killed him. You might be surprised that he didn't want to give you up at first."

"Poor Pietr. He really wasn't very good at being evil. I assume that the Vienna sniper was Finnish as well?"

"Yes. He was quite put out when his shot missed you. Wind gusts are so unpredictable." She buffed her finger nails on her lapel. I wondered where she'd picked up that mannerism.

"Wait, you mean that was you?"

"I can't have my favourite human being punctured for no good reason."

"Then why did you shoot arrows at me?"

She clapped her hands in delight. "Well done. I was wondering when you would figure that out. That wasn't *actually* me, though. I had a friend do it. He was told to be very careful not to hurt you."

"I suppose that's nice to know. But why shoot at me at all?"

"Incentive. I wanted to be sure you'd be in the right frame of mind to accept the case when it was presented to you."

"It doesn't occur to you in the least that you are a manipulative psychopath, does it?"

"As long as I get what I want, it doesn't matter."

"And the prosecution rests."

"I don't understand."

"Never mind."

"Before I forget, I'll need that credit card back."

I pulled it from my wallet and tossed it to her. It disappeared in a wisp of mist.

"If you don't mind, I need some sleep."

"Nighty night. Don't let the bed bugs bite."

"You are so weird."

After a few minutes of silence I opened my eyes. She was gone.

I wondered what the airline thought about a passenger disappearing in mid-flight. Not to mention changing sex.

Vancouver was just a three hour stop. We got in at 7:15, and did the usual shuffle through passport control and customs. The first thing I did after that was to find breakfast. The flight to Calgary left just before 10 a.m. It was an hour flight, but because of the time zone change I'd get there at noon. Two hours for a one hour flight. If I'd been going the other way it would have taken no time at all. The joys of air travel.

Calgary International was now just another airport to me, and less interesting than most. I moved placidly amid the noise and haste. Deplane, and out into the world.

Mum, Dad, and Kali had all taken time off work to come to welcome me home. We spotted each other at the same time.

Dad got to me slightly before everyone else and wrapped me in a big hug. Mum and Kali did likewise. It felt really good.

"Welcome home, Princess," Dad said by my ear. I hoped he hadn't bought me anything pink.

"It's so good to have you back," Mum said.

"Is that all your luggage?" Kali asked.

"Yeah, we jet setters travel light."

Mum looked closely. "That isn't my suitcase."

"Um, yeah. There's a funny story there."

Dad gave me a final squeeze. "You're invited over for supper tonight. You can tell us all about it."

"Thanks. I'd like to go home first and clean up, though."

"Six o'clock?"

"Cool."

Mum hugged me again. "That'll give me a chance to finish some work at the office."

Kali took my carry-on. "I'll drive you. My boss will want me back at work, but I don't care."

I snorted. "That's what happens when you're self employed."

We made it outside and headed for the short-term parking area. It's funny how people bustle while they are in the terminal, and then slow down as soon as they get outside. The sun was shining and the air was a reasonable temperature—I didn't immediately start dripping with sweat.

A scruffy-looking man was striding toward us. My internal alarm went off. In my experience people who look like him don't stride purposefully unless they are up to no good.

"Mum—," was as far as I got before things got busy.

He reached under the front of his jacket and I saw the grip of a pistol.

"Gun!" Mum and I yelled simultaneously.

I pushed Kali behind one of the concrete pillars holding up the canopy over the walkway. She didn't know what was happening and resisted at first.

Mum was less gentle with Dad. She threw him through the open automatic door into the terminal. He collided with somebody coming out. She took cover partially behind a concrete buttress by the door.

Civilians started to clue in that something was wrong and were running, screaming, and freezing. I couldn't see anything behind the pillar, and I needed to know where the gunman was.

I poked my head out and found myself face-to-face with the end of a gun barrel. It's funny how you can notice useless details in a split second. It was a right-handed Glock 22, the same as Mum's, and he was holding it in his left hand. The right hand that was trying to steady it was badly burned. Recently.

"Police!" Mum yelled. "Drop your weapon! Drop it now!"

"My brother is dead because of you." His words were quieter than you'd expect under the circumstances. He moved his finger from the trigger guard to the trigger.

I burst forward and pushed his arms up. It was the only direction where there were no targets. The gun fired into the canopy. He turned as I moved, so I lost my chance to pound him in the throat a few times before really getting medieval on him.

A male voice joined Mum's in telling him to drop his weapon and put his hands on his head.

The gun clubbed the back of my head as I stumbled, which at least robbed it of some force. I converted the stumble into a clumsy roll.

Two closely-spaced shots sounded in my already ringing ears.

Instead of rolling up onto my feet to fight, I stayed down in case whoever had fired still needed a clear line. The shooter was already on the ground. Mum and another officer approached him from opposite directions, their guns trained on the motionless body. The male constable stepped on the shooter's gun to secure it while Mum holstered her weapon and checked his pulse.

She looked up at her colleague. "Good shooting. Thanks." He put his gun away and called in the incident. He wasn't looking well.

I got to my feet and checked Kali. She was huddled on the ground behind the pillar.

"Are you hurt?"

"No," she said with a quaver in her voice. I helped her to her feet.

"Who was that guy?"

I looked at him and didn't mention the Finnish accent. It made no difference now. "I have no idea."

Mum motioned Dad that it was safe, and he came out of the terminal. He was holding the side of his face.

"Are you injured?"

"Not really." Mum took his hand away. There was a developing bruise and some scrapes. "You threw me into some hard-shelled luggage."

Mum took charge. "Veronica, go secure the scene." She pointed to where the constable had been standing. SIU and Ident would want the shell casings undisturbed. Mum pushed the spectators back, keeping the primary scene intact.

The constable was squatting by the terminal wall, his face supported by his hands.

Other police began to arrive within a few minutes. One of them, fortunately somebody who knew me, relieved me from guard duty. Before SIU arrived I squatted down beside the constable.

"I'm Veronica. What's your name?"

His voice was muffled behind his hands. "Chiang."

I poked the name tag on his uniform. "I got that. What's your first name?"

"Sherman."

"How are you doing, Sherman?"

Tears rolled down his cheeks.

"I'm going to say something that you won't believe: I know how you feel."

He looked up at me.

"I also know what you're thinking: How could a young civilian like me possibly know how you feel? When I was 16 I had to shoot a drug addict who was threatening to kill me, the officer I was with, and anybody else who came near him. Do you know Danielle Shuemaker?"

He shook his head. I saw a constable I didn't know heading toward us. Mum intercepted him, shook her head, and said, "blue wall." He went by without appearing to see us.

"She's a detective now. This guy smashed into our car with a stolen vehicle after he'd beaten the owner to death. He got Danielle with a baseball bat and was trying to get to me when I grabbed her pistol and ended the threat. Fortunately, I had a good therapist who helped me to see that it wasn't my fault." I put my hand on his shoulder. "You did your job today. If you hadn't, my Mother would have had to, and I might not be talking to you. You had a good line of fire on him and you saved a lot of lives without endangering any. Hold onto that thought, and see someone after SIU gets done with you. If you want I can give you the name of the psychologist who helped me. She talks to a lot of cops and she understands."

SIU arrived on the scene, and the guy who headed toward us was not happy that Sherman was talking to somebody.

The Special Investigations Unit was a civilian agency that got involved in any case where an officer had to discharge their firearm. The subject of their investigation was supposed to be sequestered until SIU had done their interview.

"Miss, you can't talk to the officer."

"Hello, Sam. Remember me?"

That stopped him for a moment.

"You're that girl..."

"Who shot the drug addict four years ago. Yes. We weren't discussing this incident. He's not doing very well, and I suggested he see the counsellor I went to after my line-of-duty incident."

He looked around and spotted Mum, all of three or four metres away.

"Are you in charge here?"

"Detective Janet Chandler."

"Samuel Larson, SIU. This young lady should not have been speaking with the sequestered constable."

"Good heavens," Mum said in a completely unconvincing tone, "how *ever* did that happen? Veronica, you should know better. I'm sorry, Mr. Larson. You know how busy it can be at crime scenes. I'm *sure* it won't happen again." I almost expected her to bat her eyes at him.

"See that it doesn't." He is tone was stern, but didn't look angry.

He helped Sherman Chiang to his feet, and led him off to the car.

"Thank you," Larson said on the way by. He was a decent guy.

"Perhaps we should postpone dinner," Dad said after we'd given our witness statements.

"Not a hope. I'm starving and the only thing at my place is cold cereal and cat food."

"I'm with Veronica," Kali said. "I don't want to sit at home alone after this either."

"All right, it looks like I'm cooking supper."

"I'll bring dessert," I said.

⁂

We finally got out of there around three. The gun really was like Mum's.

They finally found the constable it belonged to, unconscious behind some bushes. The ambulance that had come for the body took him to hospital.

Mum had to stay and do paperwork, of course, but she'd be home for supper.

Yoko Geri was lying on the sofa when we got to my apartment. He was in the middle of stretching when the door opened, and immediately ran over to me. He wove between my legs, purring like a crazy cat.

Kali humphed. "I've been feeding him for two months and he never did that."

I bent down to pet him. "You aren't the love of his life. Hi, fuzz butt. I missed you." He chirped and fell over on his back. I rubbed his tummy and he closed his eyes in bliss.

"I was worried, you know."

"When? While I was in Europe?"

"Your e-mails got kind of sparse after Poland."

"I was busy trying to survive. It was nothing personal."

"I'm really glad you succeeded. It would be a lot of work to train a new sister."

"I love you too, *Miquita*."

"What are you going to tell the parentals tonight?"

"Nothing about demons, if that's what you mean."

"Don't you think they deserve to know?"

"Maybe. But I don't see how it'll make their lives any better, even assuming they believe it. What's Dad going to do? Offer restaurant discounts for demons? Suppose Mum gets a weird case. What's she going to do, tell her team to start looking for demonic influences? She'd be sent for a psych evaluation and then kicked off the force."

"Just be careful. I hope you don't regret this."

"I already do."

○○○

I filled Kali in on the details that happened after Europe, then we went over to the parental house.

Dad made us steaks, roasted potatoes, and creamy scrambled eggs. I thought I'd died and gone to heaven. On the way there I'd stopped to pick up a cheesecake and strawberries. While he finished the eggs I turned the fruit into a sauce.

There was one conspicuous absence at the table—Kali's boyfriend.

"Where's George? Didn't he come home this summer?"

"He's at a job interview in Edmonton. He'll be back tomorrow."

"Does that mean you'll be moving?"

"No, the job's in Calgary."

"That's kind of weird. You'd think he'd interview here."

She got a dreamy look on her face. "I'm just glad he's home for the summer."

Time to change the topic before she started swooning. I hoped that I would find a guy who could do that to me someday. Or guys. Whoever.

After dessert we gathered in the living room for story time. I began at the beginning, with my adventures in London. I left out the sniper. That's when I brought out everybody's presents.

The first was Kali's. "This is a replica of a piece in the British Museum."

She stared at the Isis statue for a long time. "She's beautiful. Thank you."

"Mum, something you've really needed for a long time."

She laughed as she tried on the deerstalker cap. "I think I'll wear this at work."

I looked at Dad. "I tried to find recipe collections in Europe, but they were all in Finnish, Polish, or Slovakian. I did get you this." I handed him a book on native Hawaiian cuisine. None of that pineapple on pizza tourist stuff, but the real thing. He buried his nose in it and stayed there all evening.

I handed a small, heavy wrapped box to Kali. "This is for George."

She shook the box, but I'd wrapped the silver nugget in foam. There was also a pointed note: "This would make a nice ring." It was about time those two went where they were obviously going. I'd once caught Kali looking at wedding sites, so I knew she was thinking about it.

I told the rest of the story more or less the way it had happened, but leaving out the gory details. Grigor became a random mugger. The car crash never happened. Pietr lived, and nobody got shot in Vienna.

The Sampo became a piece of jewellery that was returned to its rightful owners, and we flew back via the Pacific because my clients were so impressed that they paid for a few days in Hawaii.

In the New Improved Version, the closest we got to Kilauea was the tourist overlook at the Museum.

Around ten p.m. I gave up and called it a night. Kali offered to drive me home again. As soon as we were in the car, she started asking questions.

"By the way, what did the guy this afternoon mean by you killing his brother?"

Oh damn.

"I didn't know anybody heard that."

"*Idiota*, I was right beside you."

"He was one of the Finnish nationalists I told you about. I guess his brother was one of the others who didn't make it off the mountain."

"Are there any more we should be worried about?"

"I don't think so. Maybe one. I should warn Lana."

I texted her a warning about a possible problem when she landed. She responded almost immediately that she would be careful. I also told her I'd send her an e-mail outlining my New Improved Version of the case. If anybody asked her questions I wanted our stories to match.

Just as we were pulling up to my building, I got another text from her. Her sources indicated that a man identified as a Finnish national had been found dead of second and third degree burns in Hawaii the day after the fireworks. It was assumed that he'd been hiking when the eruption caught him.

Kali didn't say anything until I'd finished reading.

"What?"

"It's over. There's nobody left to come after us."

Yoko Geri was already on the bed when I got in. I did the usual things and crawled under the covers. He burrowed underneath, then surfaced on my chest. His golden eyes searched my hazel ones.

I took a deep breath, which is not easy with a cat on your chest. "Well, I'm back," I said.

GLOSSARY

Amiga	Spanish	Female friend
Anteeksi	Finnish	Excuse me
Blini ja sienisalaattia ja hirven ulkofilee	Finnish	Blini and mushroom salad and elk sirloin
Czechá republika	Slovenian	Czech Republic
Czescz	Polish	Hello
De nada	Spanish	It's nothing
Fromage fort	French	Old cheese. One of the few French phrases Canadian Anglophones recognize
Gomen nasai	Japanese	I'm sorry
Guten tag Herr Professor. Sprechen sie Deutsch?	German	Good day, professor. Do you speak German?
Idiota	Spanish	Female idiot
Kahvi	Finnish	Coffee
Kalevala	Finnish	The Land of Heroes; a poetic name for Finland
Keskusta	Finnish	Centrum. Points toward city centre
Konsertit	Finnish	Concert
Kyllä	Finnish	Yes
Lantmil	Swedish	A distance of 10.69 km (6.64 mi)
Miquita	Spanish	Literally, little monkey girl
Mitä tapahtui?	Finnish	What happened?
Ojców	Polish	Fathers
Ojcowski Park Narodowy	Polish	Fathers National Park
Parlez vous français?	French	Do you speak French?
Pichar	Spanish	Fuck

Przepraszam. Nie rozumiem.	Polish	Excuse me. I do not understand
Ravintola	Finnish	Restaurant
Siltakatu	Finnish	Bridge Street
Thaler	German	A large denomination coin. Origin of the English word dollar.
Tōdai	Japanese	University of Tokyo nickname

ABOUT THE AUTHOR

G. W. Renshaw is a writer, martial artist, Linux druid, and actor who lives in Calgary, Alberta with his lovely wife, and the twin cats Romulus and Remus. He has a wide range of interests, from flint knapping to quantum cosmology. He will happily watch just about any film with tentacles in it.

You can connect with him at:

Facebook:
www.facebook.com/pages/GW-Renshaw/287045931461429

Website:
www.gwrenshaw.ca/

Made in the USA
Charleston, SC
23 September 2016